THE NUMBERS GAME

By Danielle Steel

THE NUMBERS GAME • MORAL COMPASS • SPY • CHILD'S PLAY
THE DARK SIDE • LOST AND FOUND • BLESSING IN DISGUISE
SILENT NIGHT • TURNING POINT • BEAUCHAMP HALL
IN HIS FATHER'S FOOTSTEPS • THE GOOD FIGHT • THE CAST
ACCIDENTAL HEROES • FALL FROM GRACE • PAST PERFECT
FAIRYTALE • THE RIGHT TIME • THE DUCHESS
AGAINST ALL ODDS • DANGEROUS GAMES • THE MISTRESS • THE AWARD
RUSHING WATERS • MAGIC • THE APARTMENT
PROPERTY OF A NOBLEWOMAN • BLUE • PRECIOUS GIFTS
UNDERCOVER • COUNTRY • PRODIGAL SON • PEGASUS
A PERFECT LIFE • POWER PLAY • WINNERS • FIRST SIGHT
UNTIL THE END OF TIME • THE SINS OF THE MOTHER
FRIENDS FOREVER • BETRAYAL • HOTEL VENDÔME • HAPPY BIRTHDAY
44 CHARLES STREET • LEGACY • FAMILY TIES • BIG GIRL
SOUTHERN LIGHTS • MATTERS OF THE HEART • ONE DAY AT A TIME
A GOOD WOMAN • ROGUE • HONOR THYSELF • AMAZING GRACE
BUNGALOW 2 • SISTERS • H.R.H. • COMING OUT • THE HOUSE
TOXIC BACHELORS • MIRACLE • IMPOSSIBLE • ECHOES • SECOND CHANCE
RANSOM • SAFE HARBOUR • JOHNNY ANGEL • DATING GAME
ANSWERED PRAYERS • SUNSET IN ST. TROPEZ • THE COTTAGE • THE KISS
LEAP OF FAITH • LONE EAGLE • JOURNEY • THE HOUSE ON HOPE STREET
THE WEDDING • IRRESISTIBLE FORCES • GRANNY DAN • BITTERSWEET
MIRROR IMAGE • THE KLONE AND I • THE LONG ROAD HOME • THE GHOST
SPECIAL DELIVERY • THE RANCH • SILENT HONOR • MALICE
FIVE DAYS IN PARIS • LIGHTNING • WINGS • THE GIFT • ACCIDENT
VANISHED • MIXED BLESSINGS • JEWELS • NO GREATER LOVE
HEARTBEAT • MESSAGE FROM NAM • DADDY • STAR • ZOYA
KALEIDOSCOPE • FINE THINGS • WANDERLUST • SECRETS
FAMILY ALBUM • FULL CIRCLE • CHANGES • THURSTON HOUSE
CROSSINGS • ONCE IN A LIFETIME • A PERFECT STRANGER
REMEMBRANCE • PALOMINO • LOVE: *POEMS* • THE RING • LOVING
TO LOVE AGAIN • SUMMER'S END • SEASON OF PASSION • THE PROMISE
NOW AND FOREVER • PASSION'S PROMISE • GOING HOME

Nonfiction
PURE JOY: *The Dogs We Love*
A GIFT OF HOPE: *Helping the Homeless*
HIS BRIGHT LIGHT: *The Story of Nick Traina*

For Children
PRETTY MINNIE IN HOLLYWOOD
PRETTY MINNIE IN PARIS

Danielle Steel

The Numbers Game

A Novel

Delacorte Press | New York

Published in the United States by Delacorte Press, an imprint of Random House, a division of Penguin Random House LLC, New York.

DELACORTE PRESS and the HOUSE colophon are registered trademarks of Penguin Random House LLC.

LIBRARY OF CONGRESS CATALOGING-IN-PUBLICATION DATA
Names: Steel, Danielle, author.
Title: The numbers game : a novel / Danielle Steel.
Description: New York : Delacorte Press, 2020
Identifiers: LCCN 2019038117 (print) | LCCN 2019038118 (ebook) |
ISBN 9780399179563 (hardcover) | ISBN 9780399179570 (ebook)
Subjects: LCSH: Domestic fiction.
Classification: LCC PS3569.T33828 N86 2020 (print) |
LCC PS3569.T33828 (ebook) | DDC 813/.54--dc23
LC record available at https://lccn.loc.gov/2019038117
LC ebook record available at https://lccn.loc.gov/2019038118

Printed in the United States of America on acid-free paper

randomhousebooks.com

2 4 6 8 9 7 5 3

Book design by Virginia Norey

To my darling children,
Beatrix, Trevor, Todd, Nick,
Sam, Victoria, Vanessa,
Maxx, and Zara,

May you be ageless forever,
fill your life with rewarding
work, good people, and great joy!

I wish you each
long life and great love and happiness,

with all my love,
Mom/d.s.

The Wisdom of the Ages

At 17: You chafe in frustration. When are you going to be an adult and treated like one? At 18? It feels like never.

At 27: Your 20s are so annoying! Now you're finally an adult. No one takes you seriously. Will turning 30 finally convince them?

At 39: Is life over? Does life begin at 40, or end at 40? Or does youth end at 40? Is the best part over or just beginning? It's up to you now. You have the winning cards in your hand—play them!

At 56: Is everything waning? Your career, your looks? Where are the men, the opportunities, the jobs, the excitement? Is it really over or is there time left? How much time? How much can you still do and have and be before you turn 60? And what then? There might still be one-third left! Enjoy it!

At 92: You have figured it out or are still working on it. You know what matters, you're not confused. Every moment counts. You know who you want to be with, you recognize true beauty. You are wiser and more creative than ever. You exude an inner beauty so powerful that you are beautiful on the outside. You're alternately gentle and fierce. You know the answers and share them fearlessly. You have the wisdom of the ages, the humor of a lifetime. You are brave to have come this far. And now, onward to 100 without stopping or faltering or slowing down. You wear your age like a crown and are to be learned from, and loved, celebrated, and envied. We worship at your feet.

—d.s.

THE NUMBERS GAME

Chapter 1

P ennie Jackson had just finished her junior year at one of the best
private high schools in Greenwich, Connecticut. It prepared its
students for admission into the finest colleges in the country, and
required a high standard of academic excellence. Community projects and additional activities were encouraged to strengthen their
college applications. As a result, the list of colleges they got into was
impressive.

Pennie had turned seventeen in December and would be entering
her senior year in the fall. Her boyfriend, Tim Blake, had just graduated two weeks before. With Tim leaving for college at the end of
August, Pennie wasn't looking forward to senior year. They'd been
dating for almost three years and it was going to be lonely without
him. He'd been accepted at Stanford, in California. He'd had top
grades, perfect board scores, had been captain of the basketball
team, and had worked as an intern for a senator in Washington,
D.C., in the summer for two years in a row.

Pennie and Tim had been dating since her freshman year, and she couldn't imagine her daily life without him. In spite of their serious relationship, they had both remained diligent about school, sports, extracurricular activities, and maintaining their grades. Pennie had volunteered with children at a homeless shelter since freshman year, and had created and run a toy drive for them every Christmas. She loved kids and they all loved her. She never missed a Saturday at the shelter.

She had watched Tim throw his mortarboard in the air with the rest of his class, with a sadness she had hidden well. They both knew what it meant. They had made the decision when he'd been accepted in early admissions at Stanford. They had considered it carefully, and felt it was the right choice for both of them. They wanted to be sensible, neither of them wanted a long-distance relationship and the hardships it entailed, pining for each other, only seeing each other at Thanksgiving, Christmas, and spring break, and probably disappointing each other at some point. They had promised that they would break up after Tim's graduation. He was going to spend the summer traveling in China, which was his parents' graduation gift to him, and she was going to be a junior counselor at the summer camp she had attended for five years. It would be her first summer as a junior counselor. In August, Tim would be off to Stanford, and she'd be back at their old school, without him, missing him, applying to college, and doing her volunteer work.

They had made their agreement and stuck to it. They had broken up three days before, and were both leaving for the summer in two weeks. They didn't want to drag it out in the end. They had cried like children when they left each other, but true to their word, they hadn't called, texted, or spoken to each other for the past three days. It was much harder than she'd expected. They wanted to stay friends, but for now, they were trying to get used to being apart. She felt as though her heart had been torn in half as he drove away from her house after he'd come to say goodbye. They had been inseparable for the past three years, and now suddenly, she was on her own. He was not only her boyfriend, but her confidant and best friend. It was so much to lose, letting him go was the hardest and most adult thing she'd ever done.

Pennie was a beautiful green-eyed blonde, with long, straight, wheat-colored hair, slim legs that never seemed to end, a striking figure, full breasts, and a waist Tim could almost circle with both hands. She looked like the proverbial girl next door, or the girl everyone wished lived next door. Tim had spotted her on her first day at their school, at the beginning of her freshman year and his sophomore year. By Christmas, they were already in love. They made love for the first time a month after she turned fifteen, and were responsible about it. They rarely took any chances, although they had a few times, but nothing had happened.

Tim was as handsome as she was pretty. He was tall, athletic, with broad shoulders and a chiseled face that made him look manly for his age. His blond hair was the same color as hers, and he had deep blue eyes. People often commented that they looked like brother and sister. Tim was an only child, adored by his parents. Pennie had twin brothers six years younger than she, who annoyed her much of the time. She loved them but they invaded her space, took her things and never returned them, and teased her at every opportunity. Seth was slightly more sensitive, and Mark always landed with both feet in his plate on every subject. He was tactless in the extreme. Tim thought they were funny.

Pennie and Tim had talked about marriage a few times in the past few years, what that would be like, whether or not they could keep their relationship alive long enough, until they grew up. But once college became a reality, they both realized that marriage wouldn't be possible. After his parents' constant protection and scrutiny, he was ready to spread his wings and was looking forward to college. He thought that Pennie deserved the same freedom, to grow wings of her own. She had thought about applying to Stanford to be near him, but her parents didn't want her going that far from home. They wanted her to apply to the eastern Ivy League colleges, which had always been her goal too. Her grades were as high as Tim's, and with her board scores and volunteer work, she had a good chance of getting in.

Tim wanted to be an econ major, and go to business school later. Pennie hadn't discovered her passion yet. She was strong in English, writing, and history. She was thinking about a teaching degree, or a major in English literature. Her path wasn't as clear as Tim's. His father was an investment banker in New York, and Tim wanted to work in finance too. His mother did extensive charity work and headed up several committees.

Marriage was light-years away for Tim and Pennie, and they knew it. They didn't delude themselves about that anymore. They had years ahead of them to find jobs, pursue careers, and go where life and their respective opportunities led them. Tim's parents were more conservative and older than Pennie's. They both came from reserved eastern families. They had worried that Tim and Pennie's relationship would distract him and affect his grades. But Tim had managed all his responsibilities and the relationship well. Pennie's parents were a little younger and somewhat more free-form. Pennie's mother, Eileen, knew that they had been sleeping together for two and a half years. Pennie had told her. She had always been honest and open with her mother. Tim's parents hoped they weren't sexually involved and didn't ask. His father had warned him about not getting anyone pregnant and ruining his life. The conversation had been stilted and awkward, since he and his father both knew that the "anyone" they were talking about was Pennie. But he hadn't gotten "anyone" pregnant, and his parents were relieved that he was going away to college, before his relationship with Pennie got even more serious. He had told them that they were planning to break up before he left for Stanford, which they thought was a wise decision. They liked her, and conceded that she was a nice girl, and very bright, but they made it obvious that they thought the relationship was potentially dangerous for their son, and too serious for young people their age. It worried them that the romance went on for several years. They occasionally advised him to date other girls, which Tim ignored. But inevitably he would now, at Stanford.

When Pennie turned fifteen, her mother had told her the truth about her own marriage. Eileen and Paul had met and started dating during her senior year at Boston College. Paul was at Harvard Business School then, headed for Wall Street, and eventually wanted to become an entrepreneur. He had big dreams. They both did. Immediately after graduation, Eileen got a job as an editorial assistant at a publishing house in New York, which had always been her dream.

She had three roommates in Greenwich Village, and loved her job. Once she had graduated and moved to New York, her relationship with Paul became too complicated with him in Cambridge and her in New York, and it petered out. They'd enjoyed dating, but they weren't madly in love. Eileen was more excited about starting her career than pursuing the relationship with Paul.

She'd been in her job for a few months when Eileen figured out that she was pregnant. She'd been in denial and misread all the signs. She took the train to Boston one weekend to tell Paul, not sure what to do next. The news hit both of them like a bomb. They told their parents, who were horrified. Hers were devastated, and his were outraged. Paul made his own decision to do what he felt was the right thing. Against his parents' wishes, he left business school, and he and Eileen got married at City Hall in New York. He got a job at an ad agency in the city and they rented a small, depressing, inexpensive apartment they could afford in Queens. Eileen stayed on at the publishing house until a week before Pennie was born. They were twenty-two and twenty-four when they got married, and Pennie's arrival changed everything. All their dreams went right out the window. Their families treated them like criminals or outcasts. Eileen's mother, who had been bitter and disappointed all her life, with a difficult marriage, told Eileen regularly how she had disgraced them. Neither family offered to help them and felt they deserved the hardships they were facing on their own.

Paul and Eileen discovered that childcare was expensive, compared to the low salary Eileen had been making in publishing, and it made more sense financially for her to stay home and take care of Pennie. Her dreams of a career in publishing ended with Pennie's birth. Instead she became a housewife with a baby. She loved Pennie, but missed her job and friends. Eventually, they moved out of the city. Paul didn't love his job, but he did well at it. He was a responsible young man, and worked hard to support his wife and daughter. It was never a great love affair, and the responsibilities of marriage made it harder, but they were both determined to make the best of it. Paul had a knack for advertising, whether he liked his job or not, and Eileen took on some freelance editing when she had the chance, but most of the time she was busy keeping house and with the baby. Her mother never let her forget that she had given up her dreams to get married because she was pregnant. She seemed to want Eileen to be as unhappy as she was.

In spite of the challenges they faced, with unsupportive families and a baby to take care of, Paul and Eileen made it work. They never blamed each other overtly for what had happened, but it was clear to Pennie as she grew up that the way their lives had turned out wasn't what either of them had wanted, and they had paid a high price for their mistake. At fifteen, Pennie fully understood that her birth had severely impacted her parents' lives and made them shelve their dreams forever.

Another "mistake" when Pennie was six had brought not one more unexpected child into their lives, but twins. When Pennie was ten and her brothers four, in a major step up, the family had moved to the handsome Colonial house in Greenwich where they lived now, with big sunny bedrooms, a front garden, and a backyard. Eileen had never gone back to work, and with the arrival of the twins, she had no time even for the freelance editing she enjoyed. She had three children to take care of, and Paul had a family of five to support. He had managed it for eighteen years now, and done extremely well at the ad agency, but his life had turned out very differently from what he'd hoped. He sometimes thought that if he hadn't done the honorable thing and married Eileen, he might have been a successful entrepreneur by now. It had been his fondest hope growing up and all through college. That hope had vanished in the mists of adulthood, forced on them by an unwanted pregnancy.

Despite their rocky beginning, and their respective parents' predictions that the marriage wouldn't last because of how it started, Paul and Eileen had forged a relationship of companionship and mutual respect. Eileen appreciated how hard Paul worked, and he thought her an excellent, devoted mother. They were both good parents, and loved their kids, whether planned or not. Eileen had had her tubes tied after the twins were born, so it wouldn't happen again. She and Paul led a stable, predictable life that satisfied both of them.

Paul had stayed at the same ad agency, and was very well paid after rising from senior account executive to management. He provided them with a good life. He tried not to look back at what might have been, although it still irked him not to be an entrepreneur running his own business, and being an employee instead. Eileen still missed her brief career in publishing too, and what it could have turned into if she hadn't been obliged to quit.

At thirty-nine, Eileen was facing her fortieth birthday with dread, and feeling that she hadn't accomplished anything, except carpooling and raising three children, with a man who had married her out of duty more than love. There was no spirit of romance between them, and there never had been, but considering how awkwardly their marriage had started, it seemed to be working out surprisingly well. Eileen was grateful that Paul was a good husband and father and provided well for them. She enjoyed their life in Greenwich, and the friends they saw had children the same age. She loved their house. They had made the marriage work but she didn't want the same fate for her daughter. She wanted much more for Pennie, a career she was passionate about and a man she loved, who loved her. Eileen warned her that she would ruin her life if she ever got pregnant and had to get married. She made it clear that a life like hers was to be avoided at all cost, no matter how comfortable it looked now. She wanted Pennie to venture into the world and follow her dreams when she left for college, and not give them up for anyone. She was relieved that Pennie and Tim had been sensible and decided to break up. Their love affair had been too serious for too long for people so young, and she could tell that Pennie was tired of high school, and eager to grow up. Particularly now, knowing that Tim wouldn't be around. And once she got to college, and after, new doors would open to her that Pennie couldn't even imagine yet.

"Who knows, you and Tim might find your way back to each other years from now, after you've established your lives," she said to Pennie to console her the morning after they broke up.

"I don't think so, Mom," Pennie said sadly. "That's a long way off." Tim had big plans. He wanted to work in London for a year or two after college, or maybe Beijing or Hong Kong. He had been studying Mandarin for two years, which his father had told him might be useful for him in business. Pennie wanted to stay closer to home and live in New York. But she felt ready to be an adult now. She was tired of being treated as a child. Her three-year relationship with Tim had made her more mature than many of her peers. They were hoping to go to party schools, and have fun in college.

Pennie wanted more, just as her mother had so long ago. Eileen hoped Pennie wouldn't want to marry too young, and would give herself a chance for a real career and an exciting job before she settled down. Paul felt the same, and regularly told his daughter not to think about getting married until she was at least thirty, and to put off marriage and children for as long as she could. He always made marriage sound like a trap to be avoided. Pennie had gotten the message loud and clear. The underlying advice from both her parents was that trading career for family was not a good thing, a very bad idea, and an unwanted pregnancy would end her dreams forever. She hated the way they thought about it, and it was hard knowing that she was the cause of their disappointment, but she understood why. She had fully realized that their attitude, and their regret about the way their own marriage had started, was an antidote to love. Their relationship was solid but never tender, loving, or warm. She had seen some of her friends' parents look at each other with love and deep appreciation, a kind of affection that had never existed in her home. She was sure her parents loved each other, but they weren't *in* love, and she wondered if they ever had been. If so, it had not been in a long time. She couldn't remember her parents ever seeming passionate about each other, or really happy. They had long since accepted the limitations of their relationship and didn't expect more. They had settled for what they had. She wanted a great deal more than that from the man she loved.

Pennie thought that if she and Tim had been older, they might have had a solid basis for marriage one day. But that wouldn't happen now. It was over, after three happy, loving years with him. She knew she had to give up that dream, but it was so hard to do. Breaking up with Tim was the first big loss of her life. The pain was almost physical. She felt sick for the first few days after they broke up. And even sicker the week after.

"Did he dump you?" her brother Mark asked her, with his usual eleven-year-old lack of tact, when he noticed that Tim wasn't around. Normally he saw Tim with Pennie every day.

"Of course not, stupid. They're going to get married after college, like Mom and Dad," Seth answered for her. Pennie left the breakfast table, feeling violently sick. She didn't have the heart to tell her brothers they had broken up, or even her friends just yet. It was too painful to explain, even if it was the right thing to do and made sense for both of them, and they had planned it for months. But that didn't make it any easier.

She couldn't wait to leave for her summer job at camp, just to get away from all of them. The twins were going to be at the same camp in Vermont, but in the boys' division where she wouldn't see them very often, and she'd be busy with the girls she was assigned. She'd be sleeping in a cabin with six or eight of them, and would be too busy to think. She couldn't stand the look of sympathy in her mother's eyes now. Eileen hated to see her daughter's sadness, but there was nothing she could do about it. She knew it was part of growing up. Losing her first love was a rite of passage she would have to go through, just like Eileen had had to grow up at twenty-two, when she married Paul, and they had a baby five months later. She had told Pennie hundreds of times that she had been a colicky baby, and cried all the time, and Eileen did too. The early years of their marriage had been difficult, with too little money and responsibilities neither of them was ready for. She wanted Pennie to hear it so she wouldn't make the same mistakes. Pennie had heard it all a thousand times from both of her parents.

Eileen had been wrestling with the idea of her fortieth birthday for months. It depressed her profoundly. Forty had always sounded old to her and now she was almost there. It was middle-aged. She was halfway through her life, and what had she accomplished? Nothing much. Raising kids seemed so insignificant compared to what she could have done. She might have been a senior editor by now, working with important authors in the literary world, contributing to their work. She enjoyed cooking and the casual dinners they gave for friends occasionally. But what was that? Being able to cook a decent meal? Friends often called for her recipes, but in her mind cooking didn't take much skill. Paul loved what she cooked for them, although he was rarely home for dinner during the week. Part of his job was taking the important clients out for dinner, and wooing new ones. He regularly ate at some of the best restaurants in New York, and would get back to Greenwich on one of the last trains, or stay in a hotel in the city if it got too late. When their kids were busy, they went out for dinner on weekends, frequently with friends, which they both preferred. Alone, they often ran out of things to talk about halfway through the meal. After he'd told her about his latest accounts, and she'd filled him in on the kids' activities or problems, there wasn't much to say.

Eileen was already sad thinking about Pennie leaving for college in a year. Fortunately, the twins had another seven years at home. The time after that stretched ahead of her like a wasteland, with nothing to do. She'd been out of the workforce for too long to get a job now, and she had too little experience. She'd only worked briefly at twenty-two, and never since. She was practical, extremely well organized, and ran a smooth home, but none of that translated into a career at forty. She felt like a boring person, and when Paul had her join him for dinner with clients in the city, she felt over-the-hill, unattractive, and out of the loop. She tried to keep well informed, and read as much as she could when she had time, which wasn't often with twin eleven-year-old boys. When she picked up a book to read the current bestselling novel at night in bed, she was usually sound asleep by the second page.

She had tried to explain how she felt to Jane Ridley, her closest friend, who told her she should have an affair. It would make her feel young again. Jane had had several, and insisted it had kept her marriage alive. She was two years older than Eileen and had no children. She played bridge a lot, and shopped. They had met on a charity committee and had known each other for years. Their lives were different so they didn't see each other often, but they spoke on the phone. Jane was married to an older man who had children her age. He was generous with her.

"That's a little radical, don't you think?" Eileen answered with a rueful smile, about having an affair.

"Lots of women do it," Jane said breezily, and Eileen laughed.

"What? The tennis instructor at the club, or the golf pro? That seems like such a cliché, it's pathetic. It's not for me."

"Maybe, but it might be fun. Or you could get your eyes done, or your boobs lifted. If you're feeling old, there are remedies for that." Eileen didn't want to ask her which options Jane had employed to feel younger. But she felt like a drudge compared to Jane and some of the other women they knew. Most of the women in Greenwich seemed to fall into two categories, either the boring, domestic women like Eileen, or the jazzier ones, getting plastic surgery and having affairs, which seemed depressing to her, and anything but satisfying.

"Besides, I don't want to cheat on Paul. It makes me feel sick when I think about it. We love each other in our own way. Paul isn't demonstrative or affectionate, but I know he loves me. We've been together for almost eighteen years, and we dated before that." And they cared enough to be faithful at least, even if their marriage wasn't perfect.

"How do you know he doesn't cheat on you, or *do* you know?" A lot of men they knew cheated while their wives turned a blind eye. They took their revenge out on their husbands' credit cards, a system which seemed to work for both parties. They each got a reward. The cuckolded wife got a new wardrobe and whatever else she wanted, and the husband got a new pretty girl to play with, and got laid two or three times a day, or more often than his wife wanted after years of marriage. It was hard to keep relationships fresh and desire alive in their everyday routines.

"If you don't want the golf pro at the club, then I think some plastic surgery is in order. Maybe some fillers or laser treatments," Jane suggested. She got Botox shots regularly and fillers, and she looked great.

"Are you telling me I look old?" Eileen was horrified.

"No, not at all. You don't look your age, but you're telling me you *feel* old. That's a bad place to be. Pretty soon you convince everyone that it's true, including yourself. You need to get out more," Jane volunteered, "without Paul. You need to flirt and feel like a woman again." Eileen laughed and shook her head. It sounded like work to her, and she was comfortable as she was. She wasn't eager to make a fool of herself at her age. "When was the last time you bought sexy underwear? I mean *really* sexy!"

"When Paul stopped noticing it, and I realized he didn't care. He's never around when I get dressed, and I'm already in bed by the time he gets home. Sexy underwear would be a waste of money," Eileen said matter-of-factly. It didn't worry her. She was used to it. Their time together and their marriage centered mostly around their kids. Their sex life was adequate but not extraordinary.

"Maybe you should rethink some of that," Jane said seriously. "The boys will be gone before you know it, and then you're going to be staring at each other with nothing left to say. You're not over-the-hill, Eileen. Forty is not the end of life as we know it. It's not the end of the world. And you and Paul will have more time to yourselves when Pennie goes to college next year." Eileen nodded, unconvinced by what her friend was saying. She didn't feel sexy anymore, or womanly, or attractive to her husband. They still made love, but not often. They were both busy on weekends, with kids or doing chores, and during the week Paul spent long days in the city, and usually came home late. She used to join him more for dinner with clients in the city, but she hadn't done that in months, and he hadn't asked. He said he had no exciting clients at the moment, and told her she'd be bored, so she hadn't bothered. She couldn't remember the last time she'd been to New York. It was easier to stay in Greenwich, where she could run around in jeans or leggings, and didn't have to wear makeup or get dressed up. She hadn't worn high heels in months. She had given most of them to her daughter, who was thrilled.

Eileen was still a pretty woman, and Pennie looked a lot like her. She had been a knockout in her youth, but with time, the realities of her life, and a lukewarm marriage, she didn't really care how she looked anymore, and it showed. She didn't make the extra effort to get dressed up or wear makeup or do her hair. Paul never commented or seemed to notice what she wore or how she looked. Compliments had never been his strong suit, although he was better about it when they were dating. Now being together was like wearing an old comfortable pair of shoes, for both of them.

Paul always looked polished and well dressed when he went to work, but made as little effort as she did at home on weekends. He was still handsome, and women found him attractive. He tried harder with strangers, and Eileen was surprised sometimes by how charming and interesting, and even funny, he could be when talking with other women, but he went home with her.

The week before she was due to leave for camp, still missing Tim acutely, Pennie thought she had food poisoning or the flu. She threw up violently all morning, but felt better in the afternoon, and then suddenly something occurred to her that she hadn't thought of before. Her periods had always been irregular, but more so in the last two months. They had come and gone in a day with some minor spotting. It seemed like a ridiculous idea that something might have happened, and she wondered if she was clutching at straws, trying to hang on to Tim now that she realized how painful it was to let him go.

Feeling slightly foolish, she went to the drugstore and bought a pregnancy test. She'd done it before the few times they'd been worried, and she'd never been pregnant despite some scares. She vaguely remembered that they'd had unprotected sex once a few months before. She couldn't even remember when, it seemed so long ago, and nothing had come of it. She got her period on time afterwards, even if it was short.

She had the test in her purse when she got home. Her mother was out taking the boys to get the last of what they needed for camp. Pennie went upstairs to her bathroom, and her hands were shaking when she took the test out of the box. For an insane moment, she hoped that she might be pregnant. She didn't want it to be over with Tim. She wanted some part of him to stay with her forever, even though she knew she was in no way prepared or ready to have a child. It would ruin her life, just as it had her mother's, even more so since she was five years younger than her mother had been when she'd had Pennie. A baby at seventeen would have been a disaster in her life. She couldn't do it.

She locked the door of her bathroom, and did the test, waited the brief time for it to process, and closed her eyes for a minute before she looked. She wouldn't allow herself to wish for a positive result, no matter how much she loved him. Then she opened her eyes and stared at the test stick for a long time. It wasn't possible. It couldn't be right. She couldn't be pregnant now that they had broken up. She wanted to be an adult. She was tired of being discounted as too young for everything, but this wasn't how she wanted to demonstrate her adulthood. But want it or not, the test result was clear. She was pregnant.

Her eyes filled with tears as she put the used test back in the box and put it in her purse. She sat down on the toilet cover and stared into space. Had she wished this into being? Had she done it on purpose, subconsciously? However it had happened, it was real and she had to deal with it.

Tears slid down her cheeks as she tried to figure out what to do. She had to call Tim and tell him. What was she going to tell her parents? How was Tim going to react? Would he fall in love with her all over again, or would he be furious? They were too young to have a baby. He was leaving for China in a week and for Stanford in August. She felt a wave of panic wash over her. It was the most terrifying thing that had ever happened to her. There would be no easy way out of it for either of them. In a sudden rush, she wanted to give up her new claim to adulthood, and run back to her childhood. This wasn't how she wanted to become a grown-up. She wasn't ready for a baby, or to become a mother. All she wanted to do was fly into Tim's arms and hide. But there was no hiding from this now.

Pennie sat locked in her bathroom for an hour, trying to think about what she had to do. She couldn't call their family doctor. She was sure he would tell her parents. She had gone to Planned Parenthood for birth control advice before. But first she wanted to call Tim. He would know what to do. She had to break the silence they had agreed on. She sent him a text asking him where he was. He responded within minutes, and said he was at home, packing for the trip to China, and asked her how she was. The text was friendly but not loving.

"I need to talk to you. Can you meet me for coffee?" she texted back.

"Why? We said we wouldn't do that," he reminded her. "I'm meeting my parents for dinner."

"Can I see you before, just for a few minutes?"

"I don't think we should. It will upset us both." But not nearly as much as the news she had to tell him. She wasn't even sure how pregnant she was. But if it was due to their one slip a few months before, she would be somewhere around three or four months pregnant.

"I'll make it short. It's important."

"Something wrong? Are you okay?"

She didn't answer the question. She didn't want to lie. "Where should I meet you?"

He suggested their favorite coffee shop. He didn't think she should come to his house, they might lose their resolve. He missed her as much as she missed him, and he didn't trust himself alone with her. If she was going to beg him not to break up with her, he didn't want to be in the midst of a painful, tearful scene when his parents got home.

They agreed to meet half an hour later, and he was there when she arrived. He looked as handsome as ever, and couldn't suppress a smile when he saw her. She was so damn beautiful and he still loved her so much. His heart felt tight in his chest when she sat down, wearing sandals and pink shorts with a white T-shirt, and no makeup, her long blond hair hanging down her back. He was wearing jeans, a blue shirt, and loafers. He could see that she was nervous. She had the test in her purse in case he didn't believe her.

"What's up?" Seeing him almost took her breath away.

"I just found out something you ought to know," she said, trying to sound calmer than she felt, and not cry.

"Like what? Is something wrong? Are you sick?" He was worried and she shook her head as tears crept into her eyes in spite of her efforts not to let them.

She looked him in the eye, and spoke in a soft voice. "I'm pregnant, Tim. I think it may have been that time three or four months ago when we forgot to buy condoms." A fatal oversight, and they decided to make love anyway and told themselves nothing would happen "just once." The pill had made her sick when she tried it, and they preferred condoms.

"Oh my God. You can't be." He sounded choked.

"I am. I just did a test. What are we going to do?"

"Our parents will kill us," he said, feeling like a child faced with her devastating news. He had no ambiguous feelings about it. It was the worst thing that had ever happened to them, worse than breaking up. "We can't have a baby now. I'm leaving for Beijing next week, and Stanford in August."

"I know."

"Can you find out how pregnant you are?" She nodded.

"I'll see a doctor at Planned Parenthood."

"We have to figure this out," he said, and stood up. He wanted to be alone to digest what she had just told him. He didn't want to do it with her right there. "How could we be so stupid?" He had tears in his eyes too. "I love you," he said miserably, "but we're not ready for this, either of us. I don't want to leave you now, but I can't cancel the trip. My parents already paid for it." And there were four boys from his class going with him. The trip had been planned for months and his parents would have a fit if he didn't go. "Go to the doctor tomorrow. Do you want me to go with you?" he offered, and felt sorry for her, and for himself too.

She shook her head bravely and looked up at him as she stood up. "I'll call you after I see the doctor."

They walked out of the coffee shop together without saying a word, each of them lost in their own thoughts and fears. They could feel their world crashing around them. They felt like they'd been shot out of a cannon into an adult world neither of them was prepared for. Tim walked her to her car and kissed her cheek as she got in, but he didn't put his arms around her. He looked as if he was afraid to touch her now. As she drove away, she saw him standing there with tears rolling down his cheeks, and she was crying too.

Chapter 2

The doctor Pennie saw at Planned Parenthood the next morning told her that she was fourteen weeks pregnant. He explained to her that according to Connecticut law, an abortion could be performed until "viability," as late as twenty-four to twenty-eight weeks, but that he personally did not agree, and wouldn't perform an abortion after fourteen weeks. So if she wanted an abortion, she'd have to see another doctor. She heard the heartbeat on the fetal monitor, and she saw the baby on the sonogram screen. Everything looked normal, except for the fact that she was seventeen, Tim was eighteen, he was leaving for college soon, and they weren't married. She called Tim as soon as she left the clinic, with a bottle of prenatal vitamins in her purse. The doctor had been very matter-of-fact. Pennie had lied and said she was eighteen, and she and her boyfriend were engaged, as though it mattered.

She told Tim the news, and they agreed to meet again at a park where they went for walks sometimes. Both of their homes felt off-limits now. At the park, they were on neutral ground.

"What do you want to do?" he asked her as they sat on a bench and stared at the ducks in the pond. There were children scattering food for them, with their mothers hovering nearby.

"I don't know. We don't have a lot of options," Pennie said softly. "The doctor I saw won't do an abortion, as pregnant as I am now. And seeing the baby on the sonogram, I couldn't have gotten rid of it anyway." He nodded. He had thought about it all night. He could think of only one solution that was acceptable to him.

"We have to get married, Pen. You can't do this alone, and I don't want you to. If you're three months pregnant, it must be due around Christmas. I'd like to do the first term at Stanford, and then I'll apply for a transfer to Connecticut College. I could go to school here, and my parents will help us out." He had planned it all the night before, unable to sleep.

"I can't let you do that. You've wanted to go to Stanford for as long as I've known you. I'm not going to ruin your life. That's what happened to my parents, and they were older than we are. I don't think they've ever been really happy. They *had* to get married. I won't do that to you." She felt lifeless as she said it, but she loved him too much to rob him of his dreams.

"And what would you do? Drop out of school? Not even finish high school?" He sounded angry at her for the first time, and at himself for their stupidity. One foolish moment was about to ruin both their lives. "It's our baby. We have to step up to the plate. We both have to go to school. We'll just have to ask our parents to help us. I can get a part-time job and work at night." His mind was racing. "We can get married now. I'll cancel the trip to China, then I can stay with you till August. Just as I said, I'll do the one term at Stanford, and transfer

26

back here." It was the only plan he'd been able to come up with the night before, if she decided to keep the baby. And now she had no choice. "Is it healthy? Does it look okay?"

"It looked fine," she said somberly. This was not a happy event in her life. She felt like she was trapping him into marriage and she didn't want to do that to him, and steal his future. She was not going to blow his dreams to smithereens, even if he was willing. And her own dreams were dead now.

"Did they tell you the sex?" She shook her head. He was curious about their baby.

"They did a bunch of blood tests which will tell us." He nodded. It was suddenly all too real. They weren't breaking up after all, they were getting married and having a baby.

"I'm not going to marry you, Tim, it's not fair. This isn't your fault. It's my fault too. Don't cancel the trip to China. I'll see you when you get back. I have to go to camp anyway." She had signed a contract for the summer job. And she'd promised.

"You can't go now," he said, frowning.

"Yes, I can. I have to. I can't cancel at the last minute." It was her first real summer job, and she needed it for her college application, although she probably wouldn't go to college now.

"Won't it show by the end of the summer?" he asked innocently.

"I don't know. Maybe not. I can hide it and wear baggy clothes and tell them I'm getting fat. I don't know if they'll let me come back to school if I'm pregnant. I can go to public school this year if I have to." She had thought of that too. The consequences were already far-reaching. And she knew her parents would be furious if she had to leave her school.

"This is so fucked up, and not how it should be," he said as he ran a hand through his hair and stared at her. "I'm sorry, Pennie."

"Me too. We'll figure it out. When are you going to tell your parents?"

"Tonight. You should too. They have a right to know what's going on. And we need their help. I don't think I should go to China, but if you're going to camp anyway. . . ." His voice trailed off. There was so much to consider. And at Christmas, they would be parents, whether married or not.

They sat on the bench for a long time, and then walked for a while. They both had a difficult task to face that night. Pennie was dreading telling her parents, and so was Tim with his. Their lives had been shattered in a single instant. Their parents had warned them for three years not to let something like this happen and now it had.

"I don't think you should transfer back here," she said generously. "If we stay together, after the baby is born, maybe I could move to California with the baby." It was a whole different scenario from what he'd planned for his college life. Instead of spreading his wings, she had clipped them. He was trapped.

After she left him, Pennie drove home thinking about what she would tell her parents, trying to guess what they would say. It wasn't going to be easy for her or for them, or for Tim and his parents.

Her mother had just come home with the boys when Pennie walked in. Eileen told her that her father was having dinner in the city. Pennie knew she'd have to wait until he got back, which was better anyway, since Seth and Mark would be in bed by then, and hopefully asleep.

She went upstairs and lay down on her bed, thinking about Tim and their baby. She could just begin to understand now how her parents must have felt when they found out about her, and for the first time she felt truly sorry for them. Almost as sorry as she did for Tim, and herself. She stayed in her room and skipped dinner that night. She told her mother she'd had something to eat with friends, and Eileen was glad she had gone out for a while. She had been moping around the house since she and Tim had broken up. Meeting up with her friends was a good sign. In a week, she'd be at camp, too busy to think about him.

Pennie was in her room when she heard her father come in. The front door slammed and the boys had gone to bed an hour before. She peeked out and saw her parents come up the stairs, talking. If he'd had dinner with clients, she knew he would have had a few drinks, which might help. She had been rehearsing what she had to say all evening. She waited until they got to their bedroom, knocked on the door, and walked in two minutes later.

"Hi, can I talk to you for a few minutes?" she said, as her father put an arm around her and gave her a hug.

"How's my girl? What did you do today?" . . . *Had a sonogram . . . saw my baby . . . went for a walk in the park with Tim . . .* she thought, as she gave him a wintry smile. Watching her, Eileen could already sense that something was wrong. Pennie looked serious, even more so than she had since she and Tim had broken up.

"Come on in," her mother invited her, and Pennie sat down nervously in a big comfortable chair, as her parents watched her.

"I need to talk to you," she said softly, as they approached. Her father still looked jovial, her mother was studying Pennie's face, looking for clues about what would come next.

Her mother sat down on a small settee, and her father in the chair facing hers. Neither of them was prepared for the bomb she dropped on them a minute later.

"I'm pregnant," she said in barely more than a whisper. This was harder than she'd thought it would be. For an instant they just sat and stared at her, too stunned to react.

"Oh my God," her father said in a shocked voice, looking at her as though she had turned into a snake or grown two more heads. "Shit, Pennie, how the hell did that happen? Didn't you two know enough to use condoms or take the pill or something? I assume it's Tim's," he said to her, and she nodded.

"Of course. We had a slip, I didn't know till yesterday. I just found out."

"Well, you know what you have to do about it. You have to get an abortion. You can't have a baby at your age," he said, as though there was no relevant opinion on the subject except his own. He looked panicked, and Eileen looked devastated. It took her back instantly to when it had happened to them. Paul hadn't left a second for her to speak since Pennie told them.

"I don't want an abortion, Dad. I'm more than three months pregnant. I saw a doctor today, and he won't do abortions after twelve or fourteen weeks. I saw it on the sonogram. It looks like a baby. I can't have an abortion, Dad."

"Does Tim know?" She nodded again. "What did he say?"

"He offered to marry me, right away. I'm not going to do that," she said quietly, and her mother thought she looked suddenly like a woman and not a child, as she listened to her. Pennie seemed different. Knowing about the baby had already changed her.

"What do you mean you're not going to do that?" her father asked, raising his voice.

"I'm not going to marry him, make him leave Stanford, give up all his plans and dreams, to be a husband and father at eighteen. That's not fair."

"Life isn't fair," Paul said angrily. "It was good enough for me, it's good enough for him. Why does he get to follow his dreams, while you ruin your life and have an illegitimate baby?"

"He's eighteen, Dad. You were twenty-four. You were in business school. He hasn't even gotten to college yet. And I'm not ready to be married with a baby either."

"You should have thought of that before you got into bed," her father said harshly. "If you won't have an abortion, you have no other choice except marriage."

"She has other choices," Eileen spoke up in a clear, strong voice. "Do you want to give the baby up, Pennie?" Tears filled Pennie's eyes, and she shook her head.

"No, I don't. I don't think I could do that. I don't think I could even have an abortion, after seeing the baby on the sonogram today. I guess I'll have to have it the way I am. I can stay in school till Christmas, if they let me, or go to another school where they would. And if you help me with someone to take care of the baby, I could stay here with you and go to community college a year from now, instead of the schools I was going to apply to." Bye, bye, Ivy League.

"So he gets to go to Stanford, and you go to a second-rate school and get saddled with a baby at eighteen, without a husband or the respectability of marriage. Why the hell should he get away with that? I didn't, and neither have a million other guys like me. If you play the game, you have to be willing to pay the price. If you're having a baby, you need to get married, even if you get divorced later. He owes you at least that. This is his fault too. He can't just waltz off, and you can't let him off the hook. I'm not going to let that happen," Paul said angrily. He was determined that Tim should pay the same price he had for his youthful mistakes.

"She doesn't have to get married if she doesn't want to," Eileen said firmly. She felt as though her own sins had been visited on her daughter. This was like a painful déjà vu of what had happened to them eighteen years before. But they didn't have to resolve it in the same way. "What do *you* want, Pennie? In a perfect world." But the world was no longer perfect, as Pennie had discovered abruptly the day before. Now it would never be perfect again. She would be doomed to a marriage like her parents', where they loved each other but not enough to forget that they'd been forced into marriage eighteen years before, or to forgive each other for it. She didn't want Tim to feel that way about her in twenty years.

"Maybe we could get married one day," Pennie said softly, "if we still want to. But I don't want a baby to be the only reason why we do. He'll hate me for it in the end." There was silence in the room. No one denied what she'd said, which spoke volumes about her parents.

"I don't hate your mother because we had to get married," Paul spoke calmly, "but it gave us a rough start." And just when Eileen had wanted to go back to work again, she had gotten pregnant with the twins, and wound up in bed for months. "But we've done fine. Your mother and I love each other," he said, without looking at Eileen. "You and Tim are young to get married. It's going to mean a lot of sacrifices for both of you, but I think you should. He needs to make some of those sacrifices too. Not just you." Paul was monumentally upset by her news.

"People don't get married because they're pregnant in this day and age," Eileen reminded both of them. "And I agree you're too young. It will change your whole life. I think you should give the baby up," she said, looking at her daughter with empathy, and thinking about her own experience. "Twenty-two was too young too, but it's a lot different from seventeen. A couple desperate for a child could give the baby a wonderful home, better than you two could. The chances of a marriage working out at your age are slim. It's hard enough when you're older. As teenagers, it's more than the two of you can cope with, or should have to." She was deeply sympathetic and felt sorry for both of them.

"Would you let me live here with the baby?" Pennie asked her with tears swimming in her eyes. "Even if we get married, if Tim goes to Stanford, I'll need a place to live." The tears spilled down her cheeks and her mother got up and went to put her arms around her. Pennie melted into her mother's embrace and sobbed. Paul watched them, feeling helpless. He still couldn't believe this had happened, and they had a grandchild on the way. He was forty-one years old, and not ready to be a grandfather yet. But more important, he was heartbroken for Pennie and that she had to face the burdens of marriage and motherhood so soon. He knew only too well what that was like.

"Of course you can live here," Eileen said, wiping the tears from her own eyes. She felt as though she had doomed her daughter by example with her own mistakes. "But I really think you should think about putting the baby up for adoption. Talk to Tim about it. I think he'd be relieved."

"I won't do that, Mom," Pennie said, certain of it. She wasn't going to give their baby away. She loved Tim too much to do that, and would love their baby too.

"They *have* to get married," Paul said, sounding angry again. They were a Greek chorus, telling Pennie what to do, neither of them with the answers she wanted. All she wanted was for them to be support-ive of her, and help her with the baby as a single mother at eighteen. They weren't prepared to do that yet, but Pennie hoped that eventu-ally they'd come around, without trying to force her to do things their way. This was her first major adult decision, and she knew that it had to be her own, and Tim's. Neither of them had been prepared for it, but ready or not, it was the hand they'd been dealt in a very grown-up, high-stakes game. Now they had to pay the price, or she did.

Tim's parents were more unified in their reaction, as they were in life. They had a good solid marriage, came from the same conserva-tive upper middle–class background, and shared the same values. Bill and Barbara Blake were both furious about what had happened. They blamed Pennie for it, accused her to Tim of trying to entrap him, and his father flatly forbade him to marry her because she was pregnant. Tim's mother wholeheartedly agreed.

"You can't marry her for that. What if she has a miscarriage two months later, then you're stuck with her. How do you even know she's pregnant? Maybe she's lying so you'll marry her." Bill Blake took nothing at face value. He had never liked how seriously in-volved Tim and Pennie were at their age. Bill and Barbara were both in their early fifties. They had had trouble conceiving Tim, and Bar-bara had been a virgin when they married. The idea of Tim having a child out of wedlock was horrifying to them. But they didn't want him getting married at eighteen either. Like Pennie's mother, they thought that giving the child up for adoption was the best idea, and suggested it to him, to his dismay.

They went around and around for two hours, and when Tim finally got to his room, his head was spinning. He didn't have the heart or energy to call Pennie as he'd promised. All he could do was send her a text that his parents wanted the six of them to meet the next day. They had insisted on it. They wanted to confront the Jacksons, and come to a reasonable decision.

Pennie told her parents after she heard from Tim, and they agreed to meet with the Blakes at six the next day at the Jacksons'. Paul said he would leave work early to be there and Eileen was going to drop Seth and Mark off at a neighbor's, so they could discuss the situation openly, without worrying about the twins.

Pennie was wearing a simple pale blue cotton dress when the Blakes rang their doorbell. Tim's parents looked dour when Eileen opened the door and they walked in. Tim came in right behind them, squeezed Pennie's hand, and they all went into the living room together. Paul offered Tim's parents a drink, which they refused. They didn't consider this a social call, but rather a conference at which to state their position, and save their son from what they now considered a scheming young woman, hell-bent on destroying his life. Nothing Tim had said in the past twenty-four hours had swayed them from that position. They had known Pennie for three years but had always been uneasy about the seriousness of the relationship. It was too intense for such young people.

All six of them sat down in the living room, looking uncomfortable. The Blakes stared at the Jacksons in silence for a minute. Paul spoke first.

"Our children have certainly gotten themselves into a mess," he said. Bill Blake nodded, and Eileen smiled at Barbara but got no response.

"I think we need to make our position clear here," Bill said. "We think it would be a disaster, a grave mistake, for them to get married at their age. They have their whole lives ahead of them. Tim is leaving for college soon and we want him to do that. Of course, we're willing to share in any expenses related to the . . . uh . . . ah, pregnancy, and a small amount of monthly support if she keeps it." They didn't want the idea of her keeping the baby to be financially appealing.

"This isn't about money," Paul said quickly, "it's about their future and the life of the child they irresponsibly conceived. A child needs two parents, and I feel strongly that they should get married." Paul made no bones about it. "They're young, but they took this on by taking a risk, and now they have to see it through." He glanced at Eileen and she looked away, wondering if he was going to tell them they'd gotten married because she was pregnant, but he didn't. The chill emanating from the Blakes did not elicit confessions.

"We will do everything to oppose it, if that's their decision. We'll pay for college for Tim, of course, if they don't get married. But we intend to withdraw all financial support if they do get married," Bill said harshly, which was the first Tim had heard of it, and he looked shocked at his father's words.

"Then they can live with us," Paul said somberly, "if that's the way you want to play it." The two men looked at each other, like two male lions ready to attack. Tim's mother intervened.

"We think that Pennie should give up the baby for adoption. It's really the best solution. Neither of them knows what they're getting into. They'll have other children one day with the partners they choose. Neither of them is prepared for this one. They're children themselves. Giving the baby up is the best possible decision, for the baby too." Eileen nodded.

"I agree," Eileen spoke up. "I think forcing them into marriage would be a mistake, and spoil their lives." Pennie and Tim exchanged a look as their parents spoke, and Tim interrupted.

"That's not what Pennie and I want, and we won't agree to it. I want to marry Pennie as soon as possible," he said clearly. "It's the right thing to do." Paul could suddenly remember feeling that way too. He had questioned ever since if it was the right decision, and there were times when he bitterly regretted it.

"And I won't," Pennie said, looking around the room at their parents. "I don't want to ruin Tim's life, or destroy his future. I'm going to have the baby, and live with my parents. And this isn't about money, as Dad said. I can defer college, and get a job to pay my expenses. I don't think putting the baby up for adoption is 'the best solution.' I think it's a terrible one. I love Tim, and our baby, and I won't do that." There was silence in the room for a moment. Tim smiled at her. Even her own panic over her future hadn't changed who she was, or the values she believed in. She was a responsible person, and willing to shoulder her responsibilities alone if she had to. She was adamant about not forcing Tim into marriage. "I think we should do what we were planning to do. Tim is going to China. I have a summer job. Tim will go to Stanford. And I'll have the baby in December, and we're *not* getting married." She looked stubbornly at Tim and he frowned.

"We can discuss it when I get back from China. I'm not leaving for Stanford unless we're married when I do. Maybe I can get married-student housing, and Pennie and the baby could come out in January. Otherwise, I'll transfer back here, whether she marries me or not." He sounded definite and Paul turned to his daughter with a look of fury.

"And you're just going to throw your life away like that? Give up college, maybe not finish high school, and not even get married? What kind of future do you think you're going to have that way? What do you think you're going to do? Work as a waitress for the rest of your life? And your mother and I can't bring up the baby for you. We have our own responsibilities."

"Then I'll take care of it by myself. But I'm not going to let Tim throw his life away."

"But you're willing to throw yours away? It just proves that you're both too immature to know what you're doing," Paul shouted at her.

"Which is precisely why we won't let the marriage take place," Bill said through clenched teeth.

"I'm eighteen, Dad. You can't stop me," Tim responded.

"No, but I can," Pennie said softly to Tim. "You can't make me marry you."

Paul rolled his eyes, stormed across the room to the bar, and poured himself a drink. While he did, Eileen spoke up.

"I hope you all appreciate the fact that however foolish they might have been for this to happen, we have brought up two responsible, decent, upstanding, loving young people. They are fully prepared to take on their responsibilities, and stand by each other, and have deep love and compassion for each other. Tim is willing to marry Pennie, in spite of the impact it would have on his future, and Pennie is refusing to let him do that, because she loves him. I think we have a lot to be proud of, instead of just telling them what we want them to do. In the end, this is their decision. It has to be. Even if they're young, we have no right to make that decision for them."

"Are you insane?" Paul said to her after taking a long swallow of his drink. "Do you want your daughter to have an illegitimate child because of a half-assed 'noble' decision she makes at seventeen, with stars in her eyes? Do you want her to end up even worse off than we are? We had to get married too," he reminded her, and informed the Blakes while he addressed his wife. "You never got to pursue the career you wanted to," he said to Eileen in a disparaging tone. "You've been a housewife for nearly eighteen years, bored out of your mind. And I never had the career I should have had because I had to leave Harvard Business School and take a job I've hated for eighteen years. That's what they're facing now. But they have no other choice. And Pennie making herself an uneducated social outcast out of misguided noble motives is not the answer here." His words weren't lost on the Blakes or his wife. They fully understood how bitter Paul was about his own forced marriage, but he wanted the same fate for Tim and Pennie. Marriage was the only solution he could see to minimize the damage if Pennie wouldn't give the baby up. Eileen was silent and looked stricken after he spoke. He had exposed their whole history to the Blakes.

"That's exactly what we *don't* want for our son, or your daughter, the scenario you just described," Bill Blake said more gently. "I hope they see sense eventually, before they do something even more foolish. And I'm very sorry Pennie has to go through this, but I think our wives are right, and if Pennie insists on having the baby, I hope she'll be willing to give it up. Unless she's willing to have an abortion, which they both say they don't want at this stage, they feel it's too late. And the doctor Pennie saw felt that way morally too."

"I won't have an abortion, and if I have it, I'm keeping it," Pennie said in a strong adult voice. She wasn't budging an inch.

"And if she doesn't keep it, I will," Tim spoke up. "She needs my consent to relinquish it for adoption. I checked, and I won't give it. This is my child too." Tim moved to sit next to Pennie on the couch, took her hand in his and squeezed it. "I know this is hard, but it's our decision. You love us, and we love you too," he said, looking at both sets of parents. "Pennie and I can think about it while I'm in China, and I hope she'll agree to marry me when I get back. That is the best solution, as I see it. It's an early start for us, but the right one in the circumstances." He looked long and hard at Pennie and she shook her head. "I'll get a job on weekends and after school, and support my own child. This is my responsibility," he said directly to his parents. It had been Paul's conclusion too, eighteen years before, and he still regretted it, but he believed it was the right thing to do. Paul had paid a high price for his decision, and if their dreams for their life together hadn't come true, they still had a beautiful daughter to show for it, and their two boys. If he hadn't married Eileen, they wouldn't have the twins, and he loved his children.

Tim stood up then, and looked at his parents. "I think we've said everything we had to say, for now." They stood up reluctantly, but knew he was right. The Jacksons followed the Blakes to the front door, and Tim hung back for a moment and spoke to Pennie in a whisper.

"You know I'm right. Let's get married in August when I get back."

"No," she answered in a single word, and then kissed him, and he kissed her back. "I love you. I'm not going to wreck your life. My parents are miserable," she whispered. "They don't admit it, but they are. I don't want that for us." It was obvious to all how bitter her father was.

"We won't be miserable, I promise. Sometimes people get married at our age and it works. We've had three years together, we know each other. This didn't happen on a casual date. And we're not your parents." Tim didn't like her father, but he liked her mother.

"You're crazy," she said, smiling at him. "I hope the baby is a boy and looks just like you. Then I'll have you with me forever and ever, whatever happens," she said, with eyes full of love.

"Maybe this was meant to be. And there are better ways to have me with you forever, like getting married. I'll talk to you before I leave. Be careful at camp. Did the doctor say you could do that?" She hadn't asked, but she was young and healthy and felt sure she could.

"Just have fun on your trip," she said.

"So much for our plans to break up." He smiled at her. He didn't think she had done it on purpose, at least not consciously, but maybe they both had. Maybe this was their destiny, and their way of ensuring they had to stay together.

Tim joined his parents outside, they were waiting in the car. A few minutes later they drove away. Bill and Barbara had politely said goodbye to Pennie's parents, and hoped they wouldn't wind up related to them forever. Barbara commented that Paul seemed like a bitter, angry man, and Eileen looked depressed, but they said nothing about Pennie, and Tim sat lost in thought all the way home. He was making his peace with the idea of marrying her, and having a baby. It wasn't what he had wanted, but he loved her. It gave new meaning to his trip to China. Maybe this was going to be his last fling before he became a married man. It was an overwhelming thought, but he was willing to face it with her, if she agreed to marry him. Given the circumstances, he hoped she would, despite what his parents thought. One thing was sure, at seventeen and eighteen, overnight, their wish had come true, they were adults.

Chapter 3

Pennie's parents tried to discuss the situation with her before she left for camp, and most of the time she refused. Her father wanted her to get married, and thought Tim should shoulder his responsibilities, as Paul himself had been forced to. And Tim was willing to do that. Eileen thought she should give the baby up.

Pennie saw Tim once before he left for Beijing. Things were different now between them. Life was forcing them together, whether they married or not. For the rest of their lives, they would share a child and have a bond to each other. Tim was trying to convince her to get married as soon as he got back. For now, his plans for China and Stanford still hadn't changed. He promised to come home and see her as often as he could during his first term at Stanford, in the last trimester of her pregnancy. And if he stayed there, he wanted her to come out with the baby and live with him. They had time to make the decision, since neither of them wanted an abortion. Pennie said she just couldn't, after seeing the sonogram. Whether they married or not, they were going to have a baby in December. They both still found it an astounding idea. They were going to be parents themselves in less than six months.

Pennie left for her job at camp two days after Tim left for China. He sent her occasional texts from his trip, but he had no service at all in some of the more remote areas he went to. She hoped he was having fun with his friends.

Her job as junior counselor was more demanding and taxing than she had expected. The ten-year-old girls she was assigned to were a handful. They never left her alone even for a minute, and one of them or another always had a stomachache, a headache, a splinter, a blister, a bee sting, or a cut finger. One of the girls was suspected of having a hot appendix and was rushed to the hospital with what turned out to be indigestion from too much candy sent by her grandmother. Pennie rode horseback with them, swam with them, played tennis and badminton with them, volleyball and softball. They went rowing, kayaking, and canoeing. She accompanied them to arts and crafts, where they made presents for their parents. She had a great time, but she fell into bed exhausted every night. They had campfires and sang songs, all of which Pennie knew from her time there as a camper. They made s'mores and toasted marshmallows and told ghost stories around the campfire at night. They went on hikes and camped out under the stars. They had tugs-of-war and relay races. She helped them write letters home once a week, tucked them in at night, and taught them the words to the camp song.

She had only seen her brothers a few times, but they were happy when she did. They thought it was funny that she was a junior counselor and teased her about it.

In the last week of July, they had a track meet. She'd been coaching the girls all week to get their speed up for the running events. She was a fast runner herself. It was exhausting but her little group did well with her coaching. Afterwards, she took a short break and happened to be standing at the end of the dock at twilight when a girl from another cabin wandered down the dock, tripped and fell into the water, hit her head on one of the pilings, and sank like a rock. Pennie dove in without hesitating for an instant, pulled her up from the bottom where she'd sunk rapidly, and one of the male counselors who saw it happen helped Pennie pull the girl onto the dock. She was unconscious, and the counselor worked on her for a moment, got the water out of her, and brought her back to consciousness. He checked her pupils and thought that she had a concussion. They called 911 and the local paramedics came immediately. The girl was crying when they took her away in an ambulance, with the head of the camp with her. The male counselor commended Pennie for her fast reaction, and the strenuous effort getting the unconscious girl onto the dock.

"You did all the hard work," Pennie said, smiling at him but still shaken by the experience, and the realization of how quickly things could go wrong. If they hadn't been there to save her, the girl would have drowned. And as she said it, she saw the counselor look at her strangely.

"Are you okay?" he asked her. She felt a terrible pain slice through her, and when she looked down to where he was staring, she saw that her shorts were drenched in blood and it was running down her legs onto the ground where they were standing.

"I . . . yes . . . I'm fine," she said with a look of panic and embarrassment, and rushed back to her cabin, leaving a trail of blood.

When she took her clothes off in the bathroom, there was blood everywhere. The girls had just gone to the dining hall, and a senior counselor appeared a few minutes later, sent by the male counselor she'd been talking to. It was obvious that something serious was happening to her. She was hemorrhaging, and the female counselor suspected what it was.

"Tell me the truth, Pennie," she said, trying to help Pennie stanch the blood with towels, which were instantly drenched dark red. "Are you pregnant?"

"Yes," she said in a weak voice. Between the pain and the bleeding she could hardly stand up. "Four months," she added. The counselor helped wrap Pennie in towels and a blanket, and a moment later, drove her to the hospital after telling another counselor where they were going. It had been a strenuous day, between the track meet, running after the kids all day, and pulling the drowning girl from the bottom of the lake onto the dock.

Pennie was in excruciating pain on the way to the hospital, and by the time they got there, she was having severe contractions and losing massive amounts of blood. There was no way to stop it, so they hooked her up with a transfusion immediately and whisked her into surgery, to deliver the dead baby. When she woke up they told her it was a boy. The doctor in charge said that she could easily have bled to death. She'd already had two more transfusions by then. She was sobbing later when she called her parents and told them. Her mother drove up to Vermont that night to be with her. Pennie was deathly white and still groggy from the anesthetic, and she cried as soon as she saw her mother.

"I didn't do it on purpose . . . I guess I overdid it . . . I'm so sad . . . I didn't want to lose it." She felt guilty as well as devastated.

"I know, baby, I know," her mother said as she held her, but it was a simpler solution to a problem which could have ruined her life and Tim's, even if it could have given them much joy. It felt like a tragedy to Pennie, knowing that a tiny life had been lost. It was the death of a hope, and the symbol of their young love, even if the circumstances had been wrong. But now there would be no painful decisions to make. Fate had decided for them.

She stayed in the hospital for three days until she was stronger, and Eileen stayed with her. Pennie had to rest for the next three weeks at home. After a discreet meeting with the director at the camp, they agreed to say that Pennie had suffered a burst appendix, and had to go home to recover. It was an event which had happened at camp before, and although the girls would be disappointed, it would cause no further comment. The only person other than the director who knew what happened was the counselor who had driven her to the hospital and saved her life by doing so. She had agreed with the director and Eileen to keep the matter entirely confidential.

Eileen picked Pennie's things up at camp before picking Pennie up from the hospital. The girls in her cabin had made her a big sign with daisies on it, wishing her a speedy recovery. They had given her a copy of *Madeline* from the camp library, the story of a little girl in Paris, in a convent boarding school, whose appendix had burst too. The girls in her cabin had all written messages in it to her.

Pennie was quiet and depressed when they left. She had managed

47

to text Tim in China and tell him what had happened. He was in Shanghai by then, and it was easier to reach him. He called her in the hospital, and they had both cried, but fate had decided their destiny and the baby's and spared them difficult decisions. He promised to see her in August when he got back. And now they could both move forward with their futures as they had planned them. He was off to college and she had to finish high school. She burst into tears when she saw her father, and he told her how sorry he was that she had to go through the ordeal she had, but he was grateful she had survived. She had a month to recuperate before her brothers came home from camp.

She didn't call her friends, and didn't want to see them. No one knew about the baby except Tim and his parents. He had let them know, and they didn't communicate with Pennie or her parents. They were just relieved that the problem had been solved. They wanted no further contact with any of the Jacksons, and felt as though their son had been spared from his own noble motives, and a marriage they were convinced would have been disastrous. Pennie was just as happy not to hear from them. Tim sent her several texts while she rested at home.

He only had two days in Greenwich when he got back, but he went for a long quiet walk with Pennie and they cried together for the dreams they had lost. The page had turned, and the next chapters of their lives remained to be written. Pennie had a busy year ahead of her, while applying to college.

It was an older and wiser Pennie who began her senior year of high school in September. She was quieter and more mature. It had been a summer of coming of age. She knew she would never be quite the same again. But growing up was like that. Her parents treated her as an adult now, and she knew she could never be a child again. She was a woman, with all the joy and sorrow that entailed.

The summer hadn't been an easy one for Paul and Eileen either. They'd had endless discussions and arguments over what they thought Pennie should do about the pregnancy. And more than she'd ever realized before, it had shown Eileen how bitter Paul still was about the sacrifices he had made when he married her because she was pregnant. In a way, through what happened to Pennie, they had relived it. And the revelations had shown Eileen the fissures and scars in their marriage. Although Paul loved her and their children, she saw now that he had never fully forgiven her for the circumstances which forced him into marriage, yet he had wanted Tim to do the same thing, and perhaps ruin his life too. He wanted Tim to suffer the same life sentence he had. And when Pennie lost the baby, they were left with the things that had been said, and the anger in Paul that had been smoldering for years, like a forest fire that had been contained, but never fully extinguished.

In September, Paul started meeting with more clients for dinner again, and he didn't include Eileen. The angry words of the summer had not been forgotten yet. She was busy anyway. Seth broke his arm during recess in the first week of school, when an older boy pushed him and he tripped and fell on the playground. And Mark, seeing what had happened to his brother, punched the eighth-grader in the face, broke his two front teeth, and got suspended for two weeks. Paul and Eileen had to go to school and listen to a lecture from the headmaster. They put Mark on restriction at home. They disapproved of the act of violence, but Paul thought it was noble of him to defend his brother, which Eileen didn't entirely agree with, so more arguments ensued between them. Since Seth had broken his right arm, and was right-handed, Eileen had to do everything for him.

In the first month of school, Pennie's grades had slipped, after what she'd been through, and Eileen had to prod her constantly to fill out her college applications. Pennie had to keep up her grades, scores, and volunteer work in order to get into the caliber of college she wanted. Eileen felt as though she was running from one child to the other with never a moment's rest in between, and she was worried about Pennie. In some ways, it was easier having Paul busier than before with his clients, which gave her more time with the children. But in another sense, he was never around when she needed him to subdue the boys or even drive them around on weekends, when she was trying to encourage Pennie to fill out her college applications and work on them with her. September was so insanely busy she hadn't had time to talk to her friend Jane in weeks either. She felt like she never sat down or had a free minute.

Pennie hadn't heard from Tim since he'd started school, and Eileen thought it was for the best. They needed to get on with their lives, and Tim was busy doing that, keeping up with his classes and making new friends. For now at least, his time with Pennie was over. Who knew if, years down the road, they might start things up again. But at least they hadn't been forced to get married and become parents in their teens.

* * *

Pennie still hadn't restarted her social life after the rigors of the summer, and Eileen noticed that she went to bed early, usually watching a movie or a TV series on her computer before she went to sleep. She had become solitary without Tim. The twins always went to bed early.

The house was quiet, while Eileen was reading in bed one night, waiting for Paul to get home. It was his third client dinner that week. She hardly saw him now, except on weekends, and then he often played golf or tennis with friends. And she was too busy to object.

He got home just after eleven that night, and when he came in, she could tell that he'd been drinking. He often ordered good French wines at client dinners, and enjoyed them as much as the clients did. He was in high spirits when he came in and saw her tucked in but still awake with the book in her hands. It was a book one of the mothers at school had given her about making the best of turning forty. So far, she wasn't convinced.

"You're still up?" He looked surprised.

"I was waiting for you." She smiled at him.

"Why? Checking up on me?" he said with an edge in his voice.

"No. Should I be? Did you have a nice time tonight?" she asked innocently, happy to see him.

"Very. New clients. From Australia. Those guys know how to have a good time," he said blithely. He bent down to kiss her then, on his way to get undressed, and she got a whiff of a distinctive woman's perfume, and looked up at him, surprised.

"Did your Australian clients have a woman with them?"

"What makes you ask?" He narrowed his eyes at her.

"I could smell a woman's perfume when you bent down to kiss me."

"For chrissake, Eileen. What is this? The Inquisition? Yes, they had a woman with them. One guy brought his wife. Is there anything else you want to know? Fingerprints? Shoe sizes? Blood types?" He was instantly nasty about it. Sometimes, when he drank too much, it gave him an edge, or he could even be quite mean and not remember it the next day. She rarely questioned him about where he went and who he saw. She didn't think she had to. Even if their marriage wasn't perfect, she trusted him and had no reason not to. She'd never been concerned about him, and didn't have a jealous nature. He never flirted with other women when they went out, although he was entertaining when he wanted to be, along with his natural good looks, and women were often attracted to him. But Eileen was sure he never pursued any of them.

He stormed off to the bathroom then and slammed the door. He was back five minutes later in his pajamas, slid into bed beside her, and she could still smell the perfume on him. She leaned over to kiss him, and got a strong whiff of it on his neck. It wasn't just on the clothes he'd worn to dinner, it was on his skin. She backed away and looked at him then, as though seeing him for the first time, and she felt like there was a stranger in bed with her.

"Should I be worried?" she asked him with an open, sincere look.

"Of course not. I sold myself into slavery eighteen years ago, didn't I?" He had a nasty look in his eyes when he said it, and the comment hurt. She wasn't sure if he'd intended it to, or if "in wine, there was truth."

"That's not a nice thing to say." Pennie's dilemma that summer had brought it all back to him in vivid color and all the feelings he'd had for years about being cheated of the right career, even though the one he had had served them well.

"We all make decisions in our lives, and then we have to live with them. That's what we did, isn't it?" he said to her. "We both gave up a lot when we got married," he said quietly, acknowledging her sacrifices too.

"Are you sorry?" She was brave enough to ask, and wondered if she was treading on a minefield, not sure what he'd say.

"Sometimes," he answered honestly. "Aren't you? Don't you wish sometimes that you hadn't gotten pregnant, had had the chance to prove yourself at work for a few years, and then fallen madly in love with someone who didn't have to marry you?" She had never asked herself those questions, but apparently, he had. She wondered if they were a recurring theme to him.

"Actually, I don't. We loved each other or we wouldn't have gotten married, pregnant or not. And as far as I know, we still do. I have no regrets, and I hope you don't either." She never let herself think about it. She loved their children, and the life he had given her.

"Oh, it's nice to fantasize sometimes," he said casually, "but that's all it is. It's what men do."

"Do you fantasize about your career or women?" she asked him bluntly, curious about it now. It was the first time he had admitted it to her. And his discontent had surfaced with Pennie's pregnancy.

"Maybe both. Sometimes I wonder what it would be like not to be *so* married. We are the poster children of suburban couples. You spend your life driving car pool and chasing kids. I spend my life commuting. There's not much room for us in all that." He sounded regretful as he said it, and looked wistfully at her. He would have liked to erase their past and didn't know how.

"Maybe we should make more time," she said thoughtfully, but the children kept her so busy, as his work did for him. "We could have a date night every week, and make more effort when we go out." Most of the time, she ran a comb through her long hair like her daughter's, wound it in a knot, put a sweater on with her jeans, and sometimes even wore running shoes when they went out to dinner, because they were so comfortable, and she knew he didn't care. He did the same. She hadn't bothered to dress up for him in years, maybe since the twins. Having three children, two of them boys the same age, ate up all her spare time. She didn't have a minute for herself anymore, and maybe not enough for him.

"I think we're fine the way we are," he said with a yawn, lay down with his back to her, and turned off the light as she stared at him. She could still smell the perfume. For the very first time, she wondered if he was cheating on her. She had never considered it seriously before. And what if he was? What if he fell in love with someone else? Would she care? It was a strange question to ask herself. She would care if he cheated on her. If he did, would she leave him or pretend she didn't know, as some women did? She turned off the light on her own side of the bed, and slid down onto her pillow with an uneasy feeling. A woman's perfume had opened the door to doubt tonight, and to questions she had never faced before. She lay awake for a long time in the silent house, wondering what he was up to, and if she really knew her husband. He suddenly felt like a stranger to her, and she could hear him snoring softly next to her. She finally closed her eyes and drifted off to sleep, imagining what it would be like to sleep alone in her bed. They were still lovers, theoretically, although they didn't make love often. Or had they become just two people growing old together at the same address?

Eileen was quiet at breakfast the next morning. She and Paul rarely spoke to each other during breakfast. They both read the papers, he said goodbye and left to catch his train, and then she went to wake Pennie and the boys. Pennie usually got up on her own, to have enough time to wash her hair before school.

Paul had mumbled something about staying in the city that night, another client dinner that would probably go late. She hadn't commented and he left. As soon as the kids had left for school, in their respective car pools, Eileen called Jane.

"I know this sounds crazy and it's out of the blue, but I'm worried. I have this sick feeling that Paul may be having an affair." She felt stupid saying it, but she couldn't get the idea out of her head since the night before.

"What makes you think so? A red lace thong in his coat pocket?" Jane was the authority on all things marital among their friends. She had lots of experience, and an uncanny sense about what things meant in the relations between men and women.

"Nothing as drastic as that. I smelled perfume on him last night. On his skin, on his neck, to be precise. That's never happened before."

"It probably doesn't mean anything," Jane dismissed it.

"And he's having dinner in the city supposedly with clients, almost every night."

"Anyone specific you suspect?" Jane asked her.

"I don't even know who his clients are anymore, I'm so tied up out here with the kids. He's had a new secretary for the past year I've never even met."

"Maybe you need to 'untie' yourself a little, and have dinner with him in the city too."

"He hates having dinner with me in New York. We only go out to dinner here, so we don't have to get dressed." She realized that she had become the comfortable old shoe in his life, which had been convenient for her too, but maybe not so good for their marriage. "I think I've become lazy and boring, the classic suburban wife."

"Don't be ridiculous," Jane said and laughed. "You're a beautiful woman. Maybe you need to remind him of that, and make an effort to seduce him. Put some spice back in your marriage." Jane had said it before, but Eileen had never paid attention to her. Now she was.

"How do I do that?"

"Sexy dress, sexy underwear, perfume, candlelit dinner at a nice restaurant, and no Uggs or running shoes please. Seduce him. Treat him like a date."

"He'll think I've lost my mind. That's not how we are together."

"It's better than losing him, if he's the one you want." Jane had never found him appealing despite his looks, although she had seen him turn on the charm when he wanted. But Eileen had history with him, and kids, which counted a lot for her.

"He's the one I have," she said succinctly.

"Don't take anything for granted. A man can turn on a dime if the right woman goes after him. He's at a vulnerable age, so are you. Forty is traumatic for guys too. If some hot girl makes him feel young again, it could turn his head."

"Maybe I'm just imagining it." Eileen felt foolish at the idea of trying to seduce her own husband. He'd think she was an idiot.

"You probably aren't," Jane said seriously. "When women suspect that their husbands are cheating on them, they usually are. We come with a built-in radar system for that. Some women just turn it off. I keep mine on and finely tuned. And it can't hurt to dress up for him once in a while to let him know you care enough to try. It might bring out the Casanova in him too. Why not? Putting the romance back in your marriage at forty isn't a dumb idea. It's like putting a good solid lock on your front door. If you want to keep him, I'd suggest you put some effort into it."

Eileen smiled off and on all day, thinking of Jane's advice, and wondering if she was right. She called Paul at the office on Thursday afternoon, and suggested they have a date night on Friday.

"You called to tell me that? Are you feeling okay?" Paul said, sounding startled and amused.

"Of course. I just thought it would be nice to go out."

"I think this is the first time you've called me in ten years that wasn't to tell me that one of the kids had broken his arm, or was about to get kicked out of school, and we have an appointment with the headmaster at eight A.M. tomorrow. Sure, why not? Where do you want to go?" He named the usual places, and she suggested a fancier one, where they hadn't been in at least five years, and then only because someone else had invited them. They never ate at elegant restaurants anymore. "I'll make the reservation," he said, still sounding amused. "Did you crash the car or run over a pedestrian and you want to break the news to me gently?"

"No, I just thought it might be fun to go somewhere nice for a change." He was making her feel stupid, but she stuck to her suggestion anyway.

"I'll take care of it. Do I have to wear a tie?"

"Not if you don't want to," she said easily.

"Good. I don't. I do enough of that at work." He wore a suit and tie every day. "See you tonight. I'll try to get home at a decent hour. I don't have a client dinner tonight for a change. The one I had scheduled canceled." But he came home at ten anyway, and she had fallen asleep in bed with the TV on and a book in her hand. Pennie was up, watching a movie in her room, and the boys were already asleep. Paul only saw them now on the weekends most of the time.

The next day, he left for work in a rush, and she didn't have time to remind him about dinner, but she was sure he'd remember. It was the fanciest date they'd had in years.

She traded car pool duty with another mother. Pennie was going to work on her college essays. Eileen went to the hairdresser and got her hair and nails done, and then dressed carefully for her date with Paul. She took a black dress out of her closet that she hadn't worn in three years, and a pair of high heels, one of the few she hadn't given to Pennie yet. She wore perfume and earrings. Pennie stopped in her room to see her once she was all dressed.

"Wow, Mom, you look great. What's the occasion?"

"Dinner with your father. I thought we'd go someplace nice for a change. We're going to Chez Julien."

"Pretty fancy. Can I have those shoes when you're through with them?" She was eyeing her mother's Christian Dior shoes that Eileen had only worn twice herself.

"No! They're the last decent pair I have left. I gave you all the others."

"I'd look good in those too," Pennie teased her and left, and Eileen waited nervously for Paul to come home. He had texted her the day before that the reservation was for eight-thirty, a little late for them, but the only one he could get, and she used to like dining late, once all the children were in bed. Now they just ate with them at six if Paul was home in time, or she did if he wasn't coming home at all.

He wasn't home yet at seven-thirty, and she figured he'd be there by eight. He'd have to rush to dress, or he could wear the suit he'd worn to work and take off his tie. She was mildly worried, but not panicked yet.

Eight slipped by with no word from him.

Eight-thirty came and went. Then nine and nine-thirty. She was livid by then. She was in tears at ten. She had called him a dozen times on his cellphone. He never picked up and it went straight to voicemail. And he didn't answer her texts. She couldn't imagine he would do this to her and stand her up completely, unless he was dead. She was afraid something terrible had happened to him, like in one of those novels or a movie where the wife is all dressed, waiting, and the love of her life is dead by the side of the road somewhere. But real life was never as dramatic as that. Unless he was being held hostage by terrorists on the train. She turned on the news and nothing was reported.

He called her finally at midnight, sounding desperate. "Oh my God, Eileen, I can't believe I did that to you. I had a new client meeting at the end of the day that got organized this morning. We wound up finishing at ten. We never even ate dinner. It was too late to come home and I was exhausted, so I checked in to a hotel. I was going to call and tell you, and I fell asleep the minute I sat down on the bed. I just woke up and remembered that we were supposed to go to Chez Julien tonight. I think I thought you were kidding when you suggested it, and it went right out of my head after I booked the reservation. I'm so sorry. We'll do it another time, I promise." He sounded frantic and mortified, and she wasn't even angry by then, just sad. He had completely forgotten about her and their "date."

"Don't bother," she said in a tired voice. "I guess that's not who we are." She had taken the black dress off two hours before, handed the Dior shoes to her daughter and told her they were hers now, and she had put on her nightgown and gone to bed an hour before.

"I'll be home first thing in the morning. I'll make it up to you, I promise." But she knew he couldn't, and probably wouldn't try. They were past date nights and restaurants like Chez Julien, if he couldn't even remember a Friday night dinner plan with his wife. She'd been a fool to think otherwise and felt like one.

"Come home whenever you want," she said in a dead voice. "I'm taking the boys to soccer tomorrow."

"I'll try to come by before the end of the game."

"I won't tell them in case you don't show up, so they're not disappointed," she said without malice. She knew him well.

"I deserved that," he said humbly.

"What hotel are you staying at, by the way, in case the house burns down?"

"I'm staying at a hotel in SoHo, which is where we had the client meeting. It's a British boutique hotel. It's pretty good. We'll have to stay here sometime. The Crosby. I'll see you tomorrow, and I'm really,

really sorry I forgot our date." He sounded sincere and contrite when he said it.

"I'm not sure it matters. Good night," she said coolly, and hung up. She lay in bed with the lights on for half an hour after that, thinking about it, and how easily he'd forgotten her. So much for sexy date nights. Feeling slightly guilty, she called information and asked for the number of the Crosby hotel in Manhattan. She told the automated voice to "connect her," and a minute later, the hotel operator was on the line. She asked for Mr. Jackson's room, Paul Jackson, she said precisely, and there was a pause as the operator looked up his room number and then came back on the line.

"I'm sorry, we have no registered guest here by that name," she said, and Eileen managed to thank her and hang up. She had suspected it, or she wouldn't have called the hotel, but hearing it was entirely different. It made her fears a reality, like a bolt of lightning that went straight to her heart. She felt like she'd been turned to stone. He had lied to her and had forgotten their date. The only thing she didn't know was where he was staying that night, and in whose bed.

Chapter 4

Eileen moved through the motions of her life the next day like a robot. She made breakfast for the twins, checked in on Pennie, who was working on her applications, and took the boys to their soccer game. Mercifully, Paul didn't show up. She didn't want to see him there after the night before. And the boys hadn't been expecting him so they didn't care. It was five o'clock when she got home, and Paul was there, going through a stack of bills in his office at home, and writing checks. He looked up with an apologetic expression when Eileen came in. He stood up to kiss her and she walked past him without looking at him.

"Look, I'm sorry. I really am," he said nervously. "The client meeting went on forever, and our dinner plans went right out of my head." She paid no attention to what he said, and turned to look at him from across the room.

"Where did you stay last night?"

"I told you. The Crosby Street Hotel." For an instant she wondered if she had called the right hotel, and was almost willing to doubt herself, but she knew she had.

"I called there. You weren't registered."

"I checked out at the crack of dawn and went back to the office for a while before I came home."

"I called you there half an hour after you called me. You weren't there." He was stone-faced for a minute, not sure what to say.

"Why don't we just leave it alone for now? We've all been through a lot with Pennie's pregnancy. Let's not rock the boat again," he said. They were suddenly in dangerous waters, with sharks all around them.

"She lost the baby three months ago. That has nothing to do with where you stayed last night." Eileen homed in on him. "There's obviously another woman in your life. What do we do now?" She heard her own voice as though it were someone else's. She couldn't believe she was having this conversation with him after eighteen years and three kids, and everything they'd been through and built together. Or was it all just a house of cards that blew over in the first gust of wind? Had he done this before? She wondered now, and realized she didn't know him at all.

Paul didn't admit or deny anything. He bowed his head for a minute at his desk, looking for the right words. He didn't want to go too far, but he knew something had to be said. He looked up at her with a sigh. "Maybe we need a break. Why don't I stay in the city for a while?" It was all he could think of to say to relieve the tension.

"Stay where? With whom? I think I have a right to know." She was shaking when she asked him.

"I can get a furnished studio apartment and stay there."

"Who is she, Paul?" Eileen pressed him.

"It doesn't matter. This is the first time." She didn't believe a word he said now, but he had admitted that there was someone else. Her heart felt like it was going to stop beating. She was shocked. It wasn't the answer she'd expected. She thought he'd reassure her.

"Are you in love with her?" She wanted to know now.

"I don't want to talk about it. I love you and our kids. Can't we leave it at that for the time being? I don't want to do anything drastic."

"You already did. How long has it been going on?"

"A few months." There was no point lying to her again, he didn't want to anymore. He had been for months. "I was upset about Pennie, and I made a mistake." He made it sound so easy, but it wasn't, for either of them.

"Don't hide behind our daughter," Eileen said angrily.

"All right. We've been drifting apart for a long time. We probably never should have gotten married, but we've made the best of it. I'm just not sure what I want to do with the rest of my life. The kids are what holds us together. What happens when they leave? The boys are leaving in seven years. I'll be forty-eight then. You'll be forty-six. Do we want to continue living a mistake for another seven years?" She was shocked by his question. She'd had no idea he was thinking that way.

"They're not leaving right now as far as I can see. But it seems like you are." He was re-evaluating his life, and he hadn't mentioned it to her. And where was she in all this? Their marriage shouldn't be based on unilateral decisions. She was turning forty, and her husband had just suggested a break and was walking out on her, because she caught him cheating on her. That was major. And he wasn't suggesting they fix it. He wanted a "break," a time-out away from her. This was not the way she had expected her life to happen. She felt as though her whole world was falling apart. "When are you leaving?" She felt as though she was having an out-of-body experience, and someone else was speaking for her. It didn't even sound like her own voice. She felt strangely calm, or maybe she was just dead and didn't know it. He had killed her the night before, while he spent the night with his other woman. Now he was moving out to be with her.

"I can leave in the morning," he said quietly, "or tonight if you'd prefer." She thought about it for a minute before she answered.

"If you're involved with another woman, I don't want you to stay here," although he had been for the last four months, if the affair dated back to when Pennie told them she was pregnant, or was he lying about that too? Maybe it had gone on much longer, like years, and she'd been too big a fool to see it. They had never been blissfully happy or madly in love, but their marriage had worked well enough for eighteen years. They'd had some good times together, and raised a family, and she'd been faithful to him, even though he hadn't been to her, apparently.

"I'll leave tonight then," he said quietly, and went to pack some things. She stayed in the office, feeling dazed, and he came back a few minutes later with a small overnight bag in his hand. He said he would come back for the rest later, he didn't want to pack more now. "What are you going to tell the kids?" He was worried about that and so was she.

"I don't know. What do you say in situations like this?" This had never happened to her before.

"Maybe as little as possible until we figure it out ourselves."

"It sounds like you already have," she said in a dead voice.

"I told you, it was a mistake." But he didn't sound sorry. He was oddly matter-of-fact, even relieved.

"But you continued it anyway. Are you willing to end it?" she asked him about the affair. That was the key question. Would he give the woman up to save their marriage? It didn't sound like it.

"I don't know," he said honestly. "I wanted to several times, but the time never seemed right. I need to figure it out," he said sadly when he saw the look in Eileen's eyes. She looked broken in half by what he was doing to her. He felt better being honest now. Living a lie had been killing him. Now he felt free to make some decisions and some moves, no matter how painful it might be for both of them in the end. He was tired of living a lie, torn between two women and two lives. "Could you hold off telling the kids about her until I know what I'm doing?" It was a lot to ask, but she was an honorable woman, and he trusted her not to try and destroy his relationship with his children. She wouldn't do that.

"It depends what they ask me. I don't want to lie to them." He nodded and walked out of the office, without trying to go near her. He turned and looked at her again. "I'm sorry," was all he said, and then he hurried down the stairs and opened the front door. She heard him drive away a few minutes later, without saying goodbye to his children. He had left her to explain his disappearance.

She walked into their bedroom and lay down on their bed and stared up at the ceiling. She had no idea where to go from here, or what would happen next. She wondered what the other woman looked like and who she was. He was obviously in love with her if he was willing to leave their home for her. She had no idea if Paul would ever come back, or if she even wanted him to. She was still lying there when Pennie came to ask her a question an hour later and was surprised to find her lying down.

"Are you sick, Mom?" she asked, worried. Eileen never lay down except to go to sleep at night.

"No, just resting," she said, sat up, and swung her legs over the side of the bed.

"Where's Dad?"

"He had to go back to the city."

Pennie nodded, and handed her the draft of an essay for an application. "Could you read this for me and tell me what you think?"

"Sure."

All the children had plans for dinner that night, and she was grateful that she'd be alone to absorb what had happened. She had a lot to think about. None of it seemed real. She wondered if she should have demanded to know the woman's identity, but it was obvious Paul wasn't going to tell her and she was too stunned to force the issue. She shuffled around the house after that, with no idea what she was doing, until they left. Her life had become a shambles in an instant, and she had to try and make sense of it. Not only did she have to figure out who he was, but she had to figure out who she was, without him. What if he never came back? And did she want him now? She didn't know the answer to that either. His departure had seemed so unemotional and so bloodless. But maybe there was no blood left in the marriage. Maybe it had been dead for years and she hadn't noticed. She felt dead as she walked back up the stairs to her bedroom, trying not to wonder about where he was, and who he was with. He was a ghost in her life now, and she felt like one too.

Olivia Page was a beautiful, fiery, petite redhead, with long, luscious curly hair, big green eyes, full of energy and always in motion. She had a constant flow of exciting ideas. She was twenty-seven years old and had just started her own business. She had established an art gallery online that everyone was talking about. She represented a number of important artists, and lesser ones, and she had the connections to sell to major clients. She had worked in the contemporary art department at Christie's after she'd graduated from Yale, with a major in fine arts and a minor in art history. She had left Christie's after a year to work for a well-known gallery, and had now just started her own business.

She was the daughter of a famous Hollywood producer who had died when she was seven. He had been thirty years older than her mother, and he had been Olivia's hero until his death and long after. He was a Hollywood legend, and so was her mother, Gwen Waters. She was a major Hollywood actress, winner of two Academy Awards. She had made a slew of well-known movies, although recently she'd been working less. Olivia worshipped her mother, but she didn't envy her career. Olivia had no interest in Hollywood. The art world was her passion, and it seemed a better choice to her. Her mother was currently suffering from a lack of roles for women in their fifties, no matter how big a star she was.

She was both her parents' only child, although her mother had been married several times. She and Olivia's father had divorced before he died, but remained close, and her father had left his entire fortune to Olivia. She had a penthouse apartment on Fifth Avenue that looked like a Hollywood movie set, filled with the kind of art she sold. She had two Picassos in the living room, and a Jackson Pollock in the dining room that she had inherited from her father, and an entire wall of Andy Warhols of her mother in various hues and poses early in her career. Olivia had met countless famous people because of who her mother was, but she managed to be a real person in spite of it. She was honest and straightforward and outspoken, and had all the confidence of beauty, youth, brains, and famous parents. She was fearless and exciting and her taste in men leaned to those old enough to be her father, probably because hers had died when she was seven. She always said that men her age bored her.

The doorman buzzed her to tell her that Mr. Jackson was on his way up. She opened the door and Paul came out of the elevator looking beaten, but he came alive the moment he saw her. He felt reborn whenever he was with her. She made him feel young and daring, infused with her energy and youth. They had met in May at an event given by one of his clients at the agency, and they had been attracted to each other immediately. She didn't mind the fact that he was fourteen years older, which was younger than many men she had dated, or even that he was married. He told her that his marriage had been dead for years, and they just went through the motions for their kids. She had believed him, and didn't like the fact that he was still more engaged in it than he had led her to believe in the beginning. She felt sorry for him when his seventeen-year-old daughter told him she was pregnant. But she expected him to get out of his marriage as he had said he would. She loved older men, but not married ones. She'd made an exception for him. Their affair had gone on for five months, and she wasn't going to wait much longer. The role of the other woman in the shadows didn't suit her. The sex between them was fabulous, but she wasn't going to stay with him forever if he stayed married, and he knew it. Knowing how she felt about it had been putting tremendous pressure on him to figure things out.

He dropped his overnight bag in the front hall and put his arms around her, but before she let him kiss her, she asked him the question that had terrified him for months.

"Did you tell her?" Olivia was an honest woman, and didn't want to live a lie with him, or anyone. His being married was awkward for her.

He sighed and kissed her gently on the lips, and then they walked into the living room, with the spectacular views of the park and both rivers. "I didn't have to. She figured it out when I didn't go home last night. She asked me point blank, and I admitted there was someone else. I'm moving out. She didn't want me to stay. We're going to have to tell the kids something pretty quickly." But he had no idea where the affair with Olivia was going. She was an express train moving at jet speed, and he wasn't sure of his place in her world, or what he meant to her. She was still very young, and complained about not being taken seriously. At twenty-seven, she had the force of a woman twice her age and the energy of a girl her own age. She was the most exciting thing that had ever happened to him, and he was hanging on to her for dear life. He felt like a different person when he was with her, and acted like it. She was his fountain of youth.

"What now?" she asked him.

"I guess everything moves forward from here. I want you to meet my children," he said hopefully.

"At the right time, I will. Do you think she'll poison them against me?" She was worried about that. She had never dated a married man before, or anyone with kids. Children were not her thing.

"She's not that kind of person," he assured her. "She's a good woman. We just never should have gotten married. I'm going to rent an apartment this week, someplace where my kids can stay when they visit. It's complicated unraveling things after eighteen years," he reminded her.

"So I've noticed," she said with a knowing look, and with that, she unbuttoned his shirt, and undid his jeans, and a moment later, they were making love in front of the wall of Warhols of her mother. Then they found their way to her bed and made love again. She smiled at him and whispered, "Welcome home."

He wanted it to be true, but he felt homeless now. At least he didn't have to lie anymore about client meetings in the city, and why he came home late every night. He and Olivia could start to share a life together. All he had to do was tell Eileen the truth, that he wasn't coming back.

Olivia had brought him back to life. He had known from the beginning that his marriage to Eileen was wrong, but it had been the honorable thing to do at the time. But he had run out of gas somewhere along the way, and he just couldn't do it anymore. Maybe he could have if he'd never met Olivia. But now he had, and this was where he wanted to be. He wanted to be a better man for her. He still couldn't believe that she wanted him. She was so young and beautiful, so full of fire and excitement. He felt like he was on a rocket ship heading toward the moon every time he was with her. He wondered sometimes how long it would last. But for the past five months, it had gotten better and better. It had gotten harder and harder to go home to Greenwich, and lead the life he had there. He felt dead when he was with Eileen, and had for years. Everything about their marriage felt wrong to him now that he had Olivia to compare it to. She made him feel brave and young and strong, instead of like a failure who had missed all the right opportunities, in the wrong job, with the wrong wife. Secretly, he had always blamed Eileen, not himself.

He didn't know what to tell Eileen about her. How did one explain a woman like Olivia? She was part girl, part woman of mystery, a force of nature, a whirlwind or tornado that had engulfed him and moved him to another place, another world. And now he was about to be free from the life that had been drowning him for years. He loved Eileen, but he couldn't lead the dreary life he had shared with her anymore. He had to tell her and their children that he had to move on. He knew it was selfish of him, but a woman like Olivia came along once in a lifetime. It was his time now.

They made dinner together in her kitchen that night out of what was in the fridge, and then climbed back into her bed to watch films that her mother had given her of new releases that weren't in theaters yet. Olivia lived in a rarefied world. He got dizzy from the altitude at times, but with her, he felt like anything was possible. And now he was here, and at last a free man, or he would be soon. He didn't have to leave her to go back to Greenwich again. He had felt torn limb from limb for the past five months. At least that was over, and he could concentrate on Olivia now, and spend every night with her.

They watched two of the movies and fell asleep in each other's arms. For once, he didn't have to go anywhere.

"What are we doing tomorrow?" he mumbled happily before they fell asleep. He didn't miss his children yet, and he had the day to spend with her since it was Sunday.

"I don't know about you, but I'm having lunch with my mother. We can do something after that."

"Am I coming with you?" he asked. He was fascinated that her mother was Gwen Waters, and dying to meet her. He couldn't wait to tell his kids, once they knew about Olivia.

"She doesn't know about you yet. Now that you've moved out, I can tell her." He nodded, and then they drifted off to sleep. He felt as though he had died and gone to heaven. He snuggled up next to her, knowing he could spend the entire night with her. Olivia felt that way too. She could hardly wait to tell her mother about him now that he was finally on the path to freedom. It took him five months to get there, but Olivia thought it had been worth the wait, or she was sure he would be. He told her he had been dormant for eighteen years and she had brought him back to life. It was a heady feeling for her, to be that important to someone. She had always been with powerful older men before, some of whom had tried to dominate her. In Paul, she sensed a gentle soul, and she was the strong one, bringing him along and infusing life into him. Her only concern had been his wife, but now he had left her, which Olivia took as a sign of strength and the evidence of his love for her. She was certain it was going to work, and together they would be a winning team. What she didn't see was that he was a mirror, reflecting her own strength back at her. And the fire and passion she sensed in the relationship was her own.

Chapter 5

After a leisurely morning of reading the Sunday *Times* in bed together, Paul made breakfast for them, since Olivia admitted that she didn't like to cook for anyone. They bathed in her enormous bathtub, and dressed. Paul tried to call his children, but couldn't reach them. He wasn't sure how to explain his disappearance. He didn't know what Eileen had told them, and didn't want to call her quite so soon to ask. She was probably still in shock from his admitting to her the day before that there was someone else.

Paul had called a realtor about some listings he found, and was going to see two furnished apartments the realtor had while Olivia had lunch with her mother. He was also going to call several other real estate agents on Monday. He knew he would probably spend most of his nights with Olivia, but he needed a place of his own too, where his children could stay with him if they wanted to spend a night in the city. He had thought about getting a studio at first, but he needed at least three bedrooms for all of them, and it had to be furnished. He wasn't going to start taking furniture out of the house in Greenwich. It was their home and he didn't want to disturb it, or Eileen, who would surely want to continue living there. It was a beautiful traditional home and they'd lived there for seven years.

Olivia was expected at her mother's for lunch at one o'clock. Paul was going to see the apartments then, and they were going to meet up again at three, and maybe go to a movie, or go back to her place and cuddle up in bed. The weather was brisk and staying home appealed to both of them, now that they had the luxury of time together. Paul kept playing the scene of the day before with Eileen over in his head, wondering how it had happened and come to a head so quickly. Eileen had instigated it, but it was time. He hadn't had the guts to bring it up, but he couldn't be torn between two women and two lives any longer. The past five months had been torture. Olivia had given him a reason for being, and the strength to leave Eileen, once she confronted him.

They left each other like lovers who wouldn't meet again for years, and Olivia finally climbed into an Uber, and headed to her mother's apartment at the Dakota on Central Park West. The apartments there were legendary, as she was. Countless famous people lived there. Her apartment was on two levels, with curving staircases, a wood-paneled library that had cathedral ceilings, and antique ladders that moved on a brass rail to allow one to reach all of the books on any shelf. She had a grandiose living room, an oval dining room, and five handsome bedrooms. The art on the walls was by famous French Impressionist painters, and lesser known artists of the same school. She had a state-of-the-art kitchen and a French chef. Gwen Waters had an enviable life and lived in a precious world, with objects that were dear to her, antiques she had collected around the world, and

exquisite French fabrics. Most of it was the result of her extraordinary career, and some of it gifts from the men she had married. She
had married three times, and Olivia's father had been her second
husband. Tom Page, the famous producer. Her other two husbands
had been as famous as he was. She had been a major star for more
than thirty years, divorced once, and widowed twice, the first time
when her famous British artist husband had committed suicide. All
of her husbands had been older than she was, a tendency Olivia had
learned from her. Gwen's stays in Hollywood while filming had only
been temporary. She had been famous since her early twenties, and
the apartment in the Dakota had been the home that Olivia had
grown up in, and she always felt like a child again when she went to
visit her mother there.

Gwen's career had slowed down noticeably in the past two or
three years, and at fifty-six, still strikingly beautiful, she was frus-
trated not to be seeing better scripts. She hadn't made a movie in a
year, or seen a script she wanted in two years, and she was well
aware that her age was responsible for it. Women in their fifties were
not highly prized in Hollywood, although she was one of the few
exceptions. But she was no longer making two or three fabulous
movies a year. She hounded her agent about it constantly, and he assured her that there had been no great movies made recently, and
when he had the right part for her, she would see the script immediately. Nothing had been worthy of her lately.

Gwen was happy as soon as she saw Olivia bound down the stairs
to the living room. The two women looked nothing alike, yet both
were exceptionally beautiful. Gwen was tall and very slim, with
ebony dark hair and enormous brown eyes. She could play any part,

was willing to be transformed into characters of any age, and performed the parts convincingly, which had won her the two Academy Awards and seven nominations. She was never morbidly depressed, as some actors were when they didn't win an Oscar. In her case, there was always next year. Each of her performances was a gem, which won her the praise of the critics and her peers, and audiences loved her. She had a natural kindness which came through whatever part she played, although she did villains well too, and enjoyed them. Olivia's petite redheaded beauty was a throwback to her paternal grandmother. She collapsed onto one of the comfortable couches, and smiled at her mother.

"You're looking very happy today." Her mother smiled warmly at her. It had never particularly impressed Olivia that she had a famous mother. She was used to it.

It had annoyed her when her friends at school made a fuss about her mother being a big star. Gwen had picked Olivia up at school every day, like any other mother, when she wasn't on location. And Olivia had spent school vacations all over the world, visiting her mother on location, or her father until his death when she was seven. She was as discreet as her mother was and had taught her to be, and never talked about the things they did or stars they knew. Her mother's fame was a fact of life to her, and not something she chose to discuss with outsiders. She had already been a huge star when Olivia was born when Gwen was twenty-nine.

All of Gwen's husbands were dead now. There had been other relationships over the years, though none recently. She had been alone for the past eight years, since her last husband died, after seven happy years of marriage. He had been a major film star and died of a brain tumor. Gwen had nursed him until his final hour, and held him in her arms when he died. And now at fifty-six, she had begun to think that the good times were over, in her career and in her personal life.

Nothing exciting had happened to her since her last movie, which had been recently released and was a box office hit. But for the moment, she had nothing in the works and was tired of reading bad scripts. The time she spent with Olivia was a welcome distraction. The life of an actress at her age was not easy, and the good parts had been thinning out since she turned fifty. Gwen's mother assured her that there would still be great parts in her future, perhaps fewer but better than ever, but Gwen didn't quite believe her. As close as she was to Olivia, Gwen was equally so to her own mother.

"So tell me what's new with you," Gwen asked Olivia, as they nibbled tiny crackers with homemade pâté on them, which the cook always made when he knew Olivia was coming. They were having cheese soufflé, her favorite, for lunch.

"Well." Olivia hesitated, wondering if now was the best time to tell her mother about Paul. But she was so pleased that he had finally moved out of the house in Greenwich. It had taken him long enough, after telling her how dead the marriage was right from the beginning. "I've been seeing someone I like a lot," she admitted, looking mischievous. She always confided in her mother, and Gwen had suspected for a while that there was a new man in her life, but she didn't want to ask her, and preferred to wait until Olivia felt ready to tell her on her own.

"What's he like?" Gwen asked with interest.

"Smart, serious, quiet. Older than I am, but not too old. He's the managing director of an ad agency, and head account executive. He's very creative. And he has three kids."

"Divorced or widowed?" Olivia waited just long enough for her mother to raise a questioning eyebrow. "Please don't tell me he's married." Gwen looked worried.

"He's getting divorced. His marriage has been dead for years."

"Men who cheat on their wives always say that," Gwen said wisely. "He's not living at home with her, is he?" Olivia shook her head confidently, and Gwen was somewhat relieved. "When did he move out, before you started dating him, or after?"

"After," Olivia responded honestly. "Actually, he moved out yesterday. He's getting an apartment in the city, and a divorce."

"How old are his children?"

"He has a seventeen-year-old daughter, and eleven-year-old twin boys."

"They're young. Have you met them?"

"Not yet. He wants me to meet them soon, but I want to let the dust settle a bit first."

"How long have you known him?" Gwen questioned her.

"Five months. He's wonderful, Mama, you'll love him."

"I hope so, but I have to admit, I'm not in love with the idea of you as a home-wrecker. That's a lot of responsibility to take on, if he left his wife for you. And his kids won't thank you for it, especially the daughter."

"He says he would have left her anyway, sooner or later. He's wanted to for years, but didn't want to upset the children."

"Breaking up a family isn't a nice thing to do, if you caused him to do it. It was done to me. It doesn't make anyone a bigger, better person, and his children will be very hard on you if they blame you for the divorce. How old is he?"

"Forty-one, almost forty-two."

"What does his wife do?"

"She's just a Connecticut housewife. I think he's been bored with her for years." Olivia looked slightly supercilious as she said it, with the advantage of youth.

"If he cheated on her, which he obviously has, he might do it to you one day. That's something to think about." Gwen was not sold on the idea of this man who had left his wife for Olivia, and had cheated on her for five months until then.

"I have thought about it. I trust him. He's a good person, and it was a bad marriage. And he's never cheated on her before."

"Men say that too, but it's not always true. Well, you'll see as things progress. Keep your eyes open though, and don't lie to yourself." Olivia nodded, and the maid came to announce that lunch was ready. Brigitte, the maid, looked pleased to see Olivia. Her mother had had the same employees for many years. "Just be careful," her mother warned her again. "If he's at the beginning of a divorce, it will get ugly before it's over. Try not to get caught in his mess. Let them fight it out, and stay out of it." It was good advice, and Olivia nodded, but she was sure it wouldn't get too messy. He had told her that Eileen was a decent person, and he was planning to be generous with her. He wasn't wealthy the way Olivia was, but he made a huge salary and they lived well.

"You've had your share of wild love affairs too," Olivia reminded her as they sat down in the oval dining room.

"Not lately." Gwen smiled at her. "And never with married men.

That's one rule I've never broken. Anything else is permissible. Other people's husbands aren't."

They talked about other things then, a script Gwen had read and didn't like, two movies she'd seen, a book she'd read and would love to see made into a movie. She had her finger on the pulse of the industry. And Olivia told her about her fledgling business that was growing by leaps and bounds. Gwen was very proud of her, but as she thought about it after Olivia left, she still didn't like the idea of her with a married man. She was liable to get hurt, or hurt someone else, and there were children involved, which made it even more serious. Olivia seemed very taken with him, but Gwen wasn't convinced that she was deeply in love with him, enough so to take on two young boys and a stepdaughter only ten years younger than she was. She was infatuated certainly, but more than that? Her mother wasn't so sure. She would have to be patient if he hadn't started the divorce proceedings yet. At least he had a decent job, and had been married for almost twenty years. That said something for him. Gwen was curious about him, and wondered if Olivia would introduce him soon. She hadn't suggested it during lunch, which said something too. Gwen wondered if Olivia had doubts of her own.

On Sunday afternoon, Eileen told the children that their father had moved out. She said they were taking a break, which came as a shock to Seth and Mark, but not entirely to Pennie, who had been aware of her parents' differences in recent years. Her father's bitterness was obvious during her pregnancy. He still felt that being pressed into marriage before he was ready had impacted his life and career, and deprived him of the opportunity of greater success he believed he was capable of. He was convinced he would have been a major entrepreneur and made a fortune. He had no one else to blame for it except Eileen. Her parents weren't warm with each other, the way some of her friends' parents were. She would have liked to have parents like the others, but she didn't. Even Tim's parents, who were uptight and conservative and she didn't particularly like, seemed closer than hers. The Blakes had the same ideas and were allies, which her parents weren't, so she wasn't entirely surprised at her father moving out. Eileen and Paul never seemed affectionate toward each other. She had realized that in her teens.

After the boys went upstairs to play with their PlayStation, Pennie stayed downstairs to talk to her mother.

"Are you okay, Mom?" she asked, concerned about her. Her mother looked tired and pale, with circles under her eyes. She looked sick and sad.

"I think so. I'm still in shock. I'm kind of numb. Everything happened very quickly yesterday." She hadn't slept all night afterwards, replaying it in her head.

Pennie hesitated and then asked her the question Eileen had feared. "Do you think there's someone else?"

"I think there might be," she said as candidly as she dared without maligning Paul to his kids, which she didn't want to do, out of respect for him. "Things were never totally right with us. We got off on the wrong foot. I thought we had worked it out, but I guess your father wouldn't agree." He had made that clear when Pennie was pregnant, during their conversation with Tim's parents.

"Do you think he'll come back?" Pennie asked her.

"I don't know. I'm not sure. Maybe he doesn't know either."

"If he doesn't, you'll meet someone else. You're still young," Pennie said kindly. Pennie wasn't sure what she wished for her, for him to come back or not. He seemed harsh with Eileen at times, and disconnected, as though they had never really merged, while he blamed her for their marriage.

"No, I'm not young, or I don't feel it anyway," she said with a sigh.

"At thirty-nine, you're not old. And you're beautiful." Pennie smiled at her. She had become surprisingly mature since the baby she'd lost. It was a hard way to grow up, but she was back in good health again. Eileen could guess easily that she still missed Tim, but he was off in his new world now, without a baby or a wife, which must have been a relief to him, even if he missed her. It was harder being the one still at home. Pennie wasn't dating anyone and said she didn't want to whenever the subject came up. She was still feeling wounded by everything that had happened, and sad about the baby she'd lost. It was like losing Tim again, and all their dreams.

Eileen was worried that all of the children would be shaken by a divorce, but there was no avoiding that now, if Paul decided he was gone for good. Their marriage seemed to have ended with a whimper, although Eileen had no idea what lay ahead for all of them.

"I'm sure your father will want to see you all soon," Eileen said, and Pennie nodded. She had mixed feelings about it. She was angry at him for leaving her mother, and all of them, but he seemed so unhappy in his life that she was sorry for him.

* * *

Eileen called Jane to tell her that night too. She wasn't shocked. She had suspected that he was cheating, and she was more concerned about how Eileen was taking it. She seemed okay, but she would have rough times ahead if they got divorced, even if they were friends in the end. Being left for another woman was a brutal blow. Jane was sure that the girl he was involved with was probably younger than Eileen. And turning forty, and being left by your husband, was every woman's nightmare. They made a lunch date for the next day. Eileen said she was waiting for Paul to make the next move. She didn't feel like there was anything she could do, and now at least she knew the truth.

"How are the kids taking it?" Jane asked her.

"Pennie has been terrific. She's angry at her father, but I think it will be harder on the boys. They're younger and don't understand."

"They'll come through it. Kids always do. As long as Paul sees enough of them, and they have you and Pennie to reassure them. Most kids have divorced parents these days." It was true, but Eileen had hoped never to be one of them. She had worked hard for that, but not hard enough, and there had been a flaw in their marriage from the beginning, which in Paul's mind they had never overcome. Eileen had put past disappointments behind her, but Paul never had.

They agreed on where to meet the next day, and Eileen tried not to, but she wondered what Paul was doing and who he was with, and what she was like. She wanted to know what the competition looked like and how old she was. But even without knowing, she felt defeated. She couldn't see herself meeting another man she cared about and starting a new life. She wasn't even sure she had the energy to try. It was all so disappointing and so sad. She lay alone in her bed that night, thinking of what Paul had said. The last thing she wanted to do was get out and date again. She felt now as though the last eighteen years had been wasted, except for the kids, who were worth it all. But she was no longer sure that Paul was. And if he had been cheating on her for a while, she didn't think she could ever forgive him, and didn't want him back. She had reached a crossroads in her life. She felt her youth slipping away from her. No matter what Pennie said, she felt suddenly ancient, and as though her life as she knew it was over. The dream she had tried to build with him had come to an end. Their marriage wasn't sound enough to carry them forever. And she was turning forty, with a husband who no longer wanted her. It felt like the end of the road, with nothing to look forward to up ahead.

Chapter 6

When Gwen Waters woke up the next day, she had only one thing in mind, and one place where she wanted to go. She put on jeans and a heavy sweater, and running shoes so she wouldn't slip or fall. She ate a light breakfast of coffee and a slice of toast, and then called for an Uber and headed downtown. The car was already waiting when she got downstairs. The address was in a still-battered part of the Bowery that hadn't been gentrified yet, and she was lost in thought all the way downtown. It took them nearly an hour to get there in Monday morning traffic, but she had nothing else to do that day.

The old warehouse looked weathered when she got there, and there were bags of garbage on the sidewalk, waiting to be picked up. There were a few homeless people wandering down the street, and drunks still asleep in doorways. This wasn't SoHo or Tribeca, and was less fashionable. There were enormous doors that had been painted dark green in the façade of the building, which always reminded Gwen of Paris.

She rang the bell and waited. She knew it would take her mother time to answer, and if she was wielding her welder's torch, she wouldn't hear the doorbell and Gwen would have to call her, but she'd get there sooner or later.

She waited a full five minutes and was about to call, when one of the huge doors swung slowly open. A small disheveled woman in a heavy welder's apron, holding a torch in her hand, with a mask pushed up on her head, stood there and smiled at Gwen.

"It's you. I wasn't expecting you. I'm working on a new horse."

"I figured you were doing something like that. Hello, Mother, how are you?" She gave her a hug. There was a vague resemblance between the two women, although the older woman wasn't as tall, and their styles were entirely different. Gwen was impeccably stylish and elegant, even in jeans and a sweater. Her mother looked tousled and Bohemian. Her face was similar to Gwen's and still beautiful, though heavily lined, and her snow-white hair, which had once been as dark as Gwen's, was pulled back tightly in a bun so she didn't set it on fire with the sparks from her torch.

Gwen had given up worrying about her. Her mother did as she pleased. She was careful about her welding, but had a remarkable indifference to all other aspects of safety, and somehow got away with it. There were stacks of wood, and large odd-shaped metal objects in piles around the warehouse, electrical cords, and an obstacle course of debris, tools, and benches in various places around the building, which had been a garment factory at one time. There were also huge, spectacularly graceful horses made of steel, which would eventually be cast in bronze. Occasionally, she did wooden ones, or some with found objects. There was also a giant statue of a naked man, but Gabrielle Waters's horses were famous, and sold for a fortune.

Gwen's mother was a sculptress. She had studied at the Beaux-Arts in Paris in her youth. She was a doctor's daughter and Gwen was her only child. She looked to be about seventy-five years old, despite the lines in her face, and her eyes were a bright electric blue. Her hearing was perfect. She was surprisingly agile. She had had Gwen late in life. Gabrielle was now ninety-two years old.

She had been widowed when Gwen was only a year old. Her husband had been a famous painter, and she had never remarried. She'd had several long-term love affairs in her life, but had never wanted to marry any of her lovers. Her current lover, Federico Banducci, was a famous photographer, eight years younger than Gabrielle. He was eighty-four years old, and still working as hard as she was.

They had met at the Beaux-Arts in Paris when he was twenty and she was twenty-eight, and had only been friends then. They met again fifty years later, at seventy and seventy-eight, and had been together ever since. They had been living together for fourteen years. He'd been studying architecture at the Beaux-Arts, and gave it up for photography. Venetian by birth, of a noble family, he had gone to New York after Paris. There was a palazzo named after his family in Venice.

He had gone to the States at twenty-one, became an American citizen, was drafted and sent to Vietnam, where he had been assigned as a photographer and had taken some of the most famous photographs of the war. He had stepped into a minefield in pursuit of a photograph of frightened children and their injured mother, and half of his face was badly scarred. The other half was still perfect and looked like a Roman coin of Julius Caesar. Gabrielle saw only the beautiful half, and the beauty in life. They were deeply attached to each other, and Gwen's unconventional mother suited him perfectly. He had never been married and had no children. He adored Gabrielle and would have married her at a moment's notice. She had a conviction that marriage only made sense for people who wanted children, and she was long past that age, so she turned him down whenever he asked her, which he had many times. He still tried, particularly when he drank too much wine. But she had finally found her soul mate at seventy-eight. She was a happy, energetic, vital, brilliantly talented woman, and time had only enhanced her wisdom and creativity, and her energy seemed boundless. She was an inspiration to all who knew her. Her work had gotten larger and larger as she got older. She had the strength of a man as she created her horses, many of which were in museums around the world, and sought after by private collectors. She only made three or four a year, so they were in high demand and there was a long waiting list for her new works.

She always employed two or three young artists to help her, and there was a bustle of activity in her studio as Gwen followed her to the stairs which led to the loft where she and Federico lived. Gwen knew that he was currently in Paris setting up his latest exhibit at the Petit Palais. Gabrielle was planning to go to the opening, and Gwen had promised to go with her, since she wasn't working at the moment.

Her mother put on a kettle for tea, as the work in her studio continued without her. They were preparing the pieces she was planning to weld. Gwen settled into one of the comfortable armchairs Gabrielle and Federico had rescued from the street before it could be taken to the dump. The warehouse was filled with an eclectic collection of found objects, beautiful Italian antiques, and Federico's photographs, which hung everywhere. Their lives and their talents meshed perfectly, and the atmosphere they inspired around them was one of warmth and welcome to the diverse group of people they chose to entertain. Politicians, artists, writers, bankers, scientists. Federico was a fabulous cook and they had friends over frequently, when Gabrielle wasn't in the middle of a commission, and he wasn't on an assignment somewhere. They were always busy doing or creating something, both of them were in remarkably good health and working harder than ever.

"What brings you here today?" she asked her only child, pleased to see her, as she set down a cup of green tea in front of Gwen. She never stopped for visits during her workday, except for her daughter. She was always happy to see her. Gabrielle knew that she was out of sorts over not having any recent film work. Gwen had her mother's work ethic, but she couldn't create independently as a sculptor could. She had to find a decent script, and be hired for the movie. Gwen insisted she hadn't read a good script in a year, and was terrified her career was over due to her age.

"I missed you, and I can always use your good advice," Gwen said with a warm look. Gabrielle was more peppery than her daughter, and she disliked talking on the phone. It was easier coming to see her in person, and her mother preferred it. Gabrielle had a beautiful expressive face. She liked to remind Gwen that they had argued constantly when Gwen was in her twenties. But for the past thirty years, they had been extremely close and got along admirably. "I'm worried about Olivia. I think she's off on the wrong foot. She seems to be in love with a married man," Gwen said to her mother with a troubled expression.

"How married?" Gabrielle asked with an impish expression. She didn't look shocked. Very little shocked her at her age.

"Married enough. He just left his wife a few days ago, with the usual story about a dead marriage. He has three children, and he and Olivia have been dating for five months while he lived with his wife. I don't want her to get hurt, or hurt anyone else. And his children are liable to hate her for breaking up the marriage."

"You can't control that," her mother reminded her. "But that's not likely to happen. If I know my granddaughter, she'll get bored with him before it gets too serious. Is he respectable otherwise?"

"She says so."

"I had a few married men in my time, didn't you?" Gabrielle said, smiling at the memory of particularly one of them, a professor at the Beaux-Arts.

"Never," Gwen answered for herself.

"I was never interested in marriage until I met your father when I was thirty-five." She had Gwen a year later, and a year after that he died of cholera on a trip to India. "When one of the married men offered to leave his wife, I ran like hell. She doesn't want to marry him, does she?"

"Not yet. But you never know, she might."

"I doubt she'll stick with it. Don't be too worried. Can we get a look at him? Should we invite him to dinner here?" Gwen smiled at the suggestion, everyone loved coming to her mother's studio for Federico's pasta dinners. "I'll invite them when we get back from Paris.

Federico says the installation of the show is going well. I offered them a horse for the entrance. I have one I just finished, but they wouldn't pay to ship it over, so we didn't send it." They weighed a ton, literally, and cost a fortune to transport properly.

"I think that's a great idea about Olivia's man, to invite him here. I'd like to meet him myself."

"He's probably terrified of that. He won't be as worried about me, because I'm old," Gabrielle said and laughed. "Age is a great cover for a multitude of sins. People assume I'm innocent, which is not always the case."

"You're the youngest person I know." Gwen smiled at her. "I wish I had your energy. I still haven't seen a decent script," she complained. "It's driving me crazy."

"It will come," her mother said confidently.

"Maybe not. Actresses' careers end at my age."

"Not yours. You may not get the parts you once did, and maybe not as many, but you'll get better ones. The great roles in film are for women your age, or even older."

"Maybe I'm finished, or too old." Gabrielle laughed again when Gwen said it.

"If you're too old, what does that make me? Dead? Don't be silly. A great part will come, and a great script with it. You need a hobby in the meantime," she said. "Something to keep you busy."

"Not piano lessons again. I still can't play." Gwen grinned at her.

"Why don't you go back to painting for a while? You've got talent, you've just never had the time to develop it. You're your father's daughter."

"I haven't painted in ten years," Gwen said, and she wasn't sure she wanted to. But it was something to do while she waited for a strong script to land on her doorstep. "I'll think about it."

"Don't think. Just do it. That's the best way to get things done. The only way really." They chatted for a little while longer, until Gwen could see her mother getting restless and eager to get back to work. "You need to meet a man too. That would keep you amused," her mother said as they made their way down the stairs, back to the studio.

"I'd rather find a good script. Besides, men don't like famous women. I haven't had a real date in two years."

"The right man won't care how famous you are. Only weak men are scared off by fame, and you don't want that anyway. You need a good, normal man, like Federico. He has a very nice nephew in Venice, but he's too old for you, he's in his seventies." She kissed her daughter and put her welder's mask back in place. She was working on a horse, and the sheer size of it was impressive. There was a ladder next to it so she could do her work. Gwen had long since stopped telling her to be careful. Her mother was ageless and timeless and a miracle of some kind. "Try painting. The rest will happen at the right time," she said, and Gwen felt encouraged when she left. She had called an Uber and rode back uptown, smiling as she thought about her mother. Gabrielle had told Gwen about a new service she'd discovered to deliver food from the best restaurants in the city. She said that she and Federico had ordered dinner from La Gamine before he left, and it was fabulous. She was always up-to-date on the latest trends, and open to trying new things, more than Gwen was.

When she got back to the apartment, Gwen dug around for her

old art supplies. She pulled out an easel and a canvas. Most of the paints were dry and she needed to buy new ones. But she found a sketch pad and some charcoal, and decided to play around with that for now. As usual, her mother was right. Painting and drawing would distract her, and always made her feel peaceful. She sat down with her sketch pad after lunch, and the hours flew by until dinnertime.

Paul found a surprisingly nice furnished apartment that afternoon in a townhouse in the East Seventies, not far from Olivia's apartment. It had three bedrooms and everything he needed, including linens and kitchen equipment. The owner was in Tuscany for a year on sabbatical, and it was available immediately, in move-in condition. It was just what he needed so he could see his kids on weekends. For himself, he preferred staying at Olivia's apartment.

He called Eileen to tell her and make plans to see the children. He thought she'd be pleased that he was already organizing to see the kids, but instead they got into an argument about the twins' schedules. She wanted Pennie to work on her college applications that weekend, and he wanted all three of them to come to the city and stay overnight.

"I don't want their grades to go down the tubes in honor of your love life," she said sharply. She'd been angry at him all day, when she thought of him lying to her and sleeping with another woman while he lived with her.

"Do you want me to come and see them out there?"

"No, I don't. I'm not ready to see you yet. I need to digest what happened. You just moved out two days ago."

"I thought you'd be happy I found an apartment." He was disappointed, which was naïve of him. How could she be happy for him? He had left her for another woman.

"So you can continue cheating on me?"

"I'm not cheating now, we're separated," he reminded her, "and I told you about her."

"Five months later, and only because I asked you. You didn't come clean and volunteer it."

"Can they at least come for one night?" She grudgingly agreed and then asked him the question that had been gnawing at her all day.

"Should I be calling a lawyer? Are we getting divorced?"

"I haven't figured out what I'm doing yet. Maybe we'll get back together at some point," he said unconvincingly. He didn't believe that, but he wanted to leave the door open, in case it didn't work out with Olivia, or he found that he missed Eileen. But he hadn't so far, and she sounded hostile on the phone. He couldn't blame her. He was asking a lot of her and he knew it. "I haven't called a lawyer yet myself. I'm not sure we need one, if we can make visitation work." Jane had told her that morning that she should call a lawyer, and had given her two names, but it depressed her to think about it. She wasn't ready to call one yet, or give up hope.

She agreed to send the children to him on Friday after school, on the train, and he promised to send them back on Saturday night. That way they could catch up on homework on Sunday. And the boys wouldn't miss soccer practice. He felt jangled at the end of the conversation. If they did divorce, he wanted to stay on good terms with Eileen, but that didn't sound possible at the moment. It was still too fresh, and her emotions were raw. She had a gaping wound in her heart.

He told Olivia about it that night, and said that Eileen had been difficult.

"My mother said it would get messy eventually," she said quietly, and he looked surprised.

"You talked to her about me? You told her I'm married?"

"Obviously."

"She must think I'm a real jerk walking out on a wife and three kids."

"She wasn't crazy about it, but she's a reasonable person. When you get divorced, she'll be fine." He nodded, and didn't tell her he hadn't called a lawyer yet. But he was planning to. He just wasn't ready for the big steps. The process was harder than he'd thought it would be, even though he was madly in love with Olivia. But he felt sorry for Eileen and his kids. This was a huge change for them, and he was excited about seeing them that weekend. He was going to take them out to dinner on Friday night alone, sleep at his new apartment with them, and he invited Olivia to join them for lunch on Saturday so she could meet them.

"Are you sure about that?" she questioned him with a doubtful look. "You don't think it's too soon for them?"

"I'd rather they meet you sooner than later. We can just say we're friends for now. But that way, they won't get upset about it, and they'll see what a nice person you are."

"I don't know how great I'll be with kids. I haven't been around any. And I'm only ten years older than your daughter. She may not be crazy about that."

"She'll love it. It'll be like having a big sister or a grown-up friend," he said confidently. "And the boys are easy. All they care about are sports and video games."

"Neither of which I know anything about," Olivia said, looking worried, but he insisted it would be simple and fun. He knew his children.

They fell into bed after that, and she forgot about the children. She loved being able to sleep with him every night now, and make love whenever they wanted. He really was a free man, and he had finally left his wife after five months of promising to. He was proving to be a man of his word, and she was certain her mother's concerns were unfounded. All she had to do now was meet his kids, and it would be smooth sailing after that. That was what Paul told her, and she believed him. He believed it himself, and he didn't lie to her. Only to his wife.

Chapter 7

P aul left work early and met the children at the train at Grand
Central Station when they arrived from Greenwich on Friday
afternoon. They had taken the train after school, and arrived at five-
nineteen. They each had a tote bag, and Mark was carrying a small
suitcase that Eileen had packed with clean clothes for all of them.
The treasures they each wanted to bring and their laptops were all in
their tote bags. It was the first time their father had seen them since
he'd left the house the week before. He felt a wave of love and relief
wash over him when he saw them step off the train, the boys first,
with Pennie right behind to keep an eye on them. She had taken on
more of a parental role with them just in the past week, to help their
mother.

The boys leapt at him and hugged him, and he had an arm around
each of them as he looked into his daughter's eyes and saw the cold
disapproval and smoldering anger there. She didn't reach out to him
when he let the boys go, and she was stiff when he hugged her.

"Hi, Dad," she murmured, as they headed toward the main terminal of the station and threaded their way through the jostling crowd to the street.

The four of them got in a cab, and the boys chattered all the way to Paul's new apartment on the Upper East Side. The building was small and elegant, and the boys looked impressed.

"This is cool, Dad," Mark said, pleased. Seth was more hesitant, and Pennie had said not a word in the cab or as she looked around. The apartment was small and compact, but nicely decorated. The room he assigned to the boys had twin beds, and a large flat-screen TV on the wall. Pennie's was bigger and more feminine, done in pale blue–flowered chintz fabrics. His own room was down the hall, with a big, comfortable king-size bed, a flat-screen TV, and a view of the garden. They all reconvened in the kitchen a few minutes later, and Paul had set out guacamole and chips, which he knew they loved. No one ate at first. The vibes Pennie gave off toward her father were glacial. Her sympathies were with Eileen, not her father. She also knew that he "probably" had a girlfriend, as Eileen had said. The boys didn't know that.

"So what do you think, guys?" Paul asked them with a fatherly smile when they came back to the kitchen. He was hungry for their approval, and anxious for them to feel at home in his new digs.

"I think it was mean of you to leave Mom," Seth said quietly, and Mark gave him a shove and glanced apologetically at their father, while Pennie stood staring silently, out at the garden behind the building. It looked autumnal and bleak.

"Don't say that!" Mark scolded his twin. He wanted the visit to go well so they could see more of their father. They had talked about it on the train into the city, but Seth was hurt that they hadn't been warned of the breakup, and his father hadn't said goodbye to them when he left. "Sorry, Dad," Mark said, and helped himself to the guacamole.

"I'm sorry I didn't say goodbye to you. Things just kind of happened last Saturday, and we decided on the spur of the moment that we needed a break. I think it's been coming for a long time, but we didn't want to see it."

"Are you coming back?" Seth asked, worried. His brow was furrowed, and he looked suddenly more grown up. They were about to turn twelve, and were less rowdy than they had been. Paul hesitated before he answered.

"I don't know yet." He didn't want to lie to them. "Your mom and I need to talk."

"She's been crying a lot," Seth said, and Mark groaned. This was not what they had agreed to on the train. They were going to keep it light and have a nice visit, not grill him about his plans or make him feel guilty.

"I'm sorry to hear it. This is a big change for both of us. But maybe it will do us good. It's hard to keep a marriage on track for eighteen years. People change." *Especially if you didn't want to get married in the first place,* Pennie thought but didn't say anything. She knew she had been the catalyst for their marriage, and had carried the weight of that ever since her mother had told her at fifteen. Their separation felt like it was her fault too, because she'd gotten pregnant that summer, and her parents had been upset with each other ever since.

"I'm glad you let us come to see you," Mark said, suddenly serious. They were all reassured to see that there was room for them there, but it made the change seem more permanent, as though he was planning to stay away for a long time, or forever.

"Why don't you settle in for a little while, and then we'll go to dinner," he said. He had made a reservation at an Italian restaurant he'd been to with Olivia that he thought they'd like, with pasta and pizza and a traditional menu. He'd made a reservation at Serendipity for lunch the next day, with all the fabulous desserts. They'd been there before and loved it. There was a festive feeling to it, like a birthday party. It seemed like the perfect place for them to meet Olivia, young and light, but he didn't tell them his plan. He wanted to surprise them, and Olivia was going to just "drop by" to meet them, "casually." She was still hesitant, and nervous about it.

Pennie didn't say a word as she followed her brothers out of the kitchen, and they went back to their rooms to check them out some more. Mark turned on the TV, and Seth opened his laptop and played a game. Pennie closed her bedroom door to put on heels and a sweater she had borrowed from her mother for dinner. She looked beautiful and grown up when her father knocked on the door half an hour later, and she emerged.

"Wow, you look lovely, Pen," Paul said.

"Thank you," she said through pursed lips. She was refusing to be swept along by their father trying to put them at ease and make it all seem normal. It wasn't. She knew her mother was having a sushi dinner with Jane that night, so she wasn't alone, which made Pennie feel less guilty for coming to the city and leaving her. Even though she was angry at him, she wanted to see her father too. But it made her feel like a traitor to her mother. There were sides now, and she was on her mother's, but she loved him too. It was very confusing.

They took an Uber to the restaurant, and Paul was relieved that the kids liked it. It was nicer than the restaurants they usually went to, and made the evening feel special, and the food was very good. They were back at the house at nine o'clock. Paul gave them the Wi-Fi code, so they had access to the internet, and Seth turned on the TV in their room to watch his favorite shows, just like he did when they were at home. But none of them were sure if they were supposed to entertain their father, or could do what they wanted. They didn't know the protocol for visiting a separated parent, and were trying to take their lead from him. He was treating them more like guests than his children, and he left them for a few minutes to call Olivia. He told her it was going well, although Pennie hadn't warmed up yet. After the call, he stopped to see her in her room. She was lying on the bed, reading a magazine she had brought with her.

"Everything okay?" he asked her from the doorway, not sure if she wanted him to come in, and she wasn't sure either. He felt more like a stranger now, in the unfamiliar setting, but he was still her dad, for better or worse.

"I guess so," she said, putting down the magazine. "Why did you do it, Dad? Couldn't you have worked things out at home?" She knew their marriage hadn't been smooth, but his leaving seemed so radical, and so unnecessary. They didn't fight that much. But she couldn't judge how disconnected they'd become, and he didn't want to explain it to her. He couldn't tell her about the affair with Olivia that had changed everything and that Eileen had finally discovered it when he hadn't come home the previous Friday night. He wondered now if he had wanted her to figure it out, and had given her the necessary clues.

"Things happen," he said quietly as he walked cautiously into the room and sat down on a chair. "Just like they did with you and Tim. You don't plan them, and then you have to deal with the fallout. Your mom and I have been drifting apart for a long time, and then it suddenly all came to a head, and we both thought I should leave." It was a modified version of what had happened.

"That's what Mom said. Are you going to get divorced?"

"Maybe. I don't know. It's possible, but not a sure thing yet, that's why I'm here. To figure it out." He wouldn't have admitted that to Olivia, who thought he was on the fast track to a divorce now, and considered him a free man. So did he when he was with her. But when he saw his children, he wasn't as sure. And Eileen was part of that. Seeing them made him miss her more than he'd expected to when he left. He had thought it would be a relief to move to the city and be with Olivia all the time, and it was, but there was a piece missing too, and Eileen was it. He realized that now. "Is your mom doing okay?" he asked softly.

"She's trying to. She's very brave about it, but I've seen her crying. She doesn't say anything bad about you," she said.

"She wouldn't." And he knew she could have. "She's a wonderful person. I'm not sure how much we have in common anymore, other than the three of you. And you need more than that to make a marriage work." Pennie nodded, wanting to hate him, but she didn't. He was still the father she loved even if she was angry at him for leaving. She wanted to ask him about the girlfriend he might have, but she didn't dare. It was too awkward and painful to bring it up.

He left Pennie to check on the boys, and suggested a card game between the four of them, but there were no takers. The kids were tired and everyone went to bed early, and so did Paul. He missed Olivia in his bed that night, but this was a sacred time, and he belonged to his children. It was important to him that everything go right.

He made breakfast for them the next morning, and Pennie helped him, and warmed up a little. He made scrambled eggs and pancakes, and had bought their favorite batter and syrup. He was a good breakfast cook, although he couldn't cook much else, except the simple things he had learned from Eileen, who was a fabulous cook, and took pride in what she made for them. She was a talented chef, and had taught Pennie a few of her tricks.

After breakfast, they played around on their computers as they would have at home. Pennie washed and dried her hair and at noon Paul told them they were going to Serendipity for lunch. They loved that. He was thinking of taking them to a movie afterwards. They were catching the six o'clock train back to Greenwich. The visit had gone well so far. They took the subway to the restaurant, which was an adventure for them.

They were given a big round table at the busy restaurant, with Tiffany lamps hanging over every table, and Pennie noticed that it was set for five. She assumed it was a mistake so she didn't mention it. They ordered hot dogs and club sandwiches. The boys each ordered a banana split for dessert, Pennie ordered a frozen mochaccino, and Paul had a hot fudge sundae. They were known for their massive overindulgent desserts, which came in a bowl and were too much for anyone to finish. They chattered all through lunch, and were already excited about their costumes and plans for Halloween. Pennie said she was going to a party being given by one of the seniors. The conversation was lively as the desserts were set down, and a small redheaded young woman suddenly appeared at their table and smiled at them. Paul had meant to mention it a few minutes earlier and hadn't gotten to it. They all stared at the petite redhead as she pulled up the fifth chair and sat down.

"I'm sorry I'm late. The traffic was awful. Hi, I'm Olivia, and I'm happy to meet all of you." The children stared at her and said nothing as Paul squirmed in his seat and tried to cover the awkward moment.

"Olivia is a friend of mine, and I wanted to introduce you to her. She said she was going to be around today, and I asked her to join us."

"Without telling us?" Pennie fired at him, without acknowledging Olivia. The boys muttered embarrassed hellos and stared at their banana splits without touching them.

"Would you like dessert?" Paul offered her, as they exchanged a look, and Olivia seemed confused.

"No, I'm fine. I'll have a bite of yours," she said to Paul. It was an intimate gesture, which Pennie noticed immediately.

Olivia did her best to make small talk with them, while Paul tried to compensate for his children's silences, and the only people talking at the table were the two of them. The boys ate their banana splits without looking at her, and Pennie stared at her with a hostile expression and unconcealed fury at her father.

"I don't know why you didn't tell us you invited a friend, Dad," Pennie finally said to him, and Mark stepped into the breach, finally glancing at Olivia.

"Is she your girlfriend, Dad?" He wanted to know. They all did. Pennie assumed she was.

Paul felt like Judas denying Christ when he said she wasn't. "We're just good friends. We know each other through work. She has an art gallery online, and her mom is a famous movie star." He was groping for reasons why he'd know her, and his children weren't buying it.

"How old are you?" Seth questioned her as they all stared at her, waiting for the answer. She had worn jeans and a red sweater and sneakers, and looked Pennie's age at most.

"I'm twenty-seven," she said, smiling at them, but none of them smiled back.

"Do you have a boyfriend?" Mark asked her, and Pennie answered for her before Olivia could.

"Yes, our father. That's why she came to meet us. He didn't invite anyone else from 'work,' did he?" She had a point, and Paul didn't deny it again. It was obvious that they fully understood the purpose of the meeting. They weren't children to that degree, and he still didn't know what Eileen had said. "We're not stupid, or five years old, Dad. We get it," Pennie said, and both boys nodded in agreement and continued to stare at Olivia. She was a beautiful girl. So far, her twenties had made no mark on her. "I think it was a rotten thing to do to Mom to have her here," Pennie continued. "It makes it look to her like we're part of whatever you're doing here, and we're not. You should have asked us how we felt about it. I wouldn't have come if I'd known." Olivia wanted to crawl under the table, but she thought Pennie was right. She shot Paul a look. He was mortified by Pennie's comments and didn't know how to respond.

"Are we supposed to keep it a secret from Mom?" Mark asked innocently. It was a valid question.

"Of course not. We don't keep secrets."

"You do," Pennie said under her breath, and pushed her almost untouched dessert away. The boys had devoured theirs. Nothing affected their appetites.

"So can we tell Mom we saw her or not?" Seth questioned his father.

"Not," Mark answered for him. "She'll just cry about it, and she'll be mad at us."

"You can do whatever you like," Paul said clearly. The meeting had gotten out of hand, but he wasn't going to ask them to hide anything from their mother.

"I'm sorry this has been awkward," Olivia finally spoke up. "I know this must be hard for all of you. Your dad just left home a week ago, and now you're meeting new friends in his other life without you. I'm happy I got to meet you, but I didn't want to upset anyone. I just thought it would be fun. I've heard so much about you from your dad." She said it warmly and with a sympathetic expression. The boys thought she was nice, but Pennie didn't warm up for a second. She was furious with her father for the traitorous position he had put them in with their mother, without their knowledge or consent. He had dragged them into his new life, and his romance, and it was obvious to everyone that Olivia was his girlfriend. In other circumstances, far down the road, if the situation with their mother were clear, they might have liked her, but not this way. He had crammed her down their throats, and ambushed them.

As soon as Olivia had spoken to them, she stood up with a warm smile and looked around the table. "Well, I just wanted to come by for a few minutes, I've got to leave now. Have a great time today." She gave a little wave, which included Paul, didn't kiss him goodbye, disappeared into the crowd in the restaurant, and was gone as suddenly as she had arrived. There was silence at the table as all three of his children stared at Paul, waiting for some explanation to justify what he'd done. But there was no making it all right for them, and he knew that now. He had made the introduction to Olivia badly and prematurely. He had been foolish and naïve to think they would enjoy meeting her just because he loved her.

"How could you, Dad?" Pennie said, with eyes full of fury. "What can we say to Mom? That we had lunch with you and your girlfriend?"

"You didn't have lunch with her, she dropped by." It was a lame excuse and he knew it.

"It was all planned and you never told us, or asked us if we wanted to meet her. You made us betray Mom, and dragged us into whatever you have going on with her. It's obvious what you're doing. And you look old enough to be her father." He had salt-and-pepper hair, and lines in his face, and Olivia looked like a child next to him, but that was beside the point. There was only a fourteen-year difference between them, not thirty.

"I think we have to tell Mom," Seth said honorably. He was the deep thinker among them. Mark was more happy-go-lucky.

"I don't see why. It's just going to make her sad. I liked her. She's really hot-looking. She's nice, Dad," Mark said kindly.

"You were rude to her," Paul accused Pennie.

"What do you expect, Dad? For us to welcome her with open arms, a week after you moved out?" His daughter was more sensible than he had been, and smarter. Olivia would have been too, if he'd listened to her.

"Are you going to marry her?" Seth asked, shocked. It had just occurred to him that that might have been the purpose of the meeting.

"Of course not," Paul said rapidly. "We're friends, we've gone out a few times. I like her. I'm not marrying anyone. I'm married to your mother."

"But you're dating her?" Seth pursued it, and Paul didn't answer. He felt cornered and he was not going to make it any worse than it already was. He could imagine how Olivia was feeling. The whole mission and its purpose had been aborted. He had wanted them to make friends, way too early.

He signaled for the check and paid it, and they left the restaurant. Seth spoke up as soon as they reached the street.

"Can we go home now? I have a lot of homework to do for Monday."

"Yeah, me too," Mark added. The meeting with Olivia had been too emotionally charged for all of them, even Paul. Pennie looked like she was ready to run back to Greenwich.

"I'll look up the train schedule when we get back to the apartment. I'm sure there's one before six o'clock, if that's what you want to do." He wasn't going to force them to stay, on top of everything else. He sensed that he had some fence-mending to do with Olivia, after the awkward meeting.

They took a cab back to his apartment and none of them said a word. Paul sat staring out the window, wondering how he could have misjudged the situation so badly. It had ruined the weekend for all of them, and was a harbinger of things to come. There were opposing teams now and they were on their mother's. They saw her as the victim now that they knew he had a girlfriend.

It was two-thirty when they got back to the apartment, and there was a three-forty-eight train. They could easily be on it. Pennie called their mother and she said she'd pick them up. They were packed in five minutes, and in a cab on the way to Grand Central Station ten minutes later. Paul saw them off and the boys waved at him when they left him. Pennie didn't. She thanked him politely for the weekend, but she didn't respond when he hugged her. He had crossed an important line for her, and she wasn't ready to forgive him for it. And he'd been on thin ice with her before that.

He walked through the station with his head down after he left them. He was bitterly upset about how he had handled the meeting. He hailed a cab and went straight to Olivia's. He called her cellphone and she didn't pick up, but he suspected she was there. The doorman buzzed her when he got there, and sent him up to her apartment. He didn't have keys yet. She was waiting at the door when he got upstairs. She looked even angrier than Pennie had, the moment she saw him.

"What the fuck was that?" were her first words to him. "How could you do that, and spring me on them? I thought you had at least warned them." She went back into her apartment and he followed.

"I was going to. The right moment never happened."

"So you let me walk into it blindly like an idiot and piss them all off? They're going to hate me forever after that, and they probably would have anyway. But now we can be sure of it. You screwed everyone, Paul, them, me, your ex-wife. Even yourself."

"I know. I didn't think it would be like that. I was sure they'd fall in love with you, like I did."

"Are you crazy? They've got divided loyalties. They don't know anything about me, except now they can assume that I broke up their parents' marriage, which I did. They're going to blame me for your divorce forever. You told me the marriage was dead, but they don't know that. It's very much alive to them. I'm the interloper here, the intruder, the enemy. You put me in that position. You should have waited to introduce us, and you sure as hell should have warned them today, or even asked them if they wanted to meet me. Instead you cast me in the role of slut and home-wrecker. Shit, how do you expect that to play out after this?"

"They'll get over it. They're kids," he said, underestimating them again, but Olivia didn't. She knew better.

"They're not five years old, as Pennie said. You can't bullshit them, and you shouldn't. Pennie is not a 'kid,' she's almost a grown woman. She's nearly eighteen, and she seems to know you have a girlfriend. And thanks for denying me entirely, by the way. If you couldn't tell them I'm your girlfriend, I shouldn't have met them."

"It's too soon, I wanted to start gently."

"Well, you didn't. The way you did it couldn't have been much worse. And why are you here? Why aren't you with them?"

"They left early," he said, looking remorseful. "Right after lunch. You're right. I'm sorry. I screwed it all up. I was naïve about how they'd react."

"You were ridiculous to think you could pull that on them. I tried to warn you and you wouldn't listen. Your kids are beautiful, by the way."

"They look like their mother. Pennie is the image of her."

"Seth looks just like you." She smiled at him. She felt sorry for him. He had made a mess of the meeting, which would have been delicate anyway, and he had run roughshod over everyone's feelings, including hers.

She calmed down after that, and they talked quietly and went for a walk, but it was a warning to her that Paul didn't know what he was doing. She was flattered that he had wanted her to meet his children, but if he handled the divorce as badly as he handled their meeting, they were in for some rough times ahead. She told Paul that she wasn't eager to inherit a ready-made family of angry children who would hate her forever.

"Are you saying I'm too old for you?" he asked her, worried.

"No. I'm saying that your life is complicated, maybe more than you want to admit to me or yourself. This isn't going to be easy. I'm twenty-seven. I don't want to be in the middle of a big mess with a lot of drama. I love you, and I love being with you, but I'm scared about your kids. They're real people with their own feelings and opinions, and they love their mother. I just got off on the wrong foot with them, with your help." She was suddenly reminded of what her mother had said to her, that this wasn't just about her and Paul, there were four other people involved, his wife and three children, and inevitably there were going to be casualties. It couldn't be avoided, and was the nature of divorce. Olivia could see that now. She had gotten her first taste of it, and she didn't like it. She didn't want to hurt anyone, but she was going to, and already had. That hadn't been clear to her before. His children hadn't been real to her until she met them. Now they were. It was a sobering thought that made their relationship less fun and less appealing. There were strings attached, heavy ones, and live people. His children would be marked forever by the divorce and how he handled it. He had just bungled an important piece of it for her. It was a lot to think about. She was quiet when they got back to her apartment.

They made love that afternoon, but she was pensive and quiet, and Paul was too. He couldn't stop thinking about his children as he and Olivia lay in bed.

Three hours later, Eileen called him on his cell. He was still in bed with Olivia, watching a movie by then. She was livid.

"Do you have any idea how inappropriate it was to introduce *our* children, *my* children, to your girlfriend without my consent or theirs, a week after you left me? You haven't even told *me* anything about her yet. Are you crazy, or just a total sonofabitch?" she screamed at him, and she wasn't normally a screamer. "Where are your morals, your sense of decency? Who are you, Paul? And what kind of slut is she to be a party to this? Seth cried when he got home. He said you're never coming back, she's too young and beautiful and you'll probably marry her. And Mark had a stomachache and went to bed. You tried to drag them to your side, and make them betray me. I can tell you, all that's going to do is turn them against you, and lose me as your ally forever. I guess our marriage really is over." She didn't sound sad about it, just angry, which made her feel better and him worse. He didn't want the role of the bastard, but now he had it.

"I told them I didn't know if it was over or not. She left immediately when she saw how awkward it was and how uncomfortable they were. I don't think she was there for more than ten minutes. I made a total mess of it. I agree with you, and I'm sorry. I should have asked you. I don't know the ground rules here. I've never been in this situation before."

"Neither have I, but I never cheated on you, and I wouldn't introduce our children to my boyfriend, if I had one, a week after we split up. You disrespected everyone, me, yourself, and our children."

"It won't happen again, I promise. I'm sorry." He sounded sincerely remorseful, but she hung up on him anyway. She had never done that before either. The lines had been drawn now, and Eileen realized he had obviously lost his mind over the girl he was sleeping with. Seth was probably right, he wouldn't come back, and he'd marry her. She must be an idiot too, Eileen thought, to agree to meet them so soon. Or she was madly in love and as besotted as he was. Either way, Eileen knew now that she was fighting a losing battle to save their marriage. She had already lost him. It was why he'd been able to leave so easily and so quickly.

She talked to Jane about it that night, and Jane advised her to call one of the lawyers she'd recommended. Eileen said she would. She had no other choice now. She wanted rules he had to live by. Everything had fallen apart so quickly, she still couldn't get her mind around it. Their marriage had disintegrated. It had been rotting from the inside, like a house full of termites, until it collapsed into a pile of dust.

The boys were asleep, and she checked on Pennie before she went to bed. She was reading her college essays on her computer and looked up when her mother walked in.

"Are you okay?" Eileen asked, and Pennie nodded.

"He was such a jerk, Mom," she said, as tears filled her eyes. All illusions she'd had about her father were over.

"The boys said the girl is really beautiful and very young, and she looks like a teenager."

"She's twenty-seven, and probably a whore. I hate her." There was no question about where her loyalties lay now, and Paul knew it too. They all did. And so did Olivia. She thought it would probably turn into a full-on war soon. Pennie, Eileen, Paul, and Olivia all fell asleep that night thinking about it. Just as her mother had predicted, Olivia thought. There would be casualties. There already were, and she and his children had been the first ones. He was a fool if nothing else. Her illusions about him and how smart he was had taken a hard hit.

Chapter 8

Olivia told Paul she needed some time to herself the next morning, which concerned him. The meeting the day before with his kids had taken a heavy toll. He went back to his apartment, and she said she'd call him later. Then she dropped by her mother's apartment.

She told her about the disastrous meeting over coffee in the kitchen since the cook was off.

"You were right," she said quietly, "it gets messy."

"It's inevitable with the undoing of a marriage," Gwen said. "It's not a happy thing to be part of. You have to be awfully serious about him to want to go through it. And his children will blame you for many years, maybe forever."

"I can see that now. His daughter was looking daggers at me, and I don't blame her. I would have too, in her shoes. He misjudged it completely, and I became the sacrificial lamb. Now they hate me."

"Do you want to marry him?" her mother asked, and Olivia hesitated.

"I don't know. Not now anyway. I'm too young to get married. There's still a lot I want to do. I've seen his kids now. That's a lot to take on, especially if they hate me. I didn't understand all that before. It's different once you see them. They're very real." And so was his wife, although she'd never seen her.

"Breaking up a marriage is a big responsibility," her mother reminded her. "You'd better be ready for it if this is what you're doing and he is who you want."

"He's handsome and sexy and we have fun, but he's dragging a wagonload of baggage with him. That's the part I'm scared of."

"It comes with married men, especially if they have kids."

"I'm beginning to get that. He made it sound like everything was all free and easy, and they lived separate lives and the marriage was dead. His kids don't seem to think so, and I'll bet his wife doesn't either. He's the only one who does."

"Maybe you need to slow it down a little," her mother suggested gently, and Olivia nodded.

"Yeah. Maybe."

"Real people are going to be hurt and I'd rather you not be one of them." Olivia didn't like being hated either, especially by Paul's children. Their looks at Serendipity had sliced right through her like a knife. She knew she would never forget it, and she suspected they probably wouldn't either.

Eileen made breakfast for the kids on Sunday, and dropped them off at their various activities the day after they returned from their visit to their father. They were all in better spirits than when they got home, and none of them talked about it. Eileen took the boys to soccer practice, and gave Pennie a ride to a friend's. They only had one car now, since Paul had taken his to the city, and Eileen couldn't spare hers. She was on the move all the time.

A week later, two weeks after Paul had left, she was surprised by how efficiently things were running. She had always thought that she would be lost without him. She was startled to discover that she wasn't. It had been disorienting at first, but she had found her bearings. It was lonely at times, but she was lonely when she was living with him too. He came home late from work every night, went to client dinners without her, and most of the time he didn't talk to her when he got home, he was too tired. He played golf and tennis with friends on the weekends. He loved his children, but most of the time he didn't help her with them, so life without him wasn't very different.

She said as much to Jane too, that life without Paul was easier in a lot of ways. She had to take care of the children entirely herself, but she didn't have to take care of him too. Even after only two weeks, it was liberating, and she was coping with everything she had to do.

"Well, there's a piece of information for you," Jane said drily.

It annoyed Eileen that he was having all the fun now, with a hot new girlfriend and no family he had to come home to. He could do whatever he wanted at night, without making excuses, checking in, lying, or commuting. He had the best of the deal, while she did all the drudgery, cooking, laundry, and driving, and helped Pennie with her college applications. She had someone to come in and clean the house, but everything that related to the children had always fallen to her to do, and still did.

It had shaken her when the twins described what Olivia looked like. She was younger, but it woke Eileen up to what a drudge she'd become. She didn't care how she looked and how she dressed, and she wanted to change that. She started wearing makeup again. Pennie noticed immediately and told her she looked great. She took a little more care with how she dressed and threw her oldest running shoes away and bought new ones. It didn't make a huge difference in her appearance, but it lifted her spirits. She was thinking about her future.

She tried to impart what she was learning to her daughter, and told Pennie not to give up her dreams for anyone. She thought it was the biggest mistake she had made when she married Paul. She had given up editing and her dreams of working in publishing. They had focused on what he wanted, and what he had given up when they got married, and never on her. She was determined never to let that happen again, with Paul, or anyone else. She had to matter too, and not just as the workhorse to serve everyone else's needs.

Pennie told her that she'd only had one or two texts from Tim since he'd started school. He was busy with his new college life, and seemed to have moved on, even after losing the baby, which had brought them closer, briefly. Pennie wasn't ready to move on yet. She wasn't dating, and she didn't want to, but her mother hoped she would soon, when she felt ready. She wanted her to enjoy her senior year, especially after everything that had happened to her.

Eileen made a major effort to make it a fun Halloween for them.

She carved pumpkins with the twins, as she always did. She had their costumes ready and drove the twins around trick or treating. Pennie went to a party with friends. It had only been two weeks since Paul had moved out, but Eileen felt as though she was coming alive again. She was managing fine without him, better than she had ever thought she would. It made her wonder if they should have split up sooner. Most of the time, she was amazed to find she didn't miss him. He had wounded her so badly by cheating on her that it had killed something deep within her. She was beginning to think that she no longer loved him, which was a relief.

In the first week of November, Gwen and Gabrielle went to Paris for Federico's show at the Petit Palais. It went beautifully, the critics loved it, Gabrielle was very proud of him, and the three of them enjoyed a week in Paris, staying at the Ritz. Gwen had invited Olivia to join them, but she said she was too busy getting her online art gallery running smoothly and meeting new artists.

Things settled down with Paul again, after the disastrous meeting with his children. They were coming to the city to see him every other weekend, but sometimes they had too many plans of their own and couldn't make it. They weren't interfering in his life with Olivia, and Paul and Olivia were settling into a comfortable routine that worked for both of them. They were both busy, but he slept at her place every night, and she liked that. She was too busy to think about his divorce, and assumed he was taking care of it. They had no plans for her to see his children again. Nor for him to meet her mother.

Paul talked to Eileen about the children's Thanksgiving plans. She wanted them with her for the holidays, and they wanted to be at home in Connecticut. Paul wasn't set up to provide a real Thanksgiving meal for them, and didn't want to take them to a hotel or restaurant, so he agreed to let Eileen have them. He had no plans of his own. Olivia had already told him that she spent Thanksgiving at her mother's every year, her grandmother and Federico came, and a few old friends of her mother's, but she didn't feel comfortable asking Paul to join them. It seemed like too big a statement, and too soon to her. She wanted him to meet her mother, but not yet. And Gwen didn't approve of the fact that he was married, even if he was separated.

Olivia said she would only be gone for a few hours on Thanksgiving, and planned to meet up with him afterwards. It was the first time he wouldn't be celebrating Thanksgiving in years, and wouldn't see his children. They didn't want to come into the city during the weekend. They all had too much going on and fun plans of their own.

Olivia felt mildly guilty when she left for lunch at her mother's, but Paul was a good sport about it, went back to his own apartment, and caught up on some work.

Traditionally, Eileen's mother came to Thanksgiving in Connecticut every year. Eileen wasn't close to her. Her mother, Margaret, had always been an angry, unhappy woman, and she had never liked Paul. She made no bones about it. Her own marriage had been disappointing. She was widowed at sixty when Eileen's father died of cancer. But even after he was gone, Margaret led a small life and was a dour woman. Eileen was used to it, and called her dutifully every few weeks, but her mother was a joyless person, probably chronically depressed all her life, with no interest in Eileen or her grand-children. The children had never been close to her either, and they only saw her once a year on Thanksgiving. Eileen's father had been browbeaten by her until he died at sixty. Eileen had been thrilled to leave home and move to New York to escape both of them.

Eileen's mother lived in Massachusetts, and was only sixty-five years old, but acted as though she were ninety. She had no hobbies or interests, and watched soap operas on TV all the time. She had worked in the finance office of the same company until she retired, and had hated it for all the years she worked there. The children dreaded her visit every year. She complained about everything, and it was the one thing Paul knew he wouldn't miss over the holiday. He called her the "mother-in-law from hell," and Eileen didn't disagree with him. Eileen was an only child and her mother had been con-stantly critical of her growing up, and her father was too meek to defend her. Eileen had grown up in a suburb of Boston.

Eileen waited to tell Margaret about their separation until about a week before she came so she could make whatever negative com-ments she had to make over the phone, and not make them at dinner and ruin the holiday, which she often did anyway. The children paid no attention to her.

"What brought that on?" She seemed surprised when Eileen told her that Paul had moved out.

"I guess we'd been drifting apart for a long time, and I didn't no-tice it."

"Are you getting divorced?"

"We haven't decided yet." She wanted to give her mother as little information as possible, just the basics.

"You should try to get him back." Eileen was startled by her comment.

"You've never liked him, Mom. Why would you say that?" She was more curious than interested in what she had to say. Her mother had never given her good advice. She and Eileen's father had been a poor match, and stayed together anyway, unhappy for most of their marriage. Eileen knew from her mother that he'd had several affairs while she was growing up, but they'd never divorced.

"You're not going to find someone else at your age," she said, sounding as sour and negative as she always did.

"I'm thirty-nine, not a hundred, Mom." Eileen was annoyed by her comment, since her age was becoming a sensitive subject, with her fortieth birthday looming.

"It's all over at forty, your looks, your future, men. Does Paul have someone else?" She rang a death knell over Eileen's future, as she had always done, even in her twenties.

"Possibly." Eileen didn't want to give her the details. She always had something depressing to say.

"You can bet she's younger than you are, if he does. He's not going to want another forty-year-old. Maybe that's why he left." She hated the idea that her mother might be even partially right. And she was of course, since the woman he was involved with was considerably younger. Pennie had said she was twenty-seven. A *lot* younger. And Olivia looked like a teenager, according to her boys.

"I think he had other reasons."

"You should try to get him to come back before he marries someone else, and you wind up alone forever." Her mother's words were like a curse on her future, or a death sentence, which was why she hated talking to her, and called her as seldom as possible. Her mother had had a negative outlook on life for as long as Eileen could remember. She had insisted that Eileen marry Paul when she got pregnant, to spare them embarrassment. She had also said that no one would ever want her with an illegitimate child if Eileen wouldn't give the baby up. She never had anything good to say, and she particularly disliked Paul, but thought Eileen should stay with him nonetheless. Once Paul had realized how negative Margaret was, he paid little attention to her, which offended her. He said that listening to her diatribes was like inhaling toxic fumes. Eileen was counting on her mother being wrong about her future after forty, and did her best not to listen to her. The children always complained when they had to sit next to her. But she retired to the guest room right after dinner to watch TV, and went home the day after Thanksgiving so they didn't have to put up with her for long. It amazed Eileen that her mother wasn't old, but had given up on life years before. And all she wanted was never to be like her.

Eileen made an especially big effort and went all out for their Thanksgiving meal. She wanted it to be special to make up for their losses in the past month. Paul's absence was sorely felt, and she knew that the children were sad about it. It was only Eileen, the children, and her mother, but the dinner was exquisite. Even the children noticed it. She had made all the traditional things they loved, and added some new touches and new vegetables, a truffle stuffing, and another one with foie gras. They could hardly move when they got up from the table.

Margaret had kept her barbs to a minimum and actually enjoyed the meal. She usually upset Eileen more than the children, and Eileen was always sorry she hadn't been able to provide a better grandmother for them. Margaret made her usual comments, but Eileen did her best to ignore her. Margaret always reminded Eileen about being pregnant when she got married. But it no longer mattered. Pennie was almost grown up and Paul was gone. Her comments about Eileen's failed career fell on deaf ears and were irrelevant eighteen years later. Her criticisms were all to make Eileen feel bad, but were old news by then. Eileen was surprised to find they had no power over her anymore.

Margaret left the morning after Thanksgiving, as she always did. She said goodbye to the children, thanked Eileen, and got a cab to the train station. Eileen was grateful that they never invited her for Christmas. Margaret went to her sister's family in New Hampshire instead, whom she said she liked better. Eileen's family had paid penance for the year and done their duty. She mentioned again how good the dinner had been before she left.

"You should have been a cook," she said, which she considered a put-down, but Eileen just smiled at her.

"Thanks, Mom. I'm glad you enjoyed it." And a few minutes later, after she was gone, Pennie came downstairs in a cute short black leather skirt, a new pair of boots, and a sweater she had borrowed from her mother.

"Where are you going all dressed up?" Her mother smiled at her.

"Tim is home. We're having lunch," she said, looking nervous and excited. "He called Wednesday night when he got in. He says he loves Stanford."

"I'm glad for him," she said, studying her daughter. "Are you okay about seeing him?" Pennie nodded, and Eileen got busy with the boys after that.

Tim picked Pennie up an hour later, and drove her to a nice restaurant for lunch. They had only seen each other once briefly in a rush after his trip to China and before he left for Stanford. He wanted to do something nice for her, and she was happy to see him and impressed by the restaurant. She felt very grown up at the table with him, and he looked more mature than he had when he left in August. A lot had happened to both of them. She told him about her parents' breakup and in a way he wasn't surprised. They had never seemed that happy to him, from things Pennie had said and when he was with them.

"He has a girlfriend. I met her in New York a month ago. My father is an idiot. He tried to surprise us with her. It was a disaster. She's very pretty and very young. She's twenty-seven."

"Do you think he'll marry her?" Tim was startled to hear about the girlfriend, Paul seemed like such a family man. He was sorry for Pennie. He knew it was another blow for her.

"I don't know. He'll probably spring that on us too, if he does. We'd all be upset if he marries her, especially my mom. This has been really hard for her. She has to do everything herself. She always did, but she's really on her own now. At least before, he came home at night most of the time. She's been really good about it though. She never says bad things about him."

"I like your mom a lot," Tim said quietly. If possible, he seemed even more handsome than when he left, and Pennie was as beautiful as always. They were handsome young people. Pennie was trying to figure out what she still felt about him during lunch. She wasn't sure. He was still her best friend, although she hardly heard from him now, and she didn't have the same rush of excitement when she saw him, but they knew each other so well. That was hard to replace, and she didn't want to try, yet. "Are you dating anyone?" he asked her, and she shook her head with a serious expression.

"I was pretty depressed after . . . when . . . well, this summer." They both knew what she meant. She didn't like talking about the baby she had lost, and it was hard even with him. "I'm better now. But there's no one I want to date."

"I think things worked out the way they were meant to," he said gently, and touched her hand across the table. "We could have done it, but it would have been hard, for both of us. It would have changed our lives forever." As she looked at him, and held his hand, she knew something she hadn't before, that they really were friends. They had been through something hard together, and he had stood by her un-failingly. He would have married her if she'd agreed to, and she had a feeling he would have been more gracious than her father ever had been with her mother for the same reason. Tim wasn't a bitter, venge-ful person. He had never blamed her for a minute. He really did love her. And that love had solidified their friendship, but she had a feeling that their moment as lovers was over. The feelings had changed. They were stronger but different, what they shared now was longer lasting. He was smiling when she looked up at him, and she smiled too.

"Are you dating anyone?" she asked him.

"Kind of . . . sort of . . . not really . . . dinner or a movie here and there. No one I care about. There's no one like you, Pennie." But even with what he said, she knew they had played out their love affair, and now they were left with a friendship so strong that time and distance wouldn't change it. "I think I'd like to live in California after I graduate," he said. "Maybe work in Silicon Valley or San Francisco in venture capital. It's so small-town here in Greenwich, and New York is too extreme. I like the weather out there and the people, the way of life, the outdoors. It suits me. I love it." She could see him doing it, although California held no lure for her. She wanted to stay in the east, and be near her family, and New York. There was so much she enjoyed about the city, theater, museums, art, culture.

He drove her home after lunch, and she thanked him. The questions had been answered for her, without putting words to them. They had their separate paths. They had known that when he graduated from high school in June, and her getting pregnant had confused everything for both of them. But they weren't confused anymore. They were best friends forever and they had both grown up.

"I'll be home for Christmas. I'll see you then," he said when he dropped her off. She kissed his cheek and slid out of his car. He didn't try to kiss her on the mouth, and much to her own surprise, she didn't want him to. Best friends was better. "Take care of yourself, Pen," he called after her, and she turned with a broad smile.

"You too. See you at Christmas!" She ran into the house then and smiled as he drove away. Seeing her had been good for him too. He had felt guilty for months about what had happened, that she'd had to go through so much because of him, and he hadn't been there. He thought he owed it to her to marry her because of it. But they had been relieved of a burden neither of them was equal to. And now they could be friends, and they knew that would last, maybe longer than a marriage would have.

Chapter 9

Pennie turned eighteen two weeks before Christmas. She finished the last of her college applications the weekend before. With her mother's constant nagging, urging, help, and encouragement, she had finished them early, so she would be free over the Christmas vacation, unlike many of her classmates, who hadn't started them yet, and would have a mad scramble to get them done by the deadline. She had gone back to volunteering on Saturdays at the homeless shelter, her board scores were perfect, and her teacher recommendations were excellent. Her first choice school was still Harvard. She wanted to follow in her father's footsteps if she could get in. She wasn't sure she would. She was applying to Yale, Princeton, Dartmouth, Duke, Columbia, and NYU, although she was less excited about staying in New York for college. She wanted a completely new experience, and would like to be a little farther from home. She could always work in New York later. Tim had encouraged her to apply to Stanford. He loved it so much, but she didn't. She didn't feel like a California girl, although it would have been fun to be at the same school with him. She thought she might need a little distance from him too, so she didn't become dependent on him again. She had done that for three years, and was ready to try her own wings, not rely on his.

Eileen took Pennie and the twins and two of Pennie's girlfriends to dinner for her birthday at their favorite restaurant, and they had a lovely evening. It was a big deal for Pennie, turning eighteen. Her father had taken her out to dinner in New York to celebrate it the weekend before. They went to La Grenouille, the fanciest restaurant she'd ever been to, and she felt totally grown up, in a short black dress and heels of her mother's. They had dinner there alone, he did not suggest that Olivia join them. He made no mention of her at all. It was a father-daughter night.

After they came home from dinner on her birthday, Eileen sat down to consult with them about something. For a minute, they all thought that she was going to tell them that she had filed for divorce, but Pennie didn't think she'd announce that on her birthday, and she didn't.

"I want to ask your opinion about something," she said. "I felt like something important was missing when your father didn't spend Thanksgiving with us this year. I don't think he celebrated it. We're the only family he has."

"Wasn't he with his girlfriend?" Mark piped up, and his sister gave him a quelling look.

"It didn't sound like it," Eileen said calmly. The children hadn't seen Olivia again, and Paul had kept his love life away from them since the fateful lunch at Serendipity. "What do you think if we invite him to dinner on Christmas Eve? If you'd like that, I'll do it. If you don't care, I won't. But it might be nice for us to be together for Christmas this year." She didn't want to do it forever, but this once might be a nice transition for all of them.

"Does this mean you're getting back together?" Seth asked her, and she shook her head.

"No, it doesn't. I just thought that for Christmas, we could relax a little." Paul hadn't been back to the house since October, and she hadn't wanted him there. She hadn't seen him at all and didn't want to. They'd arranged for visitations by email and phone, but had no contact in person. He hadn't asked to see her either.

"I'd like it a lot if he comes for Christmas," Seth said, smiling broadly, and Mark seconded it.

"What about you?" she asked Pennie.

"I think it would be nice," she said softly. "Would it be hard for you?"

"Maybe, but I'm the one suggesting it. Christmas is Christmas, but I'll do whatever you like."

"Let's invite him," Mark said, grinning, and Pennie and Seth nodded. Eileen sent Paul an email that night, extending the invitation. She made it clear that there were no romantic implications to the invitation. It was a joint family invitation from her and the kids. He answered her half an hour later, said he was deeply touched by her generosity and accepted with pleasure. She had already figured out that he could sleep on the couch in his old office, which she was using now. Paul knew that Olivia would be with her family again for Christmas and hadn't invited him, so he was grateful for Eileen's invitation. He didn't want to be alone on Christmas, missing his kids.

The day after Pennie's birthday, Eileen got a large envelope in the mail that she'd been expecting for weeks. It was full of forms to fill out. It took her nearly all day to do it, but she completed all of it and sent it back the next day.

A week after Eileen had emailed Paul about spending Christmas Eve with them, Olivia was curled up in his arms after they made love, and she smiled up at him. Christmas was a week away.

"How would you like to have Christmas Eve dinner with my family?" she asked him in a husky voice fresh from their lovemaking. He smiled at her and kissed her tenderly on the lips. Their sex life had never been better, and they were happy with each other.

"I'd love to," he said gently, "but I'm spending it with my children."

"In the city? At your apartment?" She looked startled but didn't want to invite them. She wasn't ready for that, and neither were his kids. She was still smarting from their last encounter, and was sure they were too, since he had never suggested another one. And she hoped he wouldn't anytime soon.

"No, in Greenwich. Eileen emailed me about it last week, with an invitation from her and the children for Christmas Eve. I figured you would be with your family, and you haven't said anything, so I accepted."

"Why didn't you ask me first?" She was visibly disappointed, and worried.

"I didn't want to be pushy about being with your family. And to be honest, I'd love to be with my kids. I was grateful to be asked."

"Is there some deeper meaning here?" she asked, suspicious. Maybe Eileen was trying to win him back and using the nostalgia of the holiday and their children.

134

"None whatsoever. She even said so in the email, 'no romantic implications,' just a family holiday. Who knows, it might be the last Christmas I spend with them, after a divorce, so I'd like to do it."

She sat up in bed then and was wide awake. "Actually, I'd rather you didn't. I'd much prefer that you join me and my family."

"I can't now," he said gently. "I don't want to disappoint my kids."

"Or your wife?"

"She can take another disappointment. I don't want the kids to."

"Have you called your lawyer yet?" she asked him pointedly. "How's the divorce going?"

"I haven't. The separation has only been two months. I was planning to do it after the holidays. I don't need to serve her with divorce papers over Christmas. It can wait a few more weeks." Olivia didn't comment, but she didn't look pleased.

She brought up Christmas Eve dinner two more times in the next few days, but Paul was adamant. He wanted to spend it with his children. He didn't say it, but Olivia should have thought of it sooner. He very much wanted to meet her mother and grandmother, but he hadn't been invited to so far, and now it would have to wait until after Christmas. Olivia had doled out privileges slowly, and he knew that was a big one to her, and indicative of a serious commitment, so it meant a lot that she had asked him, but his children were the priority. He couldn't combine them, for now anyway. He had learned that lesson the hard way.

Olivia made several acerbic comments about his plans in the week before Christmas. She made it clear that she was unhappy he wasn't joining her, but his spending Christmas with Eileen and the kids in Greenwich was written in stone now. He gave Olivia a beautiful sapphire tennis bracelet, with small diamonds between the sapphires, and she loved it, but she was sad not to be spending Christmas with him. They were going to have dinner together on Christmas night. And she gave him an Hermès black leather jacket he loved. It fit him perfectly. They had been generous with each other.

He had a leisurely breakfast with Olivia the morning of Christmas Eve. He left at noon and took the train to Greenwich. There was a light dusting of snow on the ground when he got there, and his house looked like the image on a Christmas card. Eileen had hired someone to put up the lights on the house and in the trees around it, as they always did, and she had added new ones and a funny Santa Claus, a snowman, and a Rudolph on the front lawn, all lit up. It was corny but the kids loved it, and so did he. When he rang the doorbell and she let him in, he saw the tree decorated in the living room. It almost brought tears to his eyes to be home with them for the holiday. It was the best gift Eileen could have given him, Christmas with his children.

"Thank you for letting me come," he said to Eileen in a voice husky with emotion.

"It wouldn't be Christmas without you," she said warmly, and directed him to leave his things in his old office. It had a bathroom, so he knew he'd be fine there.

The boys jumped on him the minute they saw him. Pennie looked pleased too. Their relationship had been strained ever since she'd met Olivia, but she was warmer for the holiday, and she had bought him a black Ralph Lauren sweater with her own money. She looked happy to have him home. They all were.

He took the boys out to do a last minute errand for their mother.

There was a scarf and some gloves they wanted to buy her and didn't have the money. Pennie hadn't had time to take them.

They drove off to town, and Eileen put their Christmas music on. If you didn't know they were separated and he was in love with another woman, you would have thought that all was right in their world. In some ways, it was. And outwardly, it all looked the same.

Olivia was sad that night as she dressed for dinner at her mother's. She really wanted Paul to be there, and to spend Christmas Eve with them, but she had asked him too late. She hadn't decided until the last minute, and now he was in Greenwich with his kids and his wife. She didn't like his being there and for the first time she felt jealous of them. They were a closed circle, a unity, which didn't include her and she knew she couldn't compete with. His children were all-important to him, and he wouldn't let anything come between him and them. It was an admirable quality but she felt left out. He had finally left Eileen, and now he was back there again for Christmas, as though nothing had happened. She didn't like the fact that he hadn't filed for divorce yet. What if he didn't? But he had promised he would after Christmas.

He had texted her when he arrived in Greenwich that afternoon, and she hadn't heard from him since.

She wore a black velvet dress to dinner at her mother's that night, and Gwen saw immediately that she looked upset. Gwen was wearing a long dark green velvet skirt with a white satin blouse with full sleeves, and she looked regal as she greeted her daughter and hugged her. Her own mother and Federico hadn't arrived yet.

"Merry Christmas, darling. Is something wrong?"

"Not really. I'm just annoyed that Paul didn't come with me. I wanted you to meet him."

"Where is he? Why didn't you bring him?"

"I asked him too late. He already had plans."

"And he didn't cancel them for you?" Gwen looked surprised.

"He went to Greenwich to be with his wife and kids."

"Oh." Gwen understood the problem then and why Olivia looked unhappy. "I see. That's hard to compete with. Why didn't they come to him, the kids I mean?"

"He's not set up for it, and they wanted to be at home with their mother. So he went to them. He said it doesn't mean anything, but it bothers me anyway. He shouldn't be there."

"We'll see to it that we invite him early enough next year." Gwen smiled at her daughter as Olivia sat down on her elegant couch. A minute later, the doorbell rang and the butler opened it. Gabrielle and Federico walked in. He was wearing a black velvet dinner jacket, and she was wearing a long, dark red lace dress, which suited her. They looked adorable together, as they came down the stairs to the living room. Federico took the stairs more carefully, and Gabrielle with ease. She hugged her daughter and granddaughter, and Federico joined her seconds later. He had a mane of snow-white hair, and half of his face was still strikingly handsome and perfectly sculpted with his Roman profile, but the other half was badly scarred, which Gabrielle never noticed, and the others had gotten used to.

The waiter poured each of them a glass of champagne, and they sat down to enjoy each other's company before dinner. They talked about Federico's Paris show again, and how beautiful it had been, and Gabrielle turned to Olivia with a question.

"Where's your young man? Or not so young perhaps," she laughed.

"With his wife and children," Olivia said glumly.

"How disappointing. I was hoping to meet him. Oh well, another time." She didn't react to what Olivia had said about his wife. "Is all well?"

"Yes, he gave me a beautiful sapphire bracelet for Christmas, and he'll be back tomorrow." She held out her wrist to show her grandmother and Gabrielle nodded.

"Next year we'll have to invite him with his children." Gwen nodded, not entirely sure she liked the plan. She had valuable delicate objects in her apartment, and didn't want them broken.

They drank champagne for an hour and then went in to dinner. They had duck à l'orange, which was their tradition, with caviar first, and flaming Christmas pudding for dessert. It was a sumptuous meal.

After dinner, they exchanged gifts. Gabrielle had had her gift to her daughter delivered, and Gwen had noticed that it was incredibly heavy. They had placed it by the fireplace, near the tree. Gwen opened it and it was a miniature of one of Gabrielle's horses, which she had made for her. Gwen loved it. It was cast in bronze and a beauty. Her mother exclaimed with delight when she opened Gwen's gift to her. It was the painting she had completed since her mother had suggested she take up painting again. She had, and it was a beautiful Tuscan landscape Gwen had painted from memory. It had the feeling of a Monet.

"Oh, you're so good," her mother said with pleasure. "You should have been a painter! You are a painter!" Federico loved it too.

Gabrielle had made a tiny horse for Olivia. It fit in the palm of her hand. Her mother had given her a very pretty white fur jacket that fit her perfectly, and a fun pair of shoes. Olivia had given her grandmother a heavy warm sweater to wear while she worked, and another one for Federico, and a gold bangle bracelet for her mother. Federico had given all the ladies warm silk and cashmere Hermès scarves in a different color for each of them.

"We've been thoroughly spoiled," Gabrielle exclaimed. Federico had taken off his velvet dinner jacket and tried on the sweater from Olivia and he loved it, and Olivia wore her white fur jacket and looked adorable in it. Gwen had given Federico a warm cashmere beanie and fur-lined gloves for when he went out taking photographs at night or in the early morning, which he did frequently.

Gabrielle and Federico left around eleven-thirty. Olivia stayed until after midnight and then she went home to her empty apartment. She couldn't stop thinking about Paul, and wondered what he was doing with Eileen and the children. She missed him and was worried. It spoiled Christmas for her in spite of the pleasant evening she had spent with her family.

In Greenwich, they drank eggnog before dinner and not champagne. Eileen had cooked a turkey, and Paul carved it, as he always did. She made the black truffle and foie gras stuffings they had all loved on Thanksgiving, and Paul said they were incredible. They sat at the table for a long time and then cleared together, left it all in the kitchen to deal with later, and then opened presents. Eileen had told him what the children wanted, and he had gotten her a white cashmere sweater, which was beautiful. She had gotten him a royal blue one from Hermès. He loved the black one from Pennie. The boys had given IOUs for various services they promised to perform for all of them, like car washing and shoveling the driveway. They were all enjoying their gifts, when Eileen cleared her throat nervously, and said she had an announcement. She hesitated for a second, getting up her courage, while they waited.

"Are we getting a dog?" Mark asked.

"No, at least not right now. I'm going to do something that I've thought about for a long time. I'm going to Paris," she said. They all smiled. But there was more to it. "For three months, to study at Le Cordon Bleu professional cooking school. I've been accepted. And when I get back, I'm going to open my own catering business here in Greenwich." Paul and the children looked stunned. "I need your help, and this is important to me. Halfway through the class, you all have ski week, and I'm bringing you to Paris to spend your vacation with me." Then she looked at Paul, who was stupefied by what she was saying. She was starting a business and going to school, and had made all the decisions by herself. She had dreams again, and Eileen was determined that this time no one would take them from her. She wouldn't let them. "And I need you to stay with the kids when I'm gone," she said to Paul. "I leave on New Year's Day, and start class the next day. I'll be back on March thirty-first after I graduate. So for three months, I need you to stay in Greenwich. Tina said she'll stay overnight when you really need her to." She was the house cleaner they'd had for years, the children loved her, and she was good with them, and trustworthy and reliable. "And they'll be gone for ten days in the middle of it, so you'll get a break. But I really want to do this, and this is the only way I can." She left no room for argument, and he knew he owed it to her. He had cheated on her for five months, moved out, was continuing the affair, and after carrying the heavy load of the household and kids for eighteen years, she had managed alone for the past two months. He felt that the least he could do was move back to Greenwich for three months, and do what she did every day without complaining. He had no idea how he was going to explain it to Olivia, but he knew he had to. He didn't want to let Eileen down again.

There was a rapid babble of conversation as soon as she stopped talking. No one could believe she had applied to cooking school in Paris, been accepted, made her plans, and hadn't said a word. Their Christmas gift to her was to support her doing it. Pennie said she would help as much as she could. And Paul had agreed to move back in a week, on New Year's Day. It was a home run. She had hit one right out of the park. She realized that in some ways it was a selfish decision and didn't include them, but they were old enough to weather it for three months, and their father would be with them. He was key to the plan, but he hadn't said a word of objection. She thanked all of them and hugged them when they all went to bed. Paul still looked stunned and she thanked him profusely.

Jane called her that night on her cell when she was in bed. She was the only person Eileen had told.

"What did they say?"

"I think they're in shock," Eileen giggled, "but everyone said they'd pitch in, and Paul is going to do it. He'll move in."

"You realize, don't you, that you just screwed up his playtime royally. His girlfriend is not going to thank you for parking him in Greenwich with the kids for three months. But, oh well, isn't that too bad? And turnabout is fair play. They deserve it." Jane had no sympathy for him whatsoever, and she was delighted for her friend. She had a dream now, and a plan, and she was going to Paris to become a chef, and a caterer when she returned!

Olivia called Paul when she got home from her mother's and told him she missed him. He didn't tell her about Eileen's plans. He was going to tackle that in person. He lay on the couch where he was sleeping, after the call, and wondered how she'd take it. If he could have had her spend weekends with him in Greenwich, it would have been better for him, but he knew Eileen would never allow that, nor would his kids. Their family home was sacred to all of them, to him as well, and there was no way he could bring a woman there. He just hoped that Tina, the housekeeper, would give him a night off from time to time so he could sleep with Olivia in the city. If not, there were going to be fireworks. There might be anyway. It was a lot for her to swallow. For the next three months, he belonged to his children, on full-time duty, standing in for his absentee wife. But how could he blame her? After what he'd done, she had a right to a new life, and to train for it. He admired her no end, and wanted to do all he could to support her plan.

The next morning, they talked about Eileen's plans again over breakfast. With her usual military precision and flawless organization, she had thought of everything and covered all the bases. She assigned them specific chores that they would be responsible for. Pennie was responsible for laundry, Seth for unpacking groceries, Mark for helping their father shop for food on weekends. And they all had to tidy the living room and clean up the kitchen.

"And what am I responsible for?" Paul teased her. She was the family drill sergeant, which was familiar to him.

"Try not to lose any of the children before I get back. And . . . unfortunately for you, homework. They'll need your help with it, or the twins will." He had his work cut out for him for the next three months. He was going to be a full-time solo dad, just the way she was a full-time single mom, and had been even when they were together.

Paul left before lunch, after thanking them for a beautiful Christmas, and he took the train back to New York to meet Olivia. He had a lot to tell her. She said she'd be at her apartment. He was apprehensive about what he had to say. He couldn't tell Eileen he wouldn't cover for her, in order to protect his relationship with his girlfriend. He couldn't do that to her now. He and Olivia would just have to suck it up for three months, which wasn't the end of the world. But he knew she might think so.

Olivia was lying on her bed, watching a series on TV, when he got to her apartment. She threw her arms around his neck and was happy to see him, and wished him a merry Christmas.

"I'm so glad you're home! I missed you. It didn't feel like Christmas without you. And my mother and grandmother were very disappointed you didn't come."

"We'll work it out next year," he promised, and kissed her. She sounded like a little girl. He lay down on the bed next to her and put an arm around her. "There's something I have to tell you." He felt her stiffen next to him.

"You're not going back to her?"

"No, I'm not," he said calmly. "But I have to go back to Greenwich for three months to take care of my kids."

"With her? Is someone sick?" She looked panicked.

"Without her. That's the point. She's taking a class in Paris for three months so she can open a business. I owe this to her, Olivia. I have given her a crap deal with what we've done. And there's no one else to take care of the kids."

"Can't you hire a nanny?"

"No, I can't. They're not infants. She's leaving in a week. The housekeeper will stay with them from time to time, so I can spend the night with you. And they're going to Paris to see her for ski week in the middle of it, so we can be together then while they're with her. But other than that, I'm going to have to commute from Greenwich every day and live with my kids."

"Are you serious? For three *months*? What am I supposed to do?" She sat bolt upright in bed next to him and stared at him.

"We'll just have to live with it, and do the best we can. I have to do it. There's no one else who can. And you can't stay there with me. I wish you could." He was sincere and earnest. He didn't like the idea of being away from her either, although he was looking forward to living with his children again. He missed them, even though he loved her. They were his children, a relationship Olivia didn't understand since she had none. "Some people have to do this all the time. It's only for three months. We can manage it. And I'll stay in the city with you whenever the housekeeper stays with them, or if they stay with their friends on weekends. That's the best I can do." She could tell it was nonnegotiable.

"Can you at least spend the evenings with me before you go out there?"

"As much as I can, as long as I don't miss the last train. And I have to have dinner with them occasionally and help with homework. Eileen is a full-time hands-on mom. She's on deck for them all the time."

"And she expects you to do that in her absence? How can she sign up for a class in Paris without even asking you beforehand?"

"I guess she wanted it desperately. I've screwed up her life pretty badly. I can't stop her from doing this now. It wouldn't be right." Olivia got off the bed and paced around the room. She hadn't expected this. He was about to turn into a full-time suburban father who had to be home with his kids to do homework every night. "We can try introducing you to the children again, so you could come out there. But you can't spend the night. It's Eileen's house now, and she'd go through the roof. And I wouldn't feel right about it."

"Then she should stay home and take care of them herself. Why does this have to be your problem, *our* problem?"

"Because they're my kids too."

"I can't believe she's doing this to us."

"Think about what we've done to *her.* I can't refuse to help her out so we can spend every night together. She has a right to a life too."

"Yeah, and so do I. And not with a boyfriend babysitting for his children in Greenwich for three months."

"That's the deal, Olivia," he said quietly. "It's who I am." And who he should have been long before, he realized. She wondered suddenly as she listened to him if it was some kind of blessing, and would give her time to decide just how committed she was to the relationship, and how deep into it she wanted to be. It was going to give her a second look at him, and the fact that he had three kids, two of whom still needed him. And sometimes Pennie did too.

"You haven't even filed for divorce yet."

"I told you that I will." But he wouldn't admit to her that a part of him was glad this had happened. He was going to live with his children again for the next three months. But it was obvious how unhappy Olivia was about it. She didn't want their nights together to stop, and she could see a lot of long lonely nights ahead of her for the next three months. Why was Eileen getting to have all the fun and going to Paris? While Paul had to play babysitter.

"Can't they stay alone?" she insisted.

"No, they can't. They'd run wild, and what if there's a fire or one of them gets sick?" She hadn't thought of that. She lay back down on the bed next to him, and they made love a few minutes later. But she wasn't any happier afterwards. It all sounded like bad news to her. Between his spending Christmas Eve with Eileen and his children in Greenwich, and moving back in for the next three months, she was beginning to see what the future would look like. His children were the priority and she wasn't. Or was Eileen still a priority for him too? She wondered.

"I'm sorry, Olivia," he said again after they made love.

"I don't think you are," she said nastily. "I think you're looking forward to it." He didn't dare admit to her it was true, but he didn't want to lose her either. He hoped he wouldn't. But Eileen was pursuing her dreams now, and he wasn't going to steal them from her again. He had his own dream with Olivia. Eileen had a right to hers too.

Chapter 10

Paul and Olivia spent a quiet New Year's Eve in her apartment, making love and drinking champagne. Paul knew it was his last night of real freedom until Eileen returned at the end of March, and he wanted to enjoy it with Olivia.

He drove to Greenwich the following afternoon, on New Year's Day, and got there an hour after Eileen had left for the airport for her flight to Paris.

She had left him a nice note, thanking him again, with all the contact numbers where he could reach her. She promised to be in touch with the children every day, and he knew she would. She was a responsible person, and he wanted to be that for her now too. Olivia had been annoyed with him when he left her apartment. She had hated it when he was married and living at home in Greenwich, and now he was back there, and still married. From Olivia's perspective, their situation had just gotten worse, after two and a half happy months. Now playtime was over. He'd be rushing back to Greenwich every night.

The kids were in a bad mood when he got there too. The twins were in their room, and he noticed that Mark was sulking.

"What's up?" Paul asked, and sat down on his bed. Seth was ignoring his brother and reading a book about the life of Tolstoy. He had just read *War and Peace* and loved it.

"If you hadn't moved out, Mom wouldn't be going to Paris and trying to learn how to be a cook." Mark glared at his father.

"That's probably true. But your mom is a talented cook, and she might really enjoy it. She's earned the right to do something special."

"It's that girl's fault too. The redheaded one. Olive or whatever her name is."

"Olivia. And it's not her fault, it's mine. This is between your mom and me, no one else."

"Are you still dating her?"

"Yes, I am."

"Is she going to come here while you're staying here?"

"I don't know. I don't think so."

"Mom wouldn't like it."

"That's probably true. She might drive out to see me sometime, and we'd go out to lunch." He didn't think she should hang out around the house with him either. He wanted to respect Eileen. "What do you want for dinner? I thought I'd order pizza."

"We already had pizza this week. Can't you cook?" Mark looked irritated.

"No, I can't. Not like your mom." Mark grudgingly agreed to pizza, and when he checked with Pennie, she said she was going out to meet friends. She was eighteen now and seemed very grown up to him.

"Do you need a ride?"

"No, they're picking me up."

He was getting a taste of Eileen's life, home-cooked meals and constant chauffeuring.

He ordered the pizza and he and the twins ate it in the kitchen. Tina had agreed to cook for the kids in the evening during the week, and he would deal with their meals on the weekend. Eileen had arranged it. He was beginning to wonder how he was going to see Olivia and when. Eileen had also left him their tutoring schedule, which happened mostly in the evenings. Seth and Mark had tutors, to help them with homework. He had already warned his office that he would have to come in an hour late every day for the next three months, so he could get them all off to school. And the first thing he was going to ask Tina the next day was which nights she could stay overnight that week. He was willing to pay her handsomely for it. Peace in his relationship with Olivia was worth it. He called Tina from the office to discuss it. She said the only night she had free that week was Friday. She had promised to help a sick neighbor, and her niece had just had a baby and she was lending her a hand too. This was not going to be easy. He was wondering who he could ask to fill in.

He texted Olivia and they agreed to meet for an hour or two when he finished work. He had driven in so he wouldn't be dependent on train schedules. And as soon as he got to her apartment at six o'clock, she started complaining about how difficult it was.

"Why is it difficult for you?" he asked her, exasperated. He was doing the best he could, and it had barely started. This was only the first day.

"Because I don't even know when you can spend the night. And the rest of the time we're going to be stealing an hour here or there and that's it."

"I can spend the night on Friday," he said, trying not to get irritated with her.

"That's it? One night?"

"It's all she could give me this week. She promised to give me two nights next week." Then suddenly he remembered a notice pinned to the kitchen bulletin board. There was a college prep night at school on Friday that was mandatory for Pennie, and he had to go too. "Shit. I just remembered I can't do Friday. I have to go to school."

"So no nights this week? Is that it?" She glared at him.

"I guess so. Look, try to be patient about it. I don't like this either. They have demanding schedules, and the boys need help with homework. I don't know how the hell Eileen does it, but she covers all the bases, and so I'll have to now, for a while."

"This is like a bad movie. Why don't you try to remember that I don't have kids, and this is not how I want to live?"

"You won't. I won't be living with my kids. She will. But she's gone for three months."

"Why the hell did you agree to it, and to take her place?"

"Because I'm their father."

They spent two hours arguing and then he had to drive to Greenwich. He got home at nine-thirty, and Seth's math tutor was just leaving. Pennie came in right behind him, dropped off by a friend.

"Where have *you* been?" he asked her.

"Yearbook meeting. I'm chairman of the yearbook committee. It looked good on my applications. We meet at night, and we're way behind. I'm doing it tomorrow too."

Seth said he had a headache after the math tutor left, and Paul gave him two Tylenol. They were all in their rooms by ten-thirty, and Paul hadn't eaten yet. When he opened the fridge, there was nothing left of what Tina had cooked for dinner. He found a slice of leftover pizza from the night before and ate it cold, sitting at the kitchen table, and wondering how he was going to get through the next three months. Just keeping the kids' schedules straight was a full-time job, and he hadn't had to do homework yet, or cook a meal. And he had to keep a twenty-seven-year-old woman happy too, one who didn't give a damn about his kids and everything there was to do. It seemed like too much for just one person. It needed a team. And Paul wondered how Eileen was going to do it when she started her catering business.

She sent him a text at midnight, six A.M. in Paris, when she got up. She had to be at her first class at seven-thirty. She was making sure that everything was going smoothly, and he texted back that it was, and added, "I don't know how you do it."

"You just keep moving and it all falls into place," she said. Her first class that morning was on pans, and the afternoon class was sauces. She could hardly wait.

Paul tried to call Olivia when he got to bed, but she didn't pick up. He had some papers to read for work, turned off the light at one A.M. and set the alarm for six. He wanted to dress and get a grip on things before he made breakfast. He never knew what Eileen did in the morning after he left for work, and never cared. He suddenly realized he had a lot to learn, and a short time to do it.

He got to the office at ten, and was late for a meeting. He called Olivia afterwards, as soon as he got back to his office.

"Six o'clock?" he suggested.

"Can we make it seven? I have a five o'clock meeting and I won't be finished till then." Gone were the days of the past three months when they could meet up at the end of their day, whenever it was, and have a leisurely evening ahead of them to relax and make love. She was a pit stop now on his way home. This was actually worse than before he left Eileen, because she was there for the kids then. Now he had to be.

"I can't do seven," he said apologetically. "If I do that, I won't get home till ten, which is really too late."

"Fine, then forget it," she snapped at him.

"Olivia, please, cut me a little slack here. I'm trying to fit it all in."

"Well, you're not trying very hard to fit me in."

"I am, but I have to get home in time to see the kids. I wish you could stay there with me." But they both knew she couldn't. Even if they liked her, it wouldn't be appropriate, and he wasn't going to shack up with his girlfriend while living with his kids.

"I'll see you tomorrow," she said, annoyed with him. She complained about it to her mother when she stopped by for a visit the next day. Gwen was painting when Olivia got there.

"How's Paul?" Gwen asked casually, as she dabbed at the canvas and stood back to squint at it. It was coming together.

"Our relationship has turned to shit. His wife is taking a class in Paris for three months, and he's staying in Greenwich with the kids. He has to get home at night, and I have a feeling we're hardly going to see each other for the next three months."

"Maybe that's a good thing," her mother suggested, and Olivia nodded.

"I thought that too, but it sure isn't fun."

"Welcome to real life," her mother said to her.

"Whose real life? Not mine. I don't have kids, and I don't live in the suburbs."

"No, but he does, and right now that's the same thing. You'll get through it."

"Will I? Will *we*? I'm beginning to wonder and it's only been three days."

"It must be hard on him," Gwen said, and set her brush down. "If you add a lot of pressure, it will just make it more difficult for him."

"Why is it always about *his* schedule and *his* constraints?"

"Because he's a married man with three kids. And right now his wife is away."

"And I have to pay the price for it." She looked seriously annoyed. Her mother didn't think she was mature enough to put up with it and make allowances for him. But if she loved him enough, she would. It was a test of sorts, for both of them. "This is a lot more challenging than it originally looked. I thought his wife was the problem, having expectations of him. But it's his life."

"I told you, married men are complicated."

"It's messy." Olivia smiled at her. Her mother had said that too, and she was right.

"And you're still in love with him?" Gwen asked her.

"I think so. I'd give my right arm for his wife to come back, though, and deal with the kids."

"Three months is better than forever. Imagine if he had custody of the kids."

Olivia looked horrified. "Don't even think it. God forbid."

Paul managed to see Olivia for two hours that night and get home at nine-thirty. He didn't get dinner, but the children had eaten, been tutored, and done their homework.

He didn't see Olivia on Thursday, and he had to go to college prep night at school with Pennie on Friday, but he had organized all three children for the weekend so they were staying with friends. He had two full days with Olivia, and everything was on track again by Sunday night. Tina had agreed to stay on Monday and Wednesday nights too. He felt like he was running relay races. Every time he got a text from Eileen he told her they were doing great.

Everything fell apart again on Monday. Tina called him at the office to tell him that Mark threw up at school. She had gone to pick him up and he had a fever, and Seth texted him that he had a science project due and needed help that night. So his night with Olivia went out the window.

"Is it always going to be like this?" she commented, sounding exasperated when he called to tell her he couldn't spend the night because he had to go home for a sick child and a science project.

"Maybe, but then Eileen will come home. At least we had this weekend."

"I thought by the time kids were this age, it was easy."

"No, it's harder. There's more to do. When they're little, you put them to bed at seven and that's it. They don't do science projects and Latin homework in nursery school." But he hadn't done that with them either. Eileen had done it all with them for years.

"I guess we just have to deal with it till she gets back," Olivia said with a sigh. "How about boarding school for three months?" She seemed to be adjusting to it, and he was relieved. "Just don't sue her

156

for custody, or if you do, move them to the city." It was the commute that was killing them as much as the kids, and not having live-in help. But Eileen never wanted that and liked doing it herself. Having to juggle three children had certainly taken the romance out of his relationship with Olivia. They hardly had time to make love now, and sometimes he was so tired, stressed, and rushed, he didn't even want to. Olivia complained about that too.

In Paris, Eileen's experience was the opposite of Paul's. She found each class fascinating, each teacher demanding, but she learned something new every day. She understood the equipment better now, the tools of the trade. She had already learned to make sauces that had always been a mystery to her. She studied each lesson avidly, and each recipe, and made copious notes.

Her work partner in class was a young English boy, Hugo, twenty-three years old, whose parents owned a well-known restaurant in Nice. He was determined to get them three Michelin stars one day.

They went to restaurants together and tried to decipher the recipes. They worked well as a team, and when Eileen got home at night, she had hours to herself for the first time in eighteen years. It was a luxury for her. She could read a magazine or a book, or study recipes. She went for long walks along the Seine or in the Bois de Boulogne on Sundays. She had found a charming apartment in the Seventh Arrondissement her first week there, and the guardian brought her fresh croissants every morning. She felt like a free woman again, instead of Supermom and Wife, and she didn't have to take care of anyone but herself.

"Are you married?" Hugo asked her one day at lunch, as they ate what they'd cooked that morning. It was sea bass in a delicate sauce.

"More or less," she answered, and he laughed.

"That's not an answer. Are you married or not?"

"Are you planning to propose?" she asked him, and he laughed again.

"Definitely not. I'm gay, and I have a boyfriend in Nice. Jonathan. He's American. He paid for me to come here. It's always been my dream, but my parents couldn't afford it."

"It's been my dream too. I'm married, but we're separated."

"I'm sorry," he said.

"Me too. But I'm getting used to it. I'm going to file for divorce when I go home. To tell you the whole sad story, my husband left me for another woman. It sounds pathetic." But she was in good spirits, and loving her time at Le Cordon Bleu.

"You'll find someone else. You're beautiful, and smart and funny." She liked him. He was very earnest and hardworking and talented. Everyone in the class was. They were serious chefs. She was taking the professional course.

"According to my mother, I'm so old no one will want me. I'm forty. And I want to open a catering business in Connecticut, where I live."

"Do you have kids?"

"Three. I miss them like crazy, but I'm really enjoying this. It's the first thing I've ever done for myself."

"Good on you." He smiled at her. He liked her and they worked well together. The days were flying by too quickly.

They continued going to restaurants together, and enjoying their classes. They made friends with two other men in the class, both of them French. Eileen was shocked when six weeks had flown by, and they got their break, and her children were arriving for their ski week.

She asked Hugo where he was going to spend the break, and he said with his boyfriend in Nice. They had a villa in the hills. He had come to Paris for a few weekends, and joined them for dinner. He was about Eileen's age. He was from LA and very good-looking. They both were.

"My children are coming. I can hardly wait." She had taken three rooms at a small hotel on the Left Bank because her apartment was too small for all four of them.

She went to the airport to pick them up, and they looked tired and disheveled when they came through customs. She had rented a van and driver for them and their luggage, and their eyes were wide with wonder as they drove through Paris. The driver showed them the Champs-Élysées and the Place de la Concorde, made a quick tour of the Place Vendôme, and they drove past the Cordon Bleu building in the Fifteenth Arrondissement. Then they drove back across Paris to the Pont Alexandre III to the Left Bank, past Les Invalides where Napoleon was buried, and to their hotel nearby. It was cozy and quaint, and she took them out to dinner that night, at La Fontaine de Mars, one of the best bistros in Paris, in the Seventh, after they explored Paris some more. They had had a snack at Aux Deux Magots, one of the oldest bistros in Paris, and an ice cream at Berthillon, the best ice cream in Paris.

They loved the food at La Fontaine de Mars, and she caught up with all their news. But they had been FaceTiming every day so she knew most of it. Pennie was getting nervous about the answers to her college applications. They were only a month away. And she was working hard on the yearbook, at the homeless shelter every weekend, and helping her father with the twins.

"How's Dad doing?" Eileen asked cautiously. He had said that everything was fine in all his emails and texts.

"I think we're driving him a little crazy," Mark admitted. "He can't do all the things you do." It didn't surprise her. "He argues with his girlfriend a lot. He doesn't have much time to see her, except on weekends. She complains about it. I hear them fighting on the phone at night."

"I'll be back in six weeks," she said quietly. The time had flown so far, but she was learning everything she needed to know to run her catering business. They had even made a wedding cake. She had learned to make chocolates, and discovered she had a talent for delicate sugar work. Their professor was a master who had won many culinary awards.

"Have you had fun, Mom?" Pennie asked her. It had been hard having her mother away during her senior year, but it was a sacrifice they were all trying to make for her. She deserved it. "How are you going to run your catering business?"

"I have had fun, to answer your question. A lot of fun, and I've learned a lot. I'm going to hire an assistant to help me, and we'll subcontract out the rest, all the china and crystal rentals, tents, and staff for parties. I want to do high-end parties in Greenwich."

"I think you'll be good at it." Pennie smiled at her. Having her mother away had made her appreciate her, and everything she did to make their lives run smoothly. Paul had been struggling.

She had heard him arguing with Olivia too. Olivia wasn't happy about how busy he was, and how much time he had to spend with them. It had been nice having their father home again, and she was going to miss him when her mother came home, and so were the boys. They liked having a man in the house. But they missed their mother too.

"Have you and Dad made any decisions?" she asked Eileen, when they were alone for a minute. Eileen shook her head.

"Not that I know of. He hasn't said anything to me."

"I think he's sorry he left," Penny said wistfully.

"I'm sure he misses the three of you."

"He misses you too." Eileen missed him too, but not as much anymore. Her new life was taking off and she was excited about her new business. "Do you want him back?" Eileen sighed before she answered.

"I don't know. Sometimes things just go too far to get fixed. That might have happened to us. Life is like a river. It moves you along, whether you want to or not."

"I think that happened to me and Tim. I still love him, but I can't see us together anymore." Eileen nodded. Pennie had grown up a lot.

"That's kind of how I feel about Dad. It's sad, but it's happy too, because new horizons come into your life, and new people and experiences. I'm ready for that now. I kind of got lazy before, or distracted. I stopped doing new things. And I'm excited about that now."

"You were busy with us," Pennie excused it, but she could see that her mother had come alive again. Her eyes were bright, she smiled a lot more, and she looked comfortable and confident, excited about what she'd been doing. "Do you think Dad will marry Olivia if you get divorced?" Pennie was still sad about it, but she had accepted the idea that her parents wouldn't get back together. It didn't seem like they would.

"I don't know. You should ask him."

"She's so young. Maybe she'd want kids of her own. Do you think Dad wants more kids?" These were all the things they were worried about.

"That I don't. It would be a lot for him to take on. He's never wanted more children with me." But Pennie was right, Eileen realized. If he wanted a young woman, more than likely she'd want kids. The idea seemed strange, to think of him with a second family, but it could happen.

The vacation with her children went too quickly, and Eileen was sad to see them leave. They were equally sad to leave her. But she only had five weeks left in Paris now, and that would go even faster. She wanted to soak up all the information she could while she was there.

Paul spent the ten days they were in Paris with Olivia, and they got their relationship back on track again. They slept together every night. He didn't have to commute. Olivia took him to see her grandmother and he loved her, and enjoyed meeting Federico. Paul said they were the perfect couple. And he and Olivia had brunch one Sunday with Olivia's mother. Paul was stunned by how beautiful she was, and how interesting and intelligent and knowledgeable.

Olivia and Paul made love as often as they could while the kids were away, to make up for lost time.

By the time the children came back, things were going smoothly with Olivia again. They hadn't for the last six weeks, with too little time together. She hated to think of his children coming home. She wasn't looking forward to it, but they were in the home stretch and Eileen would be home soon, and ready to start her business. That would keep her busy too.

Paul picked them up at the airport when they got back from Paris, and they had dozens of stories to tell him about exploring Paris with their mother, and the restaurants they'd gone to with her to check out the food. Pennie had bought some clothes at Le Bon Marché near their hotel, and the boys had bought souvenirs, and brought him an Eiffel Tower that lit up, which he promised to put on his desk at the office.

He drove them back to Greenwich in a light snowfall. They all agreed Paris had been great, but it was good to be home. And their mother would be home in a little more than a month. It made Paul sad to realize that his reason for living with them was almost over. He knew Olivia would be happy about it, but he wasn't. He was going to miss them even more when he moved out again. He had gotten closer to them than he'd ever been before, being alone with them. And he'd gotten better at the chores and organization than he'd been in the beginning. But he couldn't imagine coming back to Eileen either. She had moved on, and so had he.

He didn't know if Olivia was the answer for the next chapters of his life, but he felt sure Eileen wasn't. He loved her and knew he always would, but she wasn't the future for him, she was the past, and you couldn't go back in time, only forward. When he looked ahead to his future, he saw Olivia, with her bright curly red hair. Not Eileen. He wanted a fresh start, and was ready for it. He hoped Olivia was it for him.

Chapter 11

Eileen was due back in four weeks, and the children settled down in Greenwich again. Olivia was hardly seeing Paul, when she got an email from a man with a French name, who asked for a meeting with her. She wrote back to him, asking about the nature of his business, and he said he was in the art field, and would explain it to her when he saw her. He promised not to take up too much of her time. His name was Jean-Pierre Muset, and he would only be in New York for four days.

With Paul unavailable again, she had time on her hands, and agreed to have a drink with Jean-Pierre Muset at the Mark Hotel, where he was staying. It was close to her apartment.

His email was quite formal, although his English was good, and she was surprised by how young he was when she saw him. He told her he was thirty-two. His father was a famous art dealer, in the traditional sense, and he was intrigued by her online art dealership. He said he was interested in joining her in some way, and starting a Paris branch for her, and wanted to know if the idea appealed to her. She had never thought of doing that before, but it seemed like a natural offshoot of her business.

He was tall and attractive, with dark hair and warm brown eyes, and he smiled a lot.

"I've never thought of it, but I like the idea," she admitted to him.

"I have a friend in London I went to school with, and he might be interested in a London branch. The possibilities are endless really. Ideally, I'd like to do Paris, London, Hong Kong, in that order. It could be very interesting, and expand your business considerably. If you want to pursue it, I'd like to spend a few days with you here and see how you operate, and then you could come to Paris, and help me set it up. You could spend a month in Paris, maybe two, and help me launch and set up an office there. And then come back here. Are you interested?" He was very direct and smart and she liked him. He had good ideas.

"Yes, I am interested," she said. She wanted to check him out, and if he had a good reputation, she was more than willing, and liked the idea.

"My father has a very large gallery in a mansion in Paris, which we own, and he has some spare offices he would give us for the space we would need. I talked to him about it before I left. I came here to deliver a painting for him to a client in New York. I've been working for him for the past five years. I'm ready to do something of my own, and the internet is more of our generation than his." She smiled and they talked animatedly for two hours. He left her his card, and she looked him up when she got home. His father was one of the most prestigious art dealers in Europe, Arnaud Muset, and there was a profile of Jean-Pierre on their website. His credentials were excellent for someone his age. He had gone to the Sorbonne, followed by Oxford, where he got a master's degree in art history. He had begun at Christie's, as she had. She called him after she looked him up.

"Why don't you come to my office tomorrow?" she suggested. He said he'd be there, and could spend two days with her, possibly three, before he had to get back to Europe to join his father at meetings in Madrid.

He showed up the next day in jeans with a blue shirt, a well-cut tweed jacket that looked English, and brown suede boots. He was very attractive, which she reminded herself was irrelevant. She was in love with Paul. He was tied up with his children all week, and had told her he couldn't see her until the weekend, so she had spare time to spend with Jean-Pierre, showing him everything. He represented an extraordinary opportunity for her.

"Would you be interested in a partnership eventually?" he asked her on the second day. It would involve his investing money in her business.

"Possibly. For now, let's just think of it as the Paris branch." She wanted to discuss his suggestion with her financial advisors. She had invested part of her inheritance from her father in the business, so she wasn't casual about it, and didn't want to take on a partner she didn't know well. But eventually, his proposition might be of interest to her. She enjoyed the time they spent together. He had an easy, pleasant style, but he was also businesslike and well organized. He didn't flirt with her. He was serious about their work.

He left for Paris on Friday afternoon, and she had agreed to come to Paris in a week and spend two weeks there, going over things with him. She told Paul about him that night. She hadn't mentioned it all week, because they were both busy, and she wanted to explain the plan to him at length.

"Why didn't you tell me?" Paul looked surprised.

"You didn't have time. What do you think of the idea?"

"It sounds good to me, but you should check it out with your financial people."

"I already have. So far, it all looks good. I'm going to Paris in a week to check it out with him," Olivia said, and he looked startled.

"You are? So quickly?"

"Why not?"

"Why are all the women in my life migrating to Paris?" he said, smiling. "I wish I could go with you, but I can't leave the kids. Maybe you'll run into Eileen," he said, joking, but Olivia didn't smile.

"I hope not. That would be embarrassing."

"Just don't go to Le Cordon Bleu when you're there." She had no reason to anyway. She was going to meet with an art dealer, not a cooking school.

They managed to spend one night of the weekend together, but the following week, all three of his children had midterms, and he had to be home to help them study for them. He told her he wouldn't be able to see her before the weekend. She couldn't wait for Eileen to get home. She was tired of playing second fiddle to his kids. They always came first with him, and she couldn't help wondering what their life would be like, even when he wasn't living with them. They always had a game, or a practice, or a problem, or a tutor, or were sick, or needed his attention. And with three of them, there was no time for her on the merry-go-round he lived on.

She hadn't seen him in six days when she left for Paris on Friday night. Paul was disappointed that she was leaving. He had gotten Tina to agree to stay for both weekend nights, but now Olivia would be gone.

Her flight landed in Paris on Saturday at nine A.M., and she took a cab to the Ritz, where her mother always stayed. Jean-Pierre knew when she was arriving and they had agreed to have lunch in the covered garden of L'Espadon on Saturday. He wanted her to meet his father. She was looking forward to it.

She lay down for a while to rest, and then took a bath and changed. She put on a chic black suit, and felt very sophisticated as she headed to L'Espadon downstairs at the Ritz. Jean-Pierre was waiting for her and wearing a suit and tie. He looked happy to see her.

"How was your flight?"

"Easy. I watched a movie and slept the rest of the time until we landed. I like night flights for that."

"So do I," he agreed. "My father used to send me to Asia a lot when I started working for him. I got used to sleeping on long flights."

The maître d' showed them to a table in the garden under the glass roof. He knew Jean-Pierre well. Jean-Pierre ordered champagne for them, to celebrate "their alliance" and "the Paris branch." She ordered a light lunch, and so did he. They talked nonstop for two hours, sharing ideas for the business, some of which she wanted to incorporate in New York too. He had made some excellent suggestions, and they were both in high spirits when he took her to their gallery on the rue du Faubourg Saint-Honoré, the most elegant shopping street in Paris, where his father owned a large building they had transformed into the gallery many years before.

Jean-Pierre took her upstairs in a private elevator to his father's office on the top floor. The door was open, and an imposing-looking man in his sixties was seated at an enormous Louis XV desk. He glanced up when he heard footsteps, and smiled when he saw his son with a beautiful redhead in a chic black suit. Jean-Pierre had mentioned his interest in Olivia's business in New York, but his father didn't make the connection until Jean-Pierre introduced them.

"So you are my son's new associate," Arnaud Muset said, smiling at her. They both looked so young to him, and made a handsome pair. Jean-Pierre had a weakness for very young, very sexy, somewhat cheap-looking girls. Arnaud was relieved to see him with a respectable young woman for a change. But he wasn't dating her, he wanted to go into business with her, which was an entirely different matter.

Arnaud showed her around the gallery himself, and took out some remarkable paintings for her to see. He often dealt in Old Masters and the major Impressionists, but handled the modern artists too, particularly Picasso. He pulled out two spectacular Picassos, and she quietly said that she had one from the same series herself. Arnaud was intrigued to hear it.

"My father was a big collector. I inherited two from him," she said demurely. Jean-Pierre didn't know that about her. She had been very discreet, and only spoke about business with him, or funny experiences at Christie's or in college. He didn't know who her mother was either. "My grandmother is an artist," she admitted then. "Gabrielle

Waters. She does very large bronzes, mostly horses." Arnaud looked at her in amazement and laughed.

"I have always wanted one for our country home. I've been on a waiting list for one of them for ten years. I think she only sells to old clients and her best friends. She's not impressed by me at all."

They left Jean-Pierre's father after a while and went back downstairs, so he could show her the offices his father was willing to let them use. They were very handsome spaces, which would be excellent for meeting clients. He looked at her with a smile. "You've been keeping secrets from me. You didn't tell me your grandmother is a famous artist. She's quite old now, isn't she?"

"She's ninety-two and going strong. And there have to be some surprises." She smiled at him. "She lives with a younger man of eighty-four, Federico Banducci, the photographer." Jean-Pierre's face lit up when she said it.

"I sold one of his photographs last year. We don't normally handle photography, but we had a client who wanted one and couldn't find it, so we got it for him. And I have two myself. I love his work. So you come from a long line of artists. What did your father do?" She had told him in New York that her father was deceased.

"He was a producer, Tom Page," she said proudly, and Jean-Pierre recognized the name immediately. "And my mother is an actress." She didn't explain further, but Jean-Pierre was curious about this surprisingly discreet young woman with a distinguished artistic heritage. He was interested in knowing more about her, especially if they were going into business together.

"Would I recognize your mother's name?"

"Probably." Olivia smiled innocently at him.

"Well? Are you going to tell me?" Jean-Pierre said expectantly, and she laughed.

"Gwen Waters. She's an American actress," she said, as though he might not know.

"Yes, and Renoir was a French artist. I've heard of both of them. Are you serious? Gwen Waters is your mother?" She nodded, as they stood in the space that was going to become the site of their joint venture, her Paris branch. "Now we have to go into business together. I would love to meet her."

"I'm sure you will. Actually she paints. She's pretty good. She just started painting again. She does it between films."

"I've seen all of her movies. My father would die to meet her. He has a huge crush on her." Most men did.

"So that's me. What about you?"

"You've met my father. My mother died when I was seven. I'm an only child."

"My father died when I was seven. And I'm an only child too."

"Clearly, we're twins, separated at birth, and now we've found each other and we're going into business together. Destiny." He wanted to ask her if she had a boyfriend, but he thought it too forward. They were engaged in business, not internet dating, but he was curious about her. She was so strikingly beautiful, and she certainly had an interesting family, loaded with famous people. "Are you too tired to go out tonight?" he asked her as they left the building and walked a short distance down the Faubourg Saint-Honoré. All the most luxurious stores were there. Chanel, Hermès, Saint-Laurent, and many important jewelers.

"I'm not tired at all. I slept enough on the plane."

"A client of ours has taken over a nightclub, Castel. It's a private club. He's giving a party there tonight, and I told my father I'd go. Would you like to come with me?"

"It sounds like fun." She smiled at him. "But I'm not sure I brought the right clothes."

"You can wear jeans if you want to, with a blouse or sweater of some kind. No one dresses up much in the clubs. Why don't we have dinner first, and go late? Nobody will get there till midnight or later. Or are you tired of me?"

"I'd better not be if we're going to work together," she said, smiling.

"I'll figure out some bistro for dinner. I'll pick you up at the Ritz at nine." He hailed a cab for her then to take her back to the Ritz. She'd had a wonderful time with Jean-Pierre all afternoon, having lunch, meeting his father, seeing the gallery and the space they were going to use. And their plans for the evening sounded like fun too, with dinner and the party at Castel.

She wore a sweater with rhinestones on it, jeans, high heels, and a short fur jacket she'd brought with her. It was still cold in Paris in March. He arrived promptly at nine, and took her to a small cozy bistro, then shortly before midnight, they went to Castel, which was on a narrow backstreet. It was a fashionable disco for members only, and because it was a private party, the crowd filtering in was well dressed and attractive. But there were several guests dressed as informally as she was, in jeans, and assorted creative outfits, since some were artists. There was a small, cramped restaurant on the main floor, and carpeting with an erotic design of male genitals lead-ing downstairs to the club. People were drinking and having fun. The music was techno but not too loud. Jean-Pierre introduced Olivia to their host, a very attractive man in his forties, with an equally handsome young Englishman in his twenties, whom he introduced as his partner, standing beside him. And there was a beautiful blond woman with the younger man. She was wearing a lace blouse with jeans. Hugo, the young Englishman, introduced them. Her name was Eileen Jackson, and Olivia tried not to look shocked when she heard it. Jean-Pierre introduced Olivia, and the two women stared at each other and held their breath for an instant. Then Eileen held out a hand to her, and Olivia smiled nervously. They had recognized each other's names. Olivia knew instantly who Eileen was and Eileen had heard Olivia's name a few times, so it clicked immediately as the woman who had destroyed her marriage.

"I guess fate brought us both to Paris so we could meet each other," Eileen said graciously. "You're as beautiful as my sons said." She was incredibly nice about it.

"I'm so sorry," Olivia said just loud enough for Eileen to hear her. Suddenly Eileen was real to her, as they met face-to-face. Before that she was just an idea.

"Don't be. Good things have come of it. I'm doing things I've wanted to do for years. I have my freedom. We should have ended it a long time ago. You woke us up."

"Thank you. Truly, I am sorry," Olivia said to her as the men watched, but didn't understand the exchange. "It's all much more complicated than I thought. If I could, I wouldn't do it again. I learned an enormous lesson. I'm sure Paul did too."

"I don't know if he learned anything, but he's paying penance now, running after our kids while I'm here. It's his turn! I did it for nearly twenty years."

The worst part was that Olivia really liked Eileen, and now she could see who they'd been cheating on. She almost liked her better than her husband. She seemed like the kind of person Olivia would have admired if she knew her.

"I hope everything turns out well for you," Olivia said sincerely.

"It already has," Eileen said generously, and then the crowd pushed them away from each other, and Jean-Pierre introduced Olivia to someone else.

"Who was that woman?" he asked when they were on the other side of the room. "Is she an actress? She's very beautiful."

"It's a long, very complicated story. I'll tell you about it sometime, but not here." Something happened to her when she saw Eileen. She felt as though she had woken up. She had come all this way, met her, and seeing her, Olivia knew she didn't belong with Paul. She wondered if maybe he would go back to Eileen, if she'd have him. Olivia didn't have the feeling that Eileen was unhappy. She looked comfortable and at ease at Castel.

Hugo had just asked Eileen the same question about Olivia. It was obvious that something major was happening between them. Hugo's boyfriend was hosting the party. Their meeting there that night had been a complete accident.

"That," Eileen said to Hugo, feeling strangely calm and liberated, "is the woman that my husband left me for."

"Did you know her before?" He was shocked and sorry for her.

They had become good friends in their classes together, and he had invited her to the party.

"I just met her here tonight. And the funny thing is that I think it's over, and I get the feeling he doesn't know it yet. Who was she with?"

"The son of a very important art dealer, Arnaud Muset. Jonathan buys paintings from them, so he invited him. I guess his son came instead."

"He's very good-looking," Eileen commented.

"If it's over with her, do you want your husband back?"

"No, I don't," she said without hesitating. "I like my life much more now, and it's going to get even better when I start my catering business. I'm ready. I'm filing for divorce when I go home. I already emailed the lawyer, but I haven't met him yet. I want to tell my kids before I file, and my husband."

Jean-Pierre and Olivia left the party about an hour later. It was noisy and crowded as people continued arriving. Olivia didn't see Eileen in the crowd again, but like Eileen, she had the feeling that they had been meant to meet each other, and it had freed both of them.

It felt good to get out in the air when they left the party. For a number of reasons, it had been an extraordinary evening, of chance meetings and new friendships.

Jean-Pierre drove Olivia back to the Ritz, and she was finally tired after a long day. He didn't ask her about Eileen again. From the look on Olivia's face when she met her, he had the feeling that it was a story he didn't need to know, but she might tell him one day.

* * *

For the next two weeks, Olivia and Jean-Pierre spent many hours together, discussing her business, how to set it up in Paris, who to hire, what artists they wanted to feature and would work best in the French market. They spent their days and most evenings together and were remarkably comfortable with each other. She had to go back to New York, but in April, she was planning to come back again and spend a few more weeks there. But they had already laid the foundation, and they both agreed they would be open for business in France, with offices in his father's gallery. Her lawyers were drawing up agreements between them. She was going to go back and forth to France for a while, until they were well established. And he said he'd come to New York for a few weeks, to become more involved in her New York base of operations. They wanted to add London by the end of the year.

Jean-Pierre's business acumen and expertise in the art business added immeasurably to her original business model and broadened the scope of what she'd done so far. Their meeting had been providential, and he'd known the moment he'd read about her internet gallery that it was a business he wanted to be involved in. His father was all in favor of it too.

On her last night in Paris before she went back, Jean-Pierre asked her the question he'd been wondering about since he'd met her, but felt uncomfortable asking. He got mixed messages from her and there was always something guarded about her when he got too close. He wasn't sure if she was cautious because they were working together, or another reason, and he wanted to know. He was incredibly drawn to her, and he couldn't tell if what he felt would be welcome or not, but he wanted to ask so things were clear between them.

"Olivia, are you involved with someone or not? Sometimes I think you are, and at other times, I have the feeling you're quite free." She was just as attracted to him, but she didn't want to act on it yet.

"I have been involved with someone for almost a year. It's been complicated. Too complicated. And it's over for me. I haven't told him yet. I'm going to do that when I go back to New York, regardless of anything else." She smiled at him. "And then I will be quite free, as you put it."

"I know this sounds crazy, but does it have anything to do with the woman we met at the party at Castel, the night you arrived?"

She was impressed by how astute he was. "Yes, it does." She hesitated for a minute, debating about what to tell him, and then she decided to. She didn't want to keep secrets from him, nor tell him too much. "She's his wife. They're getting divorced." He was too polite to ask her if the divorce was because of her, and he didn't want to know. "I met her for the first time that night. She was extremely nice about it."

"In that case, I think we have some other matters to discuss when you come back in April. I'll wait until then." He didn't want to approach her too soon on a personal level, and she obviously had some things to resolve. One thing at a time. But his message was clear and so was hers. Something powerful had happened between them, and they both knew it. More than just business. And something was going to happen. All in good time. In the meantime, they had much to think about, exciting plans and a whole new dimension to look forward to, at the right time.

He kissed her chastely on both cheeks when he said goodbye to her. She was leaving in the morning for New York.

"See you in a few weeks," he said gently, as he held her hand. "I can't wait."

She smiled. "Neither can I." She waved a minute later as she disappeared into the hotel.

Chapter 12

The flight to New York from Paris seemed to take forever, longer than usual. Olivia wanted to get there now, and see Paul. They had much to talk about and she had a lot to say. They had texted frequently while she was in Paris, but she had been with Jean-Pierre most of the time. And Paul was drowning in kids.

He knew she was arriving that afternoon, and had arranged for Tina to stay with the children that night. Olivia had promised to let him know once she got to her apartment. She wasn't sure she wanted to meet him there now.

When they finally landed, she got her luggage and had nothing to declare as she went through customs. She had arranged for a car and driver to pick her up. She went straight home and called Paul. He picked it up immediately, and had been waiting to hear from her. He sounded excited, and her heart sank a little. She wondered if she would feel differently when she saw him. She hoped not. She had been sure ever since she'd seen Eileen and talked to her. It probably never would have happened if she'd known her since the beginning.

She was no longer a faceless entity. She was a person, a woman, a mother, his wife. Olivia knew that she couldn't have gone on with it now. Her mother was right. It was a huge responsibility destroying someone's marriage. And maybe it wasn't too late for them after all.

"I'll be there in fifteen minutes," Paul said and hung up. She washed her face and combed her hair and he arrived minutes later. He was beaming when he saw her for the first time in two weeks. She looked stern, and a chill ran down his spine.

"Do you want a drink?" she asked him.

"Will I need one?" She looked as though she did.

"I have a lot to tell you." He hadn't kissed her yet. He wanted to. But he sensed that she was keeping her distance, and he wasn't sure why. She couldn't have fallen in love with someone else in two weeks, so he knew it wasn't that.

She sat down in the living room, and he sat in a chair facing her.

"A lot has happened since I left, mostly with my business. I've formed an alliance with an art dealer in Paris. The man I met with here before I left. We're going to open a Paris branch, and maybe one in London next year. I need to spend a lot of time in Paris for the next few months, probably through June, so I'm not going to be here much." He looked disappointed as soon as she said it. "But I want to make my business grow, and this is the right way to do it." He nodded. She left no room for argument or discussion. She had obviously made the decision, and was telling him. "I'll probably be gone most of the next few months.

"I made a decision when I was in Paris, or maybe before that, Paul. I don't want a life with someone else's children. I don't even want my own right now. It's too much for me. I feel too young to take that on.

I hate saying this to you. But your children don't want me, and the truth is I don't want them either. I can't do it. I'm not grown up enough. It terrifies me, and you don't seem to have much room for me in your life, only them, and maybe their mother. I don't want to be their mother." He felt what she said like a physical blow and she could see it. This time he argued with her. He couldn't about her business, but he could about this, or thought he could.

"You can't give up now, Olivia. Their mother will be back next week. Once she's back, I'm off the hook again, and we can go back to what we had between October and December."

"Until a problem comes up, or one of them gets sick, or Pennie gets pregnant again. All we had were stolen moments last summer too, when you were out of your head about her, understandably. I would have been too, if she were my daughter. But she isn't. I just don't want the responsibility for someone else's children, and the time they take out of your life, our life. They're a full-time job, but it's not a job I want. I didn't have them, and I don't want to bring them up or worry about them, or share you with them." It was as honest as she could be. "I compete with them for your time, and your love. That's not what I want, or who I am at this point in my life. Maybe I'm too selfish to have children. But I know I don't want to deal with someone else's. I'm not ready for that in my life." He couldn't really argue with that either. She was very sure.

"I left my wife for you, Olivia, and my family, my children," he said. "I walked out on them for you. You can't leave me now. It's not fair or right. I threw it all away for you, and now you're telling me that you don't want my kids in your life."

"I don't want anyone's kids in my life, except my own. And I'm not ready for them yet either, as I just told you. If I got pregnant, I'd have an abortion. That's why I take the pill. And what you're saying isn't entirely true. You told me that your marriage was dead and had been for years, that it was over, finished, you both knew it, and you were a free man. You lied to me and yourself about it. Your marriage wasn't over. It still isn't. It's not over for you or your kids. Your children want their mother back, and maybe you do too. You've been sleeping with me for ten months, you left your wife five months ago, and you haven't even called a lawyer yet to file a divorce. You're not sure, and I know it. And so do you. You risked your marriage with me, but you didn't throw it away. You were bored and maybe you weren't *in* love with her, but you haven't thrown anything away for me.

"Now you're up to your neck in Greenwich again. You've moved back in, and who knows what you're going to do. I think you killed it for me when you moved back in three months ago. I've hardly seen you since. And what if you have to move back in again? You still have one foot firmly planted in your marriage. You walked out the door, but then you walked back in. I think you lost me then."

"I had no other choice. I'll be out again in a week or two. Can't you wait till then before you drop-kick me out the door and give up on me?" He was pleading with her since guilt hadn't worked. And most of what she said was true. He couldn't argue with how she felt about it.

"I don't even know if you'll ever get divorced. You haven't started it yet."

"I will. I promise."

"But you didn't, and still haven't. You could be divorced by now and you haven't even started or seen a lawyer."

"I went back to the house to help Eileen out, so she could go to school in Paris. I felt like I owed it to her, we both did, because I cheated on her and then I left her."

"That's between the two of you," Olivia said coldly. She didn't think it handsome of him to try and blame her.

"You were part of it," he accused her with a mean look in his eyes.

"Yes, I was, and I shouldn't have been. We did something wrong, and we both know it. I would never do it again. I met her in Paris," Olivia said quietly.

"On purpose?" Paul looked horrified.

"No, by accident, at a party the night I got there."

"What did you tell her?" He looked panicked.

"I told her I was sorry, for all of it. And I meant it. I had no right interfering in your life. I should have left you to work it out with her. Maybe you will now."

"What did she say?"

"She was incredibly nice, and warm and gracious. She seemed fine about it, and she said it has worked out for the best. But I'm sure she cried blood until she got there. I love you, Paul. But I don't love what we did, or what it led to, or what I'd have to do to stay in it with you. I'd have to sit around forever waiting for you to get up the guts to get divorced, and maybe forever, or maybe you'll go back to her and break my heart. Or if I stayed, I'd have to run around driving car pool for someone else's kids."

"That's her job, not yours."

"It may not be hers anymore either if she's starting a catering business. She won't have time. So you'll be running around too, which is right. You should. They're your kids too, and she says she's done it all for nearly twenty years. I don't want to. I'm out of the running. I think I already was when I left for Paris. I'm going back soon. I don't want to let this drag on. I figured it out while I was away, after I saw her. I wanted to tell you as soon as I got back. She'll be home in a week, maybe you can still work it out with her. I'm sure she still loves you. And she seems like a lovely person. I liked her. And I felt guilty as hell as soon as I saw her and talked to her."

"She'll never forgive me for what we did." He was still trying to pull her into it, which she thought was inelegant of him. He wanted to blame her, as much as himself, or more. He didn't want to face up to what he had done, which Olivia didn't like. It wasn't an attractive trait and she realized now that he was weak, and a coward in some ways. At first he had blamed Eileen for the ills in his life, and now he was blaming her.

He stood up then and looked at Olivia. He could see that she meant it, and nothing was going to change her mind. It terrified him that the two women in his life had met.

"I'm sorry, Paul. Truly," she said and stood up. They faced each other for a moment, and then he turned around and walked out of her apartment. He didn't try to kiss her, or tell her he loved her. She didn't know if he did, but she knew she didn't truly love him anymore. Not enough to stay with him. She hadn't in a while, and didn't want to say that to him. She heard the door close softly and then he was gone.

She was sorry for an instant, and then she wasn't. She knew she had done the right thing, for a multitude of reasons. She would have done it even if she'd never met Jean-Pierre Muset. This was about Paul and her and Eileen and no one else, and everything she had said to Paul was true for her. She was sorry she'd ever done it. She thought that they were madly in love, his marriage was dead, and they had a future, and none of those things were true. They were in lust, not in love. His marriage was still alive and breathing then and still was now. They never had a future. It was an affair with a married man, and nothing more. A mistake, and something she should not have done. Now it was over.

She felt like she could breathe again when she unpacked her suitcase. He didn't call her or text her or tell her he was sorry. He was gone. Out of her life forever, which was what she wanted.

Olivia had dinner with her mother and grandmother the next day. She told them about her alliance with Jean-Pierre Muset, and her grandmother knew who his father was. Gabrielle also reminded them that she was having a show at the MoMA in May, of recent work, and she was pleased about it.

Gwen had read a very strong script while Olivia was in Paris and was excited about it. A well-known producer was already putting the project together and she wanted the part she'd been offered. It was a powerful role she could do a lot with. So they each had an exciting new adventure ahead.

At the end of the evening, Olivia told them that she had ended it with Paul, and that she was relieved she had. Both women were pleased. She didn't tell them about Jean-Pierre because nothing had happened yet, and maybe never would. But he was a much better choice for her than Paul had ever been. She was never going to get involved with a married man again.

Chapter 13

Eileen came home exactly as she promised she would, the day after her class ended. She was sad to leave the school and the professors, and the people she had met. She was especially sad to leave Hugo. He had become a good friend, and they promised to stay in touch.

She had earned her diploma, it had been one of the most exciting experiences of her life. She had also collected valuable information from the various chefs about how to establish her catering business. She could hardly wait to get started, and was planning to do so in the next few weeks. And she was eager to see her children, whom she hadn't seen in five weeks.

She had sent Paul an email to let him know what day she'd arrive, and what time she would land, so he could organize his own departure from the house before she got home. She assumed he would leave when he went to work in the morning. She didn't expect to see him when she returned, nor did she want to. She was planning to call him in the next day or two to let him know that she was filing for divorce. She was ready, and it was time. And she liked the idea of taking action herself, since he hadn't since he left.

She was due to land at JFK in the early afternoon, and would already be home when the kids got back from school. She knew the boys had baseball practice and Pennie had a yearbook meeting that day, so she would have time to unpack and get organized. Pennie had just learned that she was getting an award for her community service at the homeless shelter.

The car she'd ordered dropped her off at home at two-thirty, and she smiled as she walked into the house. It felt good to be back, although she already missed Paris and her life there.

Her freedom was over now. She'd have no time to herself, and she'd have to be doubly organized to start her business and still be as present as possible for the kids. She was planning to look for an assistant immediately to help her set everything up.

She was thinking about all she had to do as she walked into the house, and gave a start when she heard a sound and saw someone walk toward her. She heaved a sigh of relief when she saw that it was Paul.

"What are you doing here? I thought you were a burglar." It was nice to see him, but unexpected.

"I took the day off." He carried her suitcase up the stairs for her, and she followed him to her bedroom. Everything was in perfect order, and he had taken his things. He had cleared his papers out of the office. The house looked familiar and friendly and blissfully neat. The apartment in Paris had been harder to take care of, and she'd had to do it all herself.

"The house looks great," she complimented him, and she knew he'd done a good job with the kids, and been attentive to their needs. He hadn't kissed her hello, nor had she kissed him. They stood looking at each other like two strangers, or old acquaintances. Time had begun to separate them, they had been apart now for nearly six months. She felt like a new person after three months in Paris.

"Do you want a cup of tea?" he offered, which surprised her. He was treating her like a guest.

"No thanks. I'm fine."

"So you're a Cordon Bleu chef now. Congratulations!" She could see that he was uneasy, and she had no idea why he was hanging around. Maybe it upset him to leave their home now, but he had an apartment in New York, and she was back. He had to go. She had hoped he would have before she arrived.

"You must be happy not to have to deal with the commute anymore," she commented, and unzipped her suitcase to take out a pair of jeans.

"I think I'll miss it. It's been nice being here with the kids, and coming home to them at night." She knew he'd spent several nights in the city, but not many, according to the kids. There was always some reason why he had to come home. But she had no idea why he was lingering now. "Can we talk for a few minutes?" he asked. She was tired after the trip and didn't want to, but she didn't want to be rude after he'd helped her out for so long, and she looked up in surprise.

"Sure. Now?" He nodded, and they went to sit in her office.

"I think we need to talk," he said as she sat down.

"What about? A problem with the kids?" She thought she was up-to-date on everything concerning them, and had talked to them every day, sometimes more than once, on FaceTime and Skype.

"They're fine," he reassured her. "I mean about us."

"There's no rush. I just got back." She assumed he was going to tell her he wanted to file, but so did she. She had all her paperwork in order to serve him with the divorce, as soon as he gave her the name of his attorney. Maybe Olivia was pressuring him to do it quickly, although Eileen didn't have that impression when she met her. "I contacted my lawyer a few weeks ago. We can get things done quickly now, if that's what you want."

"It isn't." He looked at her mournfully. He had been thinking about it since Olivia got back from Paris, which changed everything for him. "I'd like to try again, if you're willing. I realized while I was here how much our marriage means to me. I lost my mind for a while, but I'm back again."

"What about Olivia?"

"We ended it when she got back from Paris." Eileen had the sudden feeling that "we" hadn't ended it, she had. It was the sense she'd gotten from Olivia in Paris when they met, that it was over for her. So she'd been right.

"And why is that?"

"It was a fling, a wild moment for both of us. I want my family, Eileen, not a young girl. I don't want to start over. I want us." That was more likely the truth if he couldn't have Olivia. In that case, he wanted to settle back in his comfortable old routine with her as his minion. Eileen was even more certain now that Olivia had dumped him, for whatever reason, maybe because of the handsome young man she'd been with, or because she didn't like Paul's situation and the mess he had created for all of them.

"I met her in Paris. She's a beautiful girl."

"She is, but so are you. We're two halves of a whole, you and I. The kids need us together, and so do we." Maybe he did, but she didn't. She had won her freedom, and she wasn't going to give it up for anyone, and least of all for him. She wasn't feeling nostalgic about their marriage. She was over it, particularly after the last three months. She was looking forward, not back. She didn't want to be put on the spot this soon, but he was giving her no other choice.

"I can't do it, Paul. Too much has happened. It's been too long."

"It's only a few months. We could go to counseling. I'd be willing to do that."

"Maybe I could have done it six months or a year ago, and I'm not even sure we could have fixed it then. Maybe if you'd given her up. But I can't do it now. I won't."

"I just gave her up." He was lying and she knew it. She knew him too well. She couldn't prove it, and it didn't matter anymore whether he lied or told the truth. She had nothing left to give him. She had given it all for eighteen years.

"I don't think you gave her up," Eileen said in a quiet voice. "And it doesn't matter now. I'm sorry for you if it didn't work out. But I can't, Paul. I just can't. I've spent the last six months trying to build a new life for myself. I'm not willing to lose that. I finally have something to look forward to again. We should have gotten divorced years ago. We were both dead for years. I think it's a blessing for both of us that it ended. Maybe Olivia did us a favor. Neither of us would have had the guts to get out of it otherwise. She came by and you went running after her. And that was the end of us. How can you want to go back to that? Now I'm alive again." He could see that she was. But he wasn't. He felt dead inside. Olivia had crushed the life out of him when she ended it, and he needed Eileen now. He needed the safe haven of their house and their kids, with her at his side.

"I must have bored you to death," she said.

"No, you didn't. I love you," he said weakly.

"I love you too. You're my family after all these years, but you never stopped resenting me because we had to get married, and punishing me for it. I can't go back to that. It would kill me."

"Please," he said to her, and started to cry, which was mortifying for both of them. She didn't want him to beg. She wasn't going back to him, no matter what he said. They never should have gotten married or stayed married. And now they needed to end it cleanly with a divorce.

"I'm going to file the divorce this week. I think we both need closure now. You're probably upset because of her. You'll get over it. She's too young anyway. Our kids must have scared her to death." She was right, but he wouldn't admit it to her. "You need something new in your life, not an old shoe like me. We're not good for each other."

"Yes, we are," he insisted, still crying, like a child begging for what he couldn't have. But he wasn't a child, he was a man who had hurt her deeply, and she didn't want him back. She couldn't say it to him, but she didn't love him anymore. She was sure of it, and had no doubts. "Will you think about it?"

"I already have, for six months. Long enough to know that we're doing the right thing ending it. It ended long ago. We just need to bury it now, and rebuild our lives."

"I want to rebuild *our* life, together."

"I don't." She couldn't say it to him more plainly. "I want a divorce."

"Our kids want us together." He was trying everything he could and none of it was working.

"Pennie will be gone in five months, and the boys in six years. I'm not giving my life up for that. I already did. They'll get over it. We'll both be happier after the divorce, which is better for them." She stood up then, unwilling to continue the conversation any longer, or to wait until it turned hostile. She was finished. "I've got to unpack and get organized," she said gently but firmly.

"Don't give up on us, Eileen, please," he was begging again.

"You gave up on us, Paul. If Olivia were still willing, you'd be out of here in five minutes flat. And I'm not willing to wait till another one comes along. We're over. Finished. Done. Now please go home." He walked out of the office without saying another word, and lumbered down the stairs like an angry bear. He had been rejected twice in the space of a week. She watched him walk out the front door without turning to look at her, and she reminded herself to have the locks changed. She didn't want him letting himself in whenever he chose.

He texted her five minutes later, "You're a bitch!" She looked at it and shook her head. And that was the guy who wanted her to try again because he loved her so much. She had made the right decision, and he had to figure out his own way now. She was grateful that he'd given her the time to go to Cordon Bleu, but their marriage was long over, and all she wanted now was to bury it.

She had dinner started when the kids came home, and it smelled delicious. Mark and Seth threw their arms around her, and they waited for Pennie to come home to sit down to dinner. It felt like a real homecoming to all of them.

She got another text from Paul later that night, "I'm sorry." She hadn't answered the first one, and didn't respond to the second one either. It was time to let go, and she had. Now he had to figure the rest out for himself. She was sure he'd have another woman in his life soon, but it wasn't going to be her.

She called her attorney the next morning after the kids left for school, and got the ball rolling. He said he would send her the papers to sign that afternoon. They decided to send them to Paul's general counsel, rather than waiting for him to hire a divorce attorney. She called a locksmith to change the locks that day. Paul didn't live there any-more, and never would again. She realized it had probably been a mistake to have him stay there while she was in Paris, but it was the only way she could have gone. And it was done now. She told her children that night that she and Paul were getting divorced. They were disappointed but not surprised. Pennie told her after the boys left the kitchen that she thought Eileen was doing the right thing.

"Thank you, sweetheart. That means a lot to me. So do I." She hugged her, and everything felt right.

The Numbers Game

* * *

Eileen was well aware of the tension her daughter was under from the moment she arrived from Paris, and even a few days before. Her college acceptance letters were due any day. She had already heard from NYU and Columbia, which were her backup schools since she didn't want to go to college in New York. The big three she was hoping for were Harvard, her first choice, Princeton, and Yale. She wasn't sure about Duke or Dartmouth. Duke was a great school, but she didn't want to spend four years in North Carolina, it was too different from the world she knew. And Dartmouth was more of a jock school, and seemed better suited to men, in her opinion. Pennie remembered how anxious Tim had been until he heard from Stanford. She felt that way now, on tenterhooks until the mail came every day.

She hadn't heard from any of her top choices yet. She knew good news came in fat envelopes with a packet of forms to fill out for her acceptance, housing, financial aid. And bad news came in thin envelopes with a single sheet, "Although your application and transcript were very impressive, we regret to inform you . . ." Many of her classmates had already been rejected by their first-choice schools.

She heard from Princeton first, a few days after her mother got home. She had a friend drive her back to the house at lunchtime, so she and her mother could open it together. The envelope was a thick one, and Pennie's hands shook as she tore it open.

"This is so much better than doing it with you on Skype. I'm glad you're home." She grinned at Eileen as she unfolded the pages.

"Me too." Eileen had tears in her eyes as she watched her. These were such important moments in her daughter's life. And then Pennie let out a scream and danced around the kitchen and hugged her mother.

"I got in! I got in! I got in! Yessss!" She had guessed from the thickness of the packet, but you could never be sure. Pennie never took good news for granted.

"Will you go?" Eileen asked her breathlessly, shaking herself, wondering if Pennie's order of preference had changed.

"I want to wait and hear what the others say." She had until May first to give them her answer. And then the schools would whittle down their lists, and move on to offer places to the students on their waiting lists. Pennie called her father and told him, and he congratulated her. No one had turned her down yet.

Duke's letter came the next day. They were coming in rapid succession now. Duke had declined her, saying that they had had nearly double the qualified applicants for the spaces available, and many worthy students had to be turned down. Pennie didn't care, she hadn't been enthusiastic about it. And she felt the same way when Dartmouth declined her too. She knew it wouldn't have been the right school for her.

Yale wait-listed her, again due to increased applications. She had one letter left to receive, the one she cared about most. It arrived five days after Eileen's return, on a Saturday. Pennie hadn't called to check, she was at a yearbook editorial meeting, and they were struggling to get all the material on time. She got home at six o'clock, and Eileen was cooking something that smelled delicious. She wandered into the kitchen, and her mother pointed to the kitchen table without a word. Her answer from Harvard was sitting there. Pennie stared at it, afraid to touch the letter or open it.

"Oh my God, what'll I do?" she asked her mother with huge eyes.

"Well, we could have it framed the way it is, unopened, and keep it the biggest mystery of your life." Her mother smiled at her. The envelope was thick, which should mean good news, but Pennie didn't want to assume anything and be crushed if they declined her. She picked it up in her hands and just held it for a minute, and then tore it open and squeezed her eyes shut.

"Will you open your eyes, for God's sake? I can't stand the suspense," her mother said to her. Pennie opened her eyes and started reading. She didn't have far to go. The letter began with a single word, "Congratulations!" Her mouth opened and her eyes opened wider. She stood still as a statue, and then leapt in the air with a bloodcurdling scream. Both her brothers hurtled down the stairs immediately, as Pennie threw her arms around her mother and lifted her off her feet.

"What happened?" Seth asked breathlessly, as he stormed into the kitchen with Mark behind him.

"I got in! I got in! I got in!" she was screaming as Seth rolled his eyes.

"We thought Mom had cut off a finger or something, or had a heart attack." They were all forbidden to touch her professional knife set, which she had in a leather case.

"So where did you get in?" Seth asked her.

"I got into Harvard!" she screamed again. Her brother beamed at her, Mark high-fived her, and Eileen stood smiling at all of them, and wiped the tears off her cheeks with her apron. It had been a beautiful and unforgettable moment.

Pennie went to call her father and all her friends, and then texted

Tim in California. He answered immediately and congratulated her. It was one of the high points of her life, and she knew she would remember it forever. She called her school advisor on his cellphone, and thanked him for his glowing recommendation.

"You did this yourself, you know," Eileen reminded her, "with all that hard work and studying, all the parties you didn't go to, and your essays were fantastic." She had done three different ones that she used for different schools. "This is a wonderful accomplishment. You should be very proud of yourself. I'm very, very proud of you." Eileen started crying again, and then laughed through her tears. They were tears of joy.

Pennie filled out the paperwork that night, including the form for housing in the dorms, and she declined all the others who had accepted and wait-listed her to free up the spaces for other students. She mailed all the envelopes on Monday morning on the way to school. She felt as though a thousand-pound weight had been lifted off her shoulders. She had been tense for a month waiting to hear. Almost all her classmates had heard by then, some with happier results than others. But most of them knew where they would be going now. It made every day bittersweet as the students thought of leaving each other. It made her think of Tim, and how he had felt when he heard from Stanford, and her own mixed feelings about breaking up with him. And then the baby had happened, and they'd almost gotten married. She wondered what their life would have been like if they had, and if they'd have stayed together after she lost the baby. It had been so overwhelming, and he had been so nice about it.

She hadn't dated anyone for all of senior year, and hadn't wanted to. She had turned a lot of nice boys down. She didn't even have a date for senior prom, and had said she wasn't going. She had wanted to put any romantic possibilities on hold. She was terrified of the risk of another pregnancy, and couldn't face it. She knew that even girls who took the pill got pregnant sometimes, if they missed one and didn't realize it, or took it at irregular hours. One girl she knew had taken an antibiotic for strep throat, which canceled out her birth control pill's effectiveness and she got pregnant. Pennie had decided to take a break for the year and stick with abstinence, although there were one or two boys she would have gone out with, if the pregnancy with Tim hadn't happened. She had never asked him again after the first time if he had a girlfriend, although she suspected he probably did, but she didn't want to know, and he never told her. He treated her with caution and compassion, and the love he still felt for her, even now. He had been deeply affected by what happened too.

But now something wonderful had happened. Her dream had come true. She was going to Harvard! It meant a lot to her father, since he had gone there as an undergraduate too, and started business school there.

Her school was bustling with news on Monday morning, and a few panicked faces of the students who hadn't gotten in anywhere, or had applied to too few schools. She had cut it close with only seven. Some of her classmates had applied to fifteen, especially if their grades and board scores weren't as good as hers. Her counselor had assured her that she had a strong shot at the Ivy Leagues, although they were unpredictable, like Duke and Dartmouth declining and Yale wait-listing her. But she was grateful Harvard hadn't declined her and didn't put her on a wait list, which extended the stress for several months. She was in! In five months she'd be a Harvard freshman! She couldn't think of a better feeling in the world, and her mother kept reminding her that she had earned it and deserved it. Eileen wanted her daughter to be proud of herself, enjoy the victory fully, and celebrate it.

Pennie went out with her friends that Saturday night, those who had their answers and were happy with their options, and they had dinner together, then Eileen took all three of her children out to dinner on Sunday night. She thought of inviting Paul to join them, but decided not to. She hadn't spoken to him since the day she got home, and his pathetic pleas to continue their marriage. She had signed the papers the next day, and by now, she was sure they had arrived at his attorney's office, but she hadn't heard a word from him and didn't want to.

She'd had lunch with Jane when she got back and told her all the news, and Jane told her she looked ten years younger after Paris. Better than Botox!

Once the college acceptances were in, and Pennie had accepted Harvard, Eileen turned her mind to other things. She called an agency for restaurant personnel that she found online and listed the job for a caterer's assistant. She wanted someone experienced, particularly with classic French cuisine. She expected it to take a while, but within two days the agency was calling her with applicants and emailing her their CVs. There were a dozen of them for her to sift through. Some of them sounded inappropriate immediately. Others went into a "maybe" pile for her to study more thoroughly late at night when she wasn't busy.

After she did, three of them stood out. She wasn't allowed to ask their ages, but she could guess in most cases from their list of previous jobs. All of them had worked in restaurants, one had been a caterer's assistant for six months, but the circumstances surrounding the end of the position sounded mysterious and didn't feel right to her. She told the agency she would meet all three applicants, and made appointments with them at a coffee shop in town. She didn't want strangers coming to her home.

The first one was a young woman who had worked at two excellent French restaurants in Boston, and was a sous-chef. She was young, had good experience and good references, but she had piercings everywhere, eyebrows, nose, ears, lips, tongue, and "sleeves" of ominous-looking tattoos on both arms. Other than that she looked neat and clean, but Eileen couldn't see her as an assistant at a high-end wedding. The second was an older man who had been a line chef in his youth, and a pastry chef at a five-star hotel for the past five years. He was very dour, but his references were excellent. He expounded for half an hour about his rigid ideas about how to manage staff. Eileen felt claustrophobic with him halfway through the interview. Their cooking experience mattered most, but their personalities factored into it too. She couldn't see herself working with either of them, no matter how good their references were. And she knew she would be spending a lot of time with her assistant if the business took off and became a success, as she wanted it to. She needed someone who would inspire confidence in the clients, didn't look scary, presented well, and could coordinate all the different kinds of staff and suppliers they'd be using, from tent rentals to dance floors, to tableware, florists, and their food wholesalers. She was looking for a person who understood fine cuisine, and could deal with guests at an event if Eileen was busy somewhere else. Eileen was hoping to garner a big portion of the wedding business in Greenwich, which would be very lucrative. People with large estates went all out when their daughters got married. The food was an important part of it, but there was a great deal more to handle. Eileen had been giving it a lot of thought since she had the idea. She'd been buying wedding books to study flowers, décor, and table settings, and had some creative ideas of her own.

The third candidate she was to see rescheduled twice, which she thought was a bad sign and suggested to her that he was unreliable, although he was pleasant on the phone and his excuses sounded valid. He was sick once with the flu, which could happen to anyone, and the second time his dog had been badly bitten so he was rushing it to the pet hospital. Eileen was sympathetic and liked dogs, but work was work. And what if they had a wedding to do? The agency had warned her that he was an excellent chef with a strong personality, which many had. They said he was good-looking and had an eye for the female staff. "He's a bit of a Don Juan," the woman at the agency warned her, "but everyone loves him." He had a strong Italian accent when Eileen talked to him, and he had worked in France, at two private châteaux and a five-star hotel. He had stayed in his jobs longer than any of the others, which was unusual for private chefs. They got bored and moved on, particularly if their employers didn't entertain enough. They liked to use their skills and show them off, which you couldn't do with a small family or an elderly couple. Eileen decided to see him anyway, even after he canceled for the dog. There was no one else she wanted to see at the moment.

He appeared ten minutes late for their appointment, and said he had gotten lost on his way to Greenwich and took the wrong turnoff. His last job was at a large private estate on Long Island. She knew the names of his employers, who were well-known socialites she had read about in magazines for many years. They also had a large and very stately home in Palm Beach. The husband had been a famous financier on Wall Street in his day. He had been with them for three years, but the wife had died suddenly, and the husband was now ninety-three and had Alzheimer's. He said there was nothing left for him to do except prepare trays for his employer and his nurses. He wasn't using his skills in the job. He felt very sorry for his employer and liked him, but it was time to move on. His employer's late wife had been full of life and loved to entertain, even at ninety, which was rare, but she had fallen down a marble staircase in high heels, had a severe head injury, and died two days later. Once she was gone, the chef had nothing to do, so he had given notice and left, and was currently unemployed.

The applicant for the job had surprised Eileen when she saw him. He was unusually tall, looked very serious at first, but was actually very funny and made her laugh several times at his descriptions of parties, events, and jobs he had had. She could see why he was a success with women. He was very charming, with expressive eyes. He looked neat and clean and presentable in his suit and expensive brown suede shoes, and he had the stylishness of Italian men and was from Milan. His parents owned a hotel in Florence, and he had grown up around food. She didn't ask the name of the hotel, but it sounded like a successful venture. But he wanted to work in the States. He had a green card, which was essential. His name was Massimiano Salvi, and he went by Max.

"I married a friend to get the green card," he explained without embarrassment. "We're divorced, and I'm legal to work here. It was the only way I could get it." He volunteered that he was thirty-three years old, since she couldn't ask him, and he seemed fit, energetic, and well spoken. His English was excellent and he was fluent in Italian, Spanish, and French.

"I hope you understand that this isn't as glamorous as many of the jobs you've had." He had worked for very wealthy people with enormous homes and big staffs, fancy restaurants, and the five-star hotel in Paris. "I'm starting a business. It isn't even set up yet. I'd like to focus on the wedding market at first, and high-end dinner parties and events. I just finished a three-month course at Cordon Bleu, and I lean to simple high-end French food." He nodded. It sounded fine to him and the kind of thing he liked to do, as well as "refined Italian cuisine," as he called it. "If I get the wedding business, we're going to have to coordinate a lot of suppliers, work hard, be ultra organized and able to keep a lot of balls in the air at once. I'm looking for an assistant to help me set up the business and juggle everything with me, and we'll need a stable of sous-chefs to call on, while you supervise the food." He nodded again, undaunted by what she was suggesting. She was offering a respectable but not enormous base salary, and a percentage of the fee of the events they catered, which she hoped would make it alluring, but was probably a lot less than he'd been earning. He thought the arrangement sounded fair.

She had really wanted to hire a woman, but she could see advantages to having a man assist her. It was going to be hard physical work, often carrying things when no one else would, and whipping things into shape in a crisis right before an event.

"We'll have to be jacks-of-all-trades, not just chefs. I don't just want to be a cook, I want to plan events."

"That is why I was bored in the job I left. Madame loved to plan grand parties, a masked ball, we transformed the house into a Venetian palace, we did a wedding that looked like Versailles for her granddaughter. Black-tie dinners for a hundred for charitable events. My first year there was wonderful, then her husband began to fail and we were a little more discreet. Then she fell, and it all ended. So sad, I loved her, she was a wonderful woman." He wiped a tear from his eye and Eileen was touched but wondered if he was too emotional. That could prove to be difficult too. "I think we can make a huge success of your business. I would like to help you." She was tempted to try him, but she wanted to think about it. She had envisioned someone more low-key and subdued, a good foot soldier. She had the feeling that Max could be flamboyant, and have his own opinions, but at worst, if it didn't work out, she could fire him, which he said too. He sounded excited about what she wanted to do, and she liked that. His references were flawless. Everyone he'd worked for had loved him. If the business was successful with the wealthy community in Greenwich, he could be the perfect assistant.

At the end of the interview, she had a good feeling about him, and decided to try him.

"How will you advertise the business when you're ready?" he asked her.

"I was hoping to do it by word of mouth. If we get a few events, it could get us started."

"Yes, excellent. But you must send emails to everyone you know. Clever ones, make it appealing, make it fun and elegant. People must talk about you, the newspapers must discover you, journalists must love you. People must beg you to do their parties and weddings and events." He was right, she realized. There was theater to it too. And she already wanted his help.

"Max, I'd like to offer you the job."

"I am very exciting to do it," he said, making an innocent mistake, and she smiled as he realized it. "No, I am not exciting. I am *excited*," he laughed at himself, and so did she.

"I have a feeling you're exciting too!"

"I get upset sometimes, when things aren't perfect. But only for five minutes. Then I make them perfect, and I'm happy again."

"I don't get upset, but I'm a perfectionist too."

"We will work well together. I am sure of it." They both stood up, and he shook her hand and beamed. He had a strong handshake. "When do we start?"

"Now. Next week, as soon as you can."

"I could work with you every day, making lists of suppliers and planning our email campaign. I can answer the phones when they start to ring. And I can be with you full-time in two weeks. I've booked a few parties until then." It was perfect, and just what she needed. He sounded flexible, willing, and creative.

"I hope the phones do ring." She gave him her address, and he promised to be there the following day. He had a small studio apartment, he said, not far from her. They shook hands on it again, and as he drove away she noticed that he drove an old Fiat. And she had an idea on the way home.

When she got home, she called the agency and said she had hired him. And when Pennie came home from school, Eileen shared her idea with her. Pennie had been looking for a summer job that didn't eat up all her time, for her last summer before college.

"I have a job for you," her mother said cautiously. "How would you like to answer phones for me, for my catering business, before you leave for Boston? That's if someone calls, of course."

"That sounds like fun, Mom." Pennie smiled at her.

"And you could help with small jobs if we get any events." It reminded her that she needed to get a phone line dedicated to the business, an email address, and had to start working on their email blast, set up a website and eventually a brochure, and they needed a name.

"I'd love to do it." Pennie was excited at the idea. And after that, Eileen went upstairs to her office to start making lists. She had an email from Max that afternoon, thanking her for the opportunity to work with her. She had told Jane about him, who wanted to know if he was cute, and Eileen laughed at her.

They were off and running. She had an assistant, and a receptionist to take calls. Now all they needed were clients, and some weddings and events. And a name. She played around with some words and names on a pad on her desk, and the simplest, most direct sounded best. Eileen Jackson Events. Simple and clear. She smiled as she stared at the name. It was happening. She had a dream. And it was coming true.

Chapter 14

Olivia spent three weeks in New York, tending to her business, getting organized to leave again, and she had dinner with her mother and grandmother and saw a few friends she hadn't seen for a while. Having an affair with a married man had driven her underground for the past year, first so no one would discover it, and then with Paul, to seize whatever stolen moments they had. She was relieved to be out of the shadows now, and no longer waiting for him to have a free hour on his way to Greenwich so she could fall into bed with him. The relationship had degenerated severely once Eileen left for Paris and Paul moved back home. Now she was free again. She missed him at first, but she was glad she had ended it before the situation got any worse, or she got in any deeper. It had been a difficult year, even though it had been exciting in the beginning. The thrill of forbidden fruit, and an older man. Now she was ready for real life again.

She heard from Jean-Pierre every day, mostly to talk about her business, and he was careful not to make romantic overtures over the phone or by text. He wanted a real relationship, not a virtual one. Too many of his friends led their emotional lives by text with people they scarcely got to know. And he thought Olivia was a fascinating woman. She thought the same about him and at times she thought she had fantasized his interest in her, because he didn't mention it on the phone.

She set the date for her return to Paris, three weeks after she'd left, and was planning to stay at the Ritz again. She wanted to spend three or four weeks there, although he explained to her that May was a difficult month to do business in France. There were four long weekends for national and religious holidays, and people tended to give up and take vacations then. But he said it was a perfect time for them to set up their office and get organized. And he had "stolen" one of his father's young female employees at the gallery as their secretary/assistant, a young French girl who spoke good English, since her mother was American. Her name was Suzanne, and Olivia had already spoken to her several times on the phone. Jean-Pierre assured her that the girl was competent.

By mid-April, Olivia was ready to go back to Paris and she didn't have to return to New York until late May for her grandmother's show at the MoMA. She had promised to be back for that, which gave her five weeks in Paris if she wanted to stay that long. She liked the idea of getting out of New York for a while. She wanted to get away from anything that reminded her of Paul. She hadn't heard from him since they'd broken up. She knew that Eileen must have been back by then, and she wondered if they had gotten back together. She had a feeling they might, once she and Paul had broken up. She didn't think he wanted to leave his children and house in

Greenwich again, and she suspected that Eileen would probably take him back. Why wouldn't she? They were her kids too. It made sense to Olivia. She didn't miss him after a while. But she was lonely in her apartment at times.

Paul had received the copy of the divorce papers Eileen had filed by then. He still couldn't believe she had rejected him and done it. He was angry at first, and then hurt, and upset with Olivia. It had been a terrible month. He missed the house in Greenwich and the children, and both women who had left him. He had played a double game for a year and lost both. It was a heavy blow. And he didn't want to believe that it wouldn't have worked with Olivia. She could have gotten used to the children and come to love them if she'd tried. Their first meeting had been unfortunate, but they would have come around. She had turned out to be flighty and young, in his opinion, and selfish. She couldn't even stick it out long enough for Eileen to come home, even though they were almost there. And from his perspective, Eileen was punishing him for the affair.

He had gone out to Greenwich a few times on the weekends to go to the boys' baseball games, and was glad Eileen wasn't there. Pennie said she was busy setting up her business and had hired an assistant. They were all moving on, and he'd been left high and dry, feeling sorry for himself. He blamed Olivia for not sticking with it, and Eileen for not forgiving him. They were both tougher than he had estimated. And in six months he'd be divorced, which he thought would never happen to him, after he'd married Eileen in the first place, and sacrificed a more exciting career for her. And now she was leaving him. He only saw his side of it, and had no one to discuss it with. Even his daughter was sympathetic to her mother.

He took Seth and Mark to several Yankees games, which cheered him up, and he drove them back to Greenwich afterwards. He stopped to buy groceries at the store in Greenwich after he dropped them off, so he didn't have to shop in New York. His apartment depressed him, and his kids never wanted to come to the city, so he was always there alone. He had taken it to be close to Olivia, which made no sense anymore. He was thinking about giving it up, and renting a house or apartment in Greenwich so he could be close to the boys, since Pennie would be gone anyway. The boys would be in Greenwich for six more years, and he didn't mind the commute. He was used to it. He was thinking about looking for something in the summer. He might even buy a house, since he was giving Eileen theirs as part of their divorce settlement. He didn't want to make her and the children move, and she couldn't afford to buy out his share, so he had done the magnanimous thing to atone for his sins, and given it to her. She'd been very appreciative, and wrote him a nice email about what the gesture meant to her and the kids, not to be forced to move to a lesser house, and to know they were secure. And he was giving her a handsome sum of money too, and child support for the kids. He had put aside the money for college for all three of them. He didn't want a war with her, and preferred to be generous. He could afford it. His career had been good to him, even if it wasn't the one he had originally planned to pursue.

He liked the idea of buying a house in Greenwich, near them, so the boys could ride their bikes over to see him on the weekend, so he called a realtor that week to see what was available. There were three in their neighborhood, which sounded good to him, although they weren't cheap.

Mathilde, the real estate agent, sounded pleasant on the phone and they agreed to meet at eleven o'clock on Saturday morning that weekend. When he got to the first house, he saw that the realtor was an attractive woman with dark hair, a good figure, and a friendly smile. She had long hair and was wearing a navy and white–striped sweater, jeans, and running shoes. She looked vaguely familiar, but he couldn't place her. He figured he had probably seen her around Greenwich, since she said she lived there too.

He hated the first house, it was beaten-up and old-fashioned inside, needed a new kitchen and bathrooms, and had no charm. It was an estate sale, previously owned by an elderly couple who hadn't remodeled it since the fifties, and it would require more work than he wanted to undertake. He wanted something new and fresh that would be cheerful to live in and his children would like.

The second house was all right and in good condition, but there was nothing special about it. And, wise in her business, the realtor had saved the best, and most expensive, for last. The first two had been reasonably priced. The third one was considerably more. And as soon as he walked in, Paul could see why. It was in perfect condition, newly remodeled, with beautiful bleached floors and big sunny windows. The house was full of light. There were three big bedrooms on the second floor, and two more on the floor above. It had a den, a dining room, a big living room, a state-of-the-art kitchen, and a gigantic playroom downstairs with a high-tech sound system. There were even curtains in every room that were part of the sale, and bathrooms that had just been redone with stylish Italian fixtures. And there was a big backyard, a pool, and a four-car garage.

"Wow!" he said, looking around. It was much nicer than their old house. It had every possible modern feature anyone could want, and nice decorating touches. It had been attractively staged, so a potential buyer could see how to do it. "Why would anyone sell this?" he asked in amazement. Did a developer do it? People redid houses all the time to sell them for a profit, and made big money in it, but this one was especially well done.

"No, it's a divorce. You know how that is. They had just finished the house, and he left with the nanny, a very pretty Swedish girl. So it's up for sale. They want to get their money out of it, within reason, but it's priced for a quick sale. They know they won't make everything back for all the expensive details they put in. They just want to put it behind them as soon as they can, and move on. The wife went back to LA, where she's from. The house has bad memories for her." He nodded. It was a familiar story, and his story wouldn't have been pretty either, if they'd sold their house. He was glad now that he hadn't made Eileen do that. It seemed like adding insult to injury in an already painful situation.

He asked Mathilde the price again, and how much negotiating room she thought there was. He didn't want to exploit their misfortunes, but he didn't want to pay a crazy price either, and she understood. The current owners had put too much money into it when they remodeled it, thinking they'd be there forever, and now they were probably going to take a loss, or at best break even on it, which the realtor said they were willing to do. They had only owned the house for three years, and spent two years remodeling it. They had moved from a smaller house in Greenwich.

"It's only been on the market for a few days and it won't last long. If you like it, why don't you make an offer you're comfortable with, and see what happens? You can always improve it if they don't accept your first offer. It's going to sell pretty quickly. Houses like this, in this kind of condition, don't come on the market often. And the owners are already gone. This is all staging. She's already back in California with the kids, and he bought a co-op in New York."

"With the nanny?" Paul couldn't resist asking, and she nodded.

"She's a lucky girl," she commented. "Not all those stories end happily. And it didn't end happily for the wife. She wants to get her money out of this as fast as she can, so she can buy in LA." It seemed so cut-and-dried to Paul, people whose lives fell apart, or were torn to shreds, sold their homes and moved on with their broken hearts or new loves. It made him sad to think about and reminded him of Olivia and Eileen. So far, none of them had come out winners, in his opinion. Eileen would have disagreed.

"I'd like to make an offer," Paul said, forcing his mind back to real estate. He could just imagine how much Seth and Mark would love it, with the giant playroom and outdoor pool they could use all summer. They would never want to leave, which was partly the idea.

"I'll write up the offer for you," the realtor said pleasantly, "and present it to their agent today. He was busy this morning, so he let me come alone. I'll drop it off at his office, once you sign it."

"Can we do it now?" Paul asked her, she nodded, and they sat down at the rented dining table to do it. He liked some of the furniture and the realtor said it was all for sale from the company that had staged it.

He made an offer just below their asking price, but not enough to insult them or blow the deal. Just low enough to feel that he had been smart about it. He signed the offer, took a last look around, and then they left, and stood outside for a minute.

"You know, you look so familiar. I keep thinking that we've met, but I don't know where." He smiled at her and she looked shy for a minute.

"School," she answered. "My middle son is in class with your boys. My older boy is starting high school in September, and my youngest is starting first grade. He's six."

"I knew I'd seen you." They both smiled. "It was driving me crazy while we walked around the house. I really hope I get it, it would be great for my boys." He hesitated for a minute and then added, "We're getting divorced too. My wife is staying in the house. My ex-wife," he corrected himself painfully. It was hard to get used to.

"I'm sorry to hear it," she said sympathetically.

"Me too. It happens, I guess." He thought she was very pretty, in a natural way. She didn't look like a model, but she wasn't plain either. He thought she was in her late thirties, or maybe forty at most, and he remembered seeing her at school now. He had an urge to invite her out for coffee or lunch, but he wanted to deal with business first. "Maybe we can get our boys together sometime," he said cautiously, and she smiled at him. She had a warm smile and perfect teeth.

"I'd love that. We have three almost the same age, my older boy is only a year and a half older than yours, and my little guy loves to tag along." The vision of five boys together would have daunted most people, but Paul liked it. Mathilde was the right age, and they both lived in Greenwich. And she had mentioned her ex-husband so he knew she was single. It all made sense and appealed to him. "I'll call you as soon as I hear back about the offer," she promised him. They shook hands and got back in their cars, and she waved as she drove away to submit the offer.

He took Mark out for ice cream then, since Pennie and Seth were out. And then he drove back to the city.

He was watching sports on TV that night, alone in his apartment with a half-empty pizza box next to him, when his cellphone rang and he picked it up absentmindedly without looking at the number. He still hoped it would be Olivia, missing him unbearably, but it never was. It was Mathilde Smith, the realtor.

"Hi, Paul. It's Mathilde." She sounded bright and cheery, which was her personality. She seemed like a positive person and enjoyed her work. "We're almost there. We need the approval of both parties. The husband accepted your offer. I know I said they were included, but his ex-wife wants ten thousand for the drapes. I got her down to five. I think it's just emotional for her. It's the only sticking point."

"You've got it. Five thousand for the drapes. I like them anyway. Done. And I'd like to look at the furniture again, and see what I'd like to buy so I don't have to run around furnishing it." He no longer had Eileen to do his decorating.

"Of course, we can go anytime. I'll just call them back about the drapes. And Paul, congratulations!" she said warmly. "You bought a beautiful home."

"I can't wait to show it to my kids. My daughter is leaving for college at the end of August, but she's going to love the pool. You'll have to bring your boys over sometime."

"They would love that," she sounded shy then, "and so would I." He wondered why he hadn't noticed her before. But he hadn't been available, and life had been different. He was married. And then he was in love with Olivia. Now he was alone, and his eyes were open and his mind clear. He was beaming when he hung up, thrilled with his new house.

He went out to Greenwich the next day to tell the kids and Eileen. He drove Pennie and the boys past the new house, and they loved it, and the idea that he would be nearby so they could see him anytime. Eileen smiled at him when he dropped them off, and gave him a thumbs-up. He had done a good thing, and was proud of himself, and she was too.

During the two weeks after Eileen hired Max, he had been at her house every day, making lists with her, and working on the email blast she was going to send. She emptied her address book into her computer, singling out people who were likely to give big parties, or even medium-sized ones, and host charitable events. She had six hundred names on the list, and they had added some fun artwork, and written an enticing email. She had put everyone on the list she could think of, including people she had met through charity committees and some of the more social parents at school. Anyone who might give a party, an event, or a wedding, or a nice dinner with some style, and good food. Max contributed some creative ideas, and was adept with the technology on her computer, and two weeks after they had met and she'd hired him, she hit the send button and sent the email for Eileen Jackson Events out into the ether. She and Max sent up a cheer, and Pennie came into her mother's office to see what was happening.

They had put up a website to which they would add photos of various events later. For now, it was all very basic. Max had been a big help to her, and he was always willing to help around the house, make a quick lunch for her while they worked, or a snack for the children when they got home from school. They liked him. He had been a terrific asset so far. They had compared recipes, and he was impressed by what Eileen had learned at Cordon Bleu, and her own natural abilities.

"You're a born chef," he complimented her. And he was a masterful one, with both experience and talent. She could hardly wait for the meals he would help her design for their events, while working with the clients.

They got their first client call three days after they sent the emails, from a woman whose name Eileen remembered, but not her face. The client said they had met on a committee for a charity to help abused women years before. The moment Eileen answered the line dedicated to her catering business, Sandra Melling breathed a sigh of relief.

"Oh, thank God . . . your email is an answer to my prayers. We haven't seen each other in years. My daughter is getting married for the second time. She just told me two days ago. She's thirty-nine and she wants a big wedding. I've called every caterer in Connecticut, they're all booked. She's insisting on getting married in June. We have eight weeks to plan a wedding for three hundred people, and she wants *everything* pink, even the wedding cake. I'm having a nervous breakdown. I got her to do it on the last Saturday in June. That's June twenty-seventh. Can you do it?" She was talking a mile a minute, and Eileen vaguely remembered that she was the widow of a very wealthy man, and had a beautiful estate. If she still had it, it would be the perfect location. And an audience of three hundred as a debut for her catering skills was a fabulous opportunity, and scary as hell. Max was in the room when she got the call, and she waved her arms frantically and pointed to the pad on her desk, where she had written the word "wedding" and the date "June 27." Max's handsome Italian face broke into a broad grin and he gave her a thumbs-up.

"As it happens, we're still free on that date," Eileen said, trying to sound businesslike and not too excited. "Mrs. Melling, we'd be happy to do it."

"You're a godsend. Call me Sandy. When can we meet?"

"Does tomorrow work for you?" Eileen suggested.

"That's perfect. I don't even know where to start. We did her first wedding in Palm Beach, but she wants this one here."

"We'll make it work," Eileen promised her, and jotted down the address for their meeting the next day. She hung up a minute later and Max whirled her around her small office. "We have a client! We're in business! It's working!" she burbled happily.

"We will look at everything," Max told her, "and then we will discuss it and give her an estimate. We agree to nothing in the meeting." He was so seasoned and so bold that sometimes she wasn't sure who was the boss and who was the assistant, but she liked him more and more. He was easy to work with so far, and a nice person, and he had excellent ideas. And they had a wedding to do in two months.

"By the way, everything has to be pink." He looked horrified after she said it.

"No. A wedding cannot be pink. It must be white."

"Second wedding. The client gets what she wants, and we get a wedding to show future clients. If she wants it green or black, we do it. Besides, it might be cute."

"We do elegant weddings, not cute ones," he said grandly.

"Ten percent of a pink wedding is still money, especially for three hundred people on a magnificent estate."

"True," he said, reconsidering, and then he broke into a smile. "I think pink is a very good idea, don't you?"

"A *very* good idea." She smiled broadly at him. They were off and running with eight weeks to plan a pink wedding.

Olivia got everything in order before she left New York in mid-April. Jean-Pierre was expecting her, and he was picking her up at the Ritz for dinner on the day she arrived. She was eager to see him. She hadn't stopped since she left Paris, and she was looking forward to setting up their office space at his father's gallery on the Faubourg Saint-Honoré. Jean-Pierre said he had a lot of plans to discuss with her over dinner.

She was at the Ritz by noon, had a quick lunch in her room, went through her emails, swam in the pool afterwards, and then had an appointment at the spa for a massage. She was back in her room at four o'clock. A vase with two dozen red roses was waiting for her in

the room, with a card. "Welcome to Paris. À ce soir. Jean-Pierre."
Until tonight. She smiled when she read it.

She went back to answering emails, and at six-thirty she bathed
and dressed carefully for dinner. She wore a short black skirt, which
showed off her legs, a white Chanel jacket, and towering high heels.
Her red hair was like a beacon and lit up her face and green eyes.

She was outside promptly at eight o'clock, and two minutes later,
he pulled up in a sleek black Ferrari. He looked incredibly handsome,
even more than she remembered, and very racy in the sports car. "It's
my father's," he confessed as they pulled away from the hotel, and
she liked that he admitted it. "He let me borrow it for the night to
impress you." There was an innocence and unpretentiousness about
him that she loved. She thanked him for the flowers, and they started
talking immediately as though they had seen each other the day before. They had spoken constantly since she left, but there was an
ease about their relationship and their meshing of ideas that made it
feel as though they had known each other forever. They were friends
and business associates now, and the same unspoken question hung
between them that had been there before.

They had dinner at a chic bistro in the Seventh, Le Voltaire, which
had been there forever, and when they got in his father's Ferrari
again afterwards, he finally addressed the question. She had been
wondering if he would ask her.

"You were going to take care of something after you left Paris. I
believe it had to do with the husband of the woman we met at Castel,
at the party." She knew exactly what he meant, and he remembered
the circumstances perfectly, as well as her explanation at the time.

"I remember," she said simply.

"Did you take care of it?" His eyes met hers when he asked her. He had waited three weeks to see her again and hear the answer.

"Yes, I did," she said, thinking of herself telling Paul all the reasons why she had decided that being with him was a mistake, and how angry he had been at her. Jean-Pierre smiled at her response and looked pleased.

"If you didn't, you know that my father's car would have turned into a pumpkin and we would become white mice," he said, and she laughed as they took off and headed toward the Right Bank in the splendor of a moonlit Paris night with the Seine beneath the bridge and Notre Dame in the background. She was surprised when he took a right turn on the Right Bank and drove her close to Notre Dame, and then parked nearby. The moon was almost full overhead. "Do you want to walk for a few minutes?" She nodded and they got out of the car and wandered close to the magnificent church. The scene looked like a postcard of Paris.

He took her hand, and they walked along the street and stood in the shadow of the church. He kissed her, as though he had always meant to, and she had expected it. He wanted the first time he kissed her to be somewhere that they would both remember. He wanted this to be different, for both of them, and had felt that way about her since the first time he saw her in New York, as though she would always be in his life from then on.

"I want us to always remember this," he said softly, and kissed her again, and then they both saw a bouquet of white balloons flying high overhead toward the stars. "It's a sign," he whispered, and she smiled at him, and then she laughed and he looked surprised. "What are you laughing at?"

"I was just thinking how pissed off your father would have been if I hadn't taken care of things when I went back, and we had to give him back a pumpkin tonight instead of his Ferrari." Jean-Pierre laughed. She looked happy and full of mischief.

"You're a terrible person," he said. It felt good to both of them to be young and happy, in Paris, carefree, and in love. Olivia knew then that he was the one she'd been waiting for, and had freed herself for. Jean-Pierre had known it from the moment they met.

Chapter 15

Olivia stayed in Paris as long as she could before her grandmother's show at the MoMA. She and Jean-Pierre spent every day together setting up the Paris branch of her business, getting their new office in order, and training their new assistant to work with the technology they used. And after being there for five weeks, she told Jean-Pierre she had to go home.

They had gone to Saint-Tropez for their first weekend together, and stayed at a house Jean-Pierre borrowed from a friend. It was beautiful and peaceful out of season there, they walked along the narrow streets and sat at outdoor cafés along the quay, as they got to know each other. Their lovemaking was gentle and loving. He spent a few nights at the Ritz with her, and she stayed at his apartment. They were discovering each other, their histories, their fears, their dreams and goals, and they were happy together. Their joy from being in each other's lives, and how well suited they were, was obvious to everyone who saw them.

Jean-Pierre's father commented on it, and was pleased to see his son with a lovely young woman. He hoped their relationship would last forever, and said so to his son.

"I'm working on it," Jean-Pierre said with a twinkle in his eye that his father had never seen before.

Olivia reminded him that she had to go to New York for her grandmother's show at the MoMA, and he hesitantly asked her if he could join her.

"I want to meet your grandmother and your mother," he said. "Would it be too awkward if I come with you?"

"No, it wouldn't." She smiled at him. "As long as you don't mind that my grandmother is very outspoken and a little eccentric. She says whatever she thinks."

"I've been around eccentric artists all my life, and I think she's earned the right to be outspoken at ninety-two. If you can't say what you think by then, when can you?" She warned him too that seeing Federico's facial scars could be shocking at first. Her family was all used to them, and he had refused to continue having plastic surgery to fix them. He had decided to live with them instead, and Gabrielle said she no longer even saw them. Olivia told Jean-Pierre that one side of his face was perfect, and the other had nearly been destroyed when the mine went off where he was standing in Vietnam. He was lucky he hadn't been killed.

They flew to New York together two days before her grandmother's show of recent works, and settled into Olivia's apartment, which he thought was spectacular. He loved the wall of Warhols of her mother that Gwen had given her, and the two Picassos she had inherited from her father.

She wanted to introduce him to her grandmother before the show, but Gabrielle told Olivia she was too busy overseeing the installation to meet him, and she'd see him at the museum.

"Is this something serious?" Gabrielle asked her.

"It might be. We haven't known each other for long, only two months." Their relationship was in its infancy, she had just turned twenty-eight and was starting to take things more seriously, not just living in the moment. She had learned a lesson from getting involved with Paul too hastily, without considering the consequences adequately.

They were no more successful seeing Gwen, who had just signed the contract for her new movie. The script she loved had been picked up by a serious producer, an important director she'd worked with before had been attached to it. A number of talented actors had been signed, and they were going to start shooting in September. Her career was taking off again, with an extraordinary part, just as her mother had predicted. The right vehicle had turned up for her talent. And she'd just been approached about another film she loved after this one.

Olivia and Jean-Pierre arrived right on time at the opening of the show, and the work her grandmother and the curator had chosen was spectacular. They had put it in just the right location in an atrium, with enough breathing space around it. Jean-Pierre couldn't decide if he was more fascinated by the work or the mesmerizing, fiery, white-haired artist. Olivia introduced him and Gabrielle narrowed her eyes as she looked at him, and then her lined face crinkled into a smile.

"You will do very nicely," she said, and spoke to him in French thereafter. She heartily approved of him, and introduced him to Federico. Jean-Pierre explained to him how he had hunted for one of his photographs for an important client, and owned two himself. Federico was immensely pleased, and Jean-Pierre was oblivious to his scars as well.

"I am Beauty and the Beast all rolled into one," Federico said, laughing at himself.

A little while later, there was a ripple throughout the room as Olivia's mother entered. There were the usual whispers that she had arrived, that she was there, who she was, from strangers who were surprised to see her and didn't know about her connection to the artist. Olivia knew how much her mother disliked the attention in her private life, and whenever she went to public places. Olivia walked up to her with Jean-Pierre and Gwen greeted him with a warm smile. He tried to treat her like any other woman, but found he couldn't, she was too beautiful and too famous. He could more easily ignore Federico's scars than Gwen's fame and stunning beauty. And unlike most people, fooled by the difference in their height and hair color, he saw an immediate resemblance to her daughter, which pleased them both. It was rare for anyone to say that they looked like each other.

The three of them stood chatting for a little while, and Gabrielle and Federico joined them.

"I signed for the second film today," Gwen told her mother proudly. "You were right. And they are both fantastic parts. I really thought for a while that my career was over and I was too old to get a decent part. At my age, the film industry can be unforgiving and quite cruel."

"Whatever age you are," her mother said tartly, "age is just a number, and numbers have no power over you, unless you allow them to. You can feel 'too old' at any age, if you let yourself. You're never too old or too young for anything, you're just the right age. It's all a numbers game invented to frighten you." Then she turned to meet someone the curator wanted to introduce her to. She was wearing a deep purple dress with a high black lace collar, black satin shoes, and a long string of pearls that she said had been her grandmother's. Jean-Pierre thought her timeless and very beautiful.

They all had dinner that night at La Grenouille with the director of the museum and the curator who had helped Gabrielle select the work for the show, and Jean-Pierre was right in his element with artists and museum people. Like Olivia, he had grown up with them, perhaps even more so because of who his father was.

Gabrielle made a comment about Gwen's painting, and Gwen laughed.

"I'm finishing the last one now," Gwen said to her mother. "I don't think I'll be painting for much longer. I'm going back to work, thank God." Olivia explained to Jean-Pierre quietly that her mother hadn't worked for about a year, and now had found two parts she loved, and would start shooting the first one in September, and the second not long after. He still felt awestruck to be standing around chatting like old friends with Gwen Waters. He told Olivia that he couldn't imagine what it was like having a mother as famous as she was.

"She's actually very normal," Olivia said with a smile. "She used to pick me up every day at school when she wasn't working. She's never been a diva. And my grandmother certainly isn't."

"Neither are you." Jean-Pierre smiled at her. She had her own opinions, but he was finding her to be reasonable and undemanding, and he was having a good time working with her and even learning from her. She was clever in business.

They went back to Olivia's apartment after dinner at La Grenouille, Gabrielle and Federico went downtown to the Bowery in an Uber, and Gwen took a cab to the Dakota.

Gwen looked at the painting she had almost finished, set up on an easel in the kitchen, when she got home. There were still a few things she wanted to add to it, and she was studying it when the phone rang. It was late for anyone to call her, and she wondered if it was Olivia. When she glanced at her cellphone, she saw that it was her mother's number. She sounded panicked when Gwen answered. Gabrielle was breathless.

"Mother, are you okay?" Gwen asked her quickly.

"It's Federico. He can't breathe. I think he's having a heart attack. I called nine-one-one, they're not here yet. I have to go. I'll text you where they take him." She hung up before Gwen could say anything. And ten minutes later, Gabrielle sent her a text that they were taking him to NYU hospital, it was the closest large medical center to where they lived. And Gabrielle was going in the ambulance with him.

Gwen had changed out of her cocktail dress the moment she got the call. She put on jeans, a black sweater, flat shoes, and the moment she got the text, she called an Uber and hurried downstairs. The car was there three minutes later, and Gwen was panicked as they sped through the night. Federico was eighty-four years old and in good health until now, but one of these days, something serious was liable to happen to him. Age was not on his side. Her mother was older, but seemed sturdier and hardier than he did. He was always full of energy, and paid no attention to his age or health, only to hers. But getting blown up years before in Vietnam had taken a toll he chose to ignore.

He had just been admitted to the emergency room when Gwen got there. They asked if she was related to him, and she said she was his daughter so they didn't prevent her from going to the room where he was being examined and her mother was waiting in the hall. Within seconds, people started to recognize Gwen. She ignored them, and went through double doors to find her mother outside the exam room, still in her purple dress with the black lace collar. She looked pale as she saw her daughter, and was standing ramrod straight while she waited to hear what the doctors would say about Federico.

Gwen put an arm around her, and they sat down on two straight-back chairs and waited.

"What happened?" Gwen asked her gently.

"I don't know. He was fine, and then suddenly he had a terrible pain in his chest and said he couldn't breathe. He was fighting for air. He can't eat rich food, or red wine, and he loves both. It usually just gives him indigestion. I thought he was having a heart attack so I called nine-one-one." It had been the right thing to do, and it occurred to Gwen that if something happened to him, and it would one day, it would devastate her mother. They relied on each other totally, and although both were independent people, their lives and hearts were intertwined inexorably. After fourteen years together, Gwen could no longer imagine either of them without the other, nor could Gabrielle.

The doctor came out twenty minutes later and said they were

going to do an angiogram on Mr. Banducci, to see what was going on. It was possible that he would need a stent for his heart, but they didn't know yet. Then they let Gabrielle in to see him, and Gwen went with her for support.

His hair was fluffed out around him and disheveled, he didn't have his glasses on, and he looked like a mad scientist in a horror movie, but Gabrielle smiled when she saw him. The color was back in his face, and he said the pain was less severe.

"I'm sorry, Gabbie," he said. "I'm fine, they should let me go home with you."

"I'm not taking you home till we know what's wrong with you," she said firmly.

"I have work to do tomorrow on my own show. I can't stay here." He tried to get up and she pushed him gently back into the bed.

"Don't make me get rough with you, Banducci," she said sternly, and he laughed.

"What are you going to do? Beat me up?"

"Of course, if I have to." She smiled at him and he chuckled again, and Gwen was watching them from the doorway with a smile.

"If you two don't behave, they'll arrest you for domestic violence." All three of them laughed, and then an attendant took him away for the angiogram. Gabrielle sobered quickly, sitting in the waiting room with Gwen. There were tears in Gabrielle's eyes.

"I don't know what I'll do if something happens to him. He's the most wonderful person I've ever known, the kindest human being on the planet."

"Why haven't the two of you ever gotten married?" Gwen asked her, curious, and Gabrielle looked blank.

"I don't want more children, why would I get married?" Gwen smiled at her answer. "I never saw the point of it. When you're young and want children, it makes sense to me. But at our age, what difference does it make? I couldn't be more committed to him if I'd given birth to him myself. He's my sun and my moon and the stars in my heaven. What could a piece of paper possibly add to that?" Her mother was her own person and always had been.

"He's religious, though, isn't he? It might make a difference to him."

"It wouldn't to me, and it's more fun living in sin with him. It keeps us on our toes and it's more romantic. Marriage might spoil that," she said, as though they were fifty or sixty years younger. Age seemed to matter to them as little as marriage. They were unimpressed by it, and it simply wasn't part of their identity or how they saw themselves or each other. Neither of them was "old" mentally, and they worked harder than people half their age.

They waited two hours for the doctor to come back. It was two in the morning by then, and he finally came to tell them that the angiogram had gone well, and Federico had come through it without any problem and was resting now.

"How's his heart?" Gwen asked him. He was well aware of who she was, and tried not to stare at her.

"Probably stronger than yours or mine." The doctor smiled. "He had indigestion and an anxiety attack." He turned to Gabrielle then. "Did he get upset about anything today?"

"He's been working very hard preparing an upcoming show of his work, and I think he carried some heavy boxes with negatives in them."

"It would be good if he'd slow down for a few days. Can't someone else carry the boxes?" The doctor was surprised by what she said.

"He won't let them. All his archives are in them."

"Well, I'd like to see him rest just for a day or two."

"He gets wound up before he has a show," Gabrielle explained. The two of them were extraordinary for their age or any other.

"You can see him now, if you like," the doctor said, "and then you should probably both get some rest." He assumed that she was about the same age as Federico. It didn't even occur to him that she was eight years older.

"Can I sleep here?" she asked. "I won't disturb anyone. I can sleep in a chair if necessary."

"We can put a cot in his room for you, if you like." He glanced at Gwen. Her parents were obviously devoted to each other, and she wasn't about to explain that Federico wasn't her father and they weren't married.

Gabrielle told Gwen to go home then, and said she was going to stay with Federico.

"Will you try to get some rest, please? Or we'll be here for you next."

"No, you won't. I don't suffer from anxiety. You know how Italian and dramatic he is." She rolled her eyes and Gwen laughed. Gabrielle and Federico had some major fights from time to time, with unbridled passion, and then it all blew over. Gabrielle got fiercely jealous if she thought he'd looked at another woman, and Federico did the same, with high drama.

"If you stay here, get some sleep, and give Federico my love." Gwen kissed her mother and a minute later Gabrielle disappeared into his room. He had an ice pack on his groin, from where they had put the catheter into his artery for the angiogram. It was a frightening, unpleasant procedure and Gabrielle felt sorry for him.

"Are you all right?" she asked gently, as a nurse slipped quietly out of the room, and Gabrielle pulled a chair up next to him and sat down.

"I'm fine, let's go home," he insisted. But he looked more tired than he wanted to admit, and he seemed suddenly small in the bed. He had such a mane of hair, and with his bulky sweaters and heavy work boots, one forgot how thin he was. He appeared frail now, which frightened her.

"They said you can go home in the morning."

"Then you go home now and get some sleep. I'm sorry I scared you."

"You just did it for attention." She smiled.

"I saw you looking at that boy tonight," he teased her about Olivia's new beau. "You don't fool me. You're a wanton woman," he accused her with a grin.

"Well, you don't need to fake a heart attack to find out how much I love you. You know I do."

"Do you, Gabbie?" he asked gently, suddenly appearing vulnerable and old to her. Seeing him that way made her feel old too, although she wouldn't have admitted it to anyone, least of all to him.

"Of course I do. I wish I could climb into bed with you," she said gently, and he smiled.

"Why don't you? It'll shock the nurses. It's good for them." He pulled back the covers for her and she laughed and tucked him in again.

"Do you want anything?" she asked him.

"Yes," he said with a smug look.

"What is it?"

"I think we should get married," he said seriously. It had been his mantra for years.

"There are no shoulds at our age. We can do whatever we want."

"Good. I *want* to marry you," he said stubbornly.

"We don't need to get married. We already are in all the ways that matter."

"Not legally. What do you have against marriage? You're such a rebel." She took it as a compliment and smiled at him.

"It's such a bourgeois institution, it's embarrassing. We're more creative than that."

"We can be creative *and* married." He never got anywhere with his arguments. She had been resistant to the idea of marriage all her life. Both before she married at thirty-five, which was considered old at the time, and after she was widowed at thirty-seven. She had never been tempted to try again. She had had lovers and long-term relationships, especially with him for fourteen years, but she had no desire to legalize it or make it official, and he did. "You might give me another anxiety attack if you refuse," he threatened with a grin.

"Oh shut up. Now go to sleep, you need to rest or they won't let you go home tomorrow."

"I'll leave anyway," he said, and reached out and held her hand. They sat that way for a long time, dozing off, until at last they both fell asleep, she in the chair and he in bed, holding hands. They slept that way all night.

The nurses smiled when they came to check on him, and left the room soundlessly.

"That's true love in there," one of them said to the other, and they exchanged a smile. "That's how it's supposed to be."

"They're cute together. I wouldn't mind finding one like that."

"I don't think they get like that till they're about a hundred," one nurse said, and the other laughed, and eventually, they just let them be, to sleep for the rest of the night. They never let go of each other's hands as they slept.

Chapter 16

Eileen's first event for Eileen Jackson Events went off seamlessly. The crystal tents arrived on time and went up without a problem. They were "crystal" because they were transparent and you could see the lush gardens through them. There were three tents on the grounds, one for eating, with tables set with gleaming crystal and silver, one for dancing, big enough for a twelve-piece band, two singers, and a dance floor that had been painted pink, and another for the ceremony, filled with pink flowers. Each tent had to accommodate all three hundred guests. There were chandeliers in each tent.

The linens were perfect, the exact shade of the bride's dress. There was a gift for each guest at their place, a Tiffany silver heart dish, engraved with the bride and groom's initials and the date. The flower arrangements on each table were spectacular, done by a florist Max had found who charged them a tenth of what everyone else wanted to. There were garlands of pink flowers, rented topiary trees, lily of the valley everywhere, among the pink flowers. The food was delicious, supervised by both Eileen and Max, and the wedding cake was a masterpiece. Max made it himself, in pink, with pink sugar work Eileen had done, and real flowers on it, tiny pink roses and more lily of the valley. Eileen had gotten the bride an appointment at Oscar de la Renta, for an exquisite pale pink organdie dress with a long train, which was ready on time and fit her like a glove.

The videographer showed up, and the wedding photographer had given them a decent rate.

Mrs. Melling, Sandy, had spent seven hundred thousand dollars on the wedding without batting an eye, and thought she got a deal because everything was so perfect, stress-free, and effortless for her. To make that happen, Max and Eileen had jumped through flaming hoops to get the best quality supplies, the prettiest décor, the freshest flowers, the most talented people willing to work for lower prices for the exposure. They had watched every single detail, pressured every supplier, tasted all the food, checked the quality of everything. Nothing had gone awry or escaped their notice. And the results were flawless. The bride wasn't beautiful in a classic sense, but she looked lovely on her wedding day, had gotten the pink wedding that she dreamed of, and said everything was more beautiful than her first wedding, which was done by a famous wedding planner, had cost her parents two million dollars for five hundred people, and wasn't nearly as nice.

Sandy Melling had thanked them a thousand times all night long. There were a few things that Eileen thought she might have done differently for efficiency's sake, and Max agreed, but they were learning.

By the end of the evening, Eileen had had four requests for meetings with new clients, three of them for weddings and one for a fifti-eth anniversary party, where they wanted everything in gold, flatware, china, crystal, tablecloths, dance floor, tents. Their business was off and running. The last guest left at four A.M., and then they had to break everything down by morning to return to the rental companies. Max and Eileen oversaw it all themselves as the men worked taking it all apart. One day, they might have staff to super-vise the breakdown, but for now it was only them. They had made a handsome profit on the wedding, and Max a healthy commission, but it wasn't the money that thrilled either of them, although that was nice. The real thrill was knowing that everything had gone per-fectly, and the client was happy. No one had failed, disappointed anyone, or not shown up. And the quality of the food had been ex-ceptional.

Everything had been broken down by eight o'clock Sunday morn-ing, including the fancy crystal tents and the chandeliers that were removed and crated. There was a long line of trucks heading out of Sandy Melling's driveway with the undoing of the party while she slept. It took as big a crew to dismantle it all as to set it up.

"We did an *amazing* job," Eileen said, sitting on a big crate with the chandelier in it from the dinner tent. She looked at Max as men in white overalls took away the Chivari ballroom chairs with silver backs and pale pink cushions that had been used in all the tents. There had been about eight hundred chairs in all with custom-made cushions. Every detail had been thought of and addressed. Max re-turned the smile as the early morning sun shone down on them. Neither of them had been to bed that night, and they were energized by their success.

"You are an *amazing* woman," he said. "You're brilliant. Your business is going to be a bigger success than you can dream of." He was thrilled that he had come to work for her. He hadn't imagined that she was so capable and efficient. She was relentless until every detail was addressed and problem solved, and always pleasant to work with. She never lost her temper, although he did, frequently. He said he was "just Italian."

He walked over to her and sat down next to her on the crate. Whatever their roles of employee and boss, they had been partners for the event, and had worked equally hard and tirelessly to ensure perfection in everything, no matter how many hours it took them.

"Your pink wedding cake was the most beautiful thing I've ever seen," she complimented him. They had saved the top of it at the bride's request, to freeze for her so the couple could have it on their first anniversary, for good luck.

"Your sugar designs made the cake," he said to her. "I'm really proud of both of us. We did a good job."

"Better than that," she said, leaning against him. Now that they'd stopped moving and running, she realized how tired she was, and knew he must be too. He put an arm around her, leaned down and kissed her on the mouth. She thought he was just being exuberant and Italian at first, and then the kiss went on and deepened and she was swept into it and kissed him back. She looked startled when he stopped. "What was that?"

"Un bacio," he said in Italian. "A kiss." He acted as though it was perfectly normal to kiss her like that.

"Did you mean to do it?" She looked shocked, not sure whether to be angry or pleased, but before she could decide, he kissed her again,

244

harder this time to show her he meant it. "Max, what are you doing?" she asked breathlessly when he stopped.

"I'm kissing you, because you're the most wonderful woman I've ever met. You're strong and brave like a man, gentle like a woman, you're a creative genius, and a fantastic chef. I want to be with you as a man and a woman, always." He made it perfectly clear as he looked at her with love in his eyes. She didn't know what to say for a minute. She hadn't expected it, and didn't know how to respond.

"I'm forty years old. You're thirty-three."

"Yes? So? Are you trying to frighten me or impress me?"

"Both." She laughed. He didn't seem to care about their ages.

"We are a man and a woman, we work brilliantly together. And I'm willing to work till I fall over to make your business a success. You deserve that, Eileen, and some happiness. Who takes care of you? Who watches over you while you take care of everyone else? I see what you do. Everything for others, nothing for you. I want to take care of you." She loved being with him and working with him, they were a fantastic team, they laughed a lot and he made everything possible. He never accepted defeat, and neither did she. He was smiling as he looked at her. "Stop looking so surprised. When was the last time a man told you he loved you?"

"I can't remember," she said softly. Everything about him was unexpected, his age, his nationality, his talent, and now he was telling her he loved her.

The men came to take away the chandelier crate they were sitting on, and he swept her into his arms and carried her to his Fiat. She didn't protest or attempt to get out of his arms. Her bag was already in the car. He set her gently down on the front seat and smiled at her.

"Dove andiamo, Principessa?" he asked her when he got in and turned the key in the ignition. "Where are we going, Princess?" They had been working together for three months, and he thought he had waited long enough. He had wanted to kiss her for the past two months.

She thought about his question for a minute. Knowing that she'd be working around the clock all weekend, she had sent the children to Paul at his new house. They loved it, and spent all the time they could in the pool now that school was out.

"Home, I guess," she answered, and grinned at Max. This was not how she had expected the wedding to end. It was an interesting twist to a perfect weekend so far, and it was getting better by the minute, with his kisses and surprise announcement.

He drove to her house, parked his Fiat in the garage, and closed the doors so no one would see it there in the early morning. He didn't want to ruin her reputation or shock her children if they drove by with their father.

"Thank you," she said, appreciating the thoughtful gesture. She was so tired she could hardly get out of the car, but they were both smiling as he followed her into the house and locked the door behind them.

Olivia spent most of June in New York, running the New York branch of her business, while Jean-Pierre ran the Paris office. At the end of the month, she left to spend July and August in France with him. They were planning to go to Saint-Tropez, Corsica, and Sardinia to see friends of his for long weekends, and then she was going to come back to New York at the end of August to spend September there. She could see a lot of commuting in her future, but it was good for the business, and good for them. They were looking forward to the summer together. She wasn't staying at the Ritz this time. She was going to stay with Jean-Pierre.

With Olivia gone over the Fourth of July weekend, and no plans to go away herself, Gwen decided to finish the last painting she'd been working on. She had work to do over the summer, studying the script, doing research, and preparing for her role in the movie she would start filming in September. It was a period role, and Gwen liked to steep herself in historical research about the character before she began a role like that. She wanted everything about it to be authentic, and her mother had been right, it was likely to be one of the most demanding and important parts she had ever played. She wanted to give it her full attention, so it was time to finish the painting, before her mind was engaged with something other than an Italian landscape. They were her favorite subjects to paint and she did them well. She was planning to give it to her mother for her ninety-third birthday, which was approaching. Gwen liked spending holidays in the city when everyone else was away.

She had just finished a particularly challenging section of the painting when Federico called her on Sunday morning, and spoke to her in barely more than a whisper. He hated talking on the phone, so she was surprised when he called her. He never did.

"I'm worried about your mother, but don't tell her I called you. She's had a bad cold for the past week. It's gone to her chest. I think she should see a doctor, but she doesn't want to. She has a terrible cough. I'm afraid that she might have bronchitis or something worse. Can you just call her casually and, when she coughs, insist that she see a doctor?" Gwen thanked him for alerting her and called her mother half an hour later, just to see how she was. Two minutes into the call, Gabrielle was hacking as Federico had described, in a fierce coughing fit that wouldn't stop.

"Wow, Mother, that doesn't sound good. Have you seen a doctor?" Gwen asked innocently. Gabrielle hated doctors and medicine and always said they killed people, and she believed it. She had avoided them all her life.

"Don't be ridiculous. You sound like Federico. It's just a summer cold. You don't go to a doctor for a cold." Gwen thought he was right. It sounded like it was deep in her chest, bronchitis at the very least.

"You don't want to wind up with pneumonia, Mother. You might need an antibiotic."

"Medicine is for children. I'm not a child." It was the kind of resistance he'd been meeting. Her mother hated any kind of medical treatment, and was rarely sick.

"I'll call you again tomorrow to see how you are. If you're not better, you should see someone tomorrow. Stay out of air-conditioning in the meantime. That's lethal in the summer, especially if you already have a cold. Let me know if you need something or if there's anything I can do to help." It was all she could do. Her mother didn't like being fussed over.

"You're not a doctor, and I don't need help." Nothing made Gabrielle crankier than being sick. She took it as a personal affront.

But on Monday morning, Federico called Gwen secretly again, and said Gabrielle was worse. He said she had a high fever and hadn't gotten out of bed. Gwen thanked him again and decided to go downtown to see for herself. The fever frightened her.

Federico let her into the warehouse where they lived, and she climbed the stairs to the loft they used as their bedroom. Gabrielle was in bed, shivering with fever and chills, her eyes were glazed and she had a racking cough that sounded even worse. Gwen and Federico exchanged a look while Gabrielle dozed between coughing fits.

Gwen sat down next to the bed and spoke gently to her. "I think you need to go to the hospital, Mother. I don't want this to get any worse." Her mother nodded and seemed distant and disconnected. She didn't argue with Gwen, which was a bad sign. She seemed semi-conscious as they bundled her up in a bathrobe over her nightgown, wrapped her in a blanket, and Gwen helped her put on shoes. She didn't even insist on getting dressed, which was unusual for her. Gwen could feel that Gabrielle was blazing with fever, while her mother shook with chills.

Ten minutes later, they had her in an Uber on the way to NYU hospital. Gwen was frightened, which she didn't say to either of them. She went to the nursing desk to check her mother in when they arrived. They had Gwen fill out several forms. They kept Gabrielle waiting for an hour to see a doctor, and then finally took her to an exam room in a wheelchair. Federico looked near tears. Gwen tried to reassure them both, but she was afraid herself.

The resident on duty, a big burly young man with a beard, examined Gabrielle. He looked over the forms and noticed Gabrielle's age.

Within five minutes he said she had pneumonia and had to be admitted. He never spoke to Gabrielle, only to Gwen, as though Gabrielle, as a coherent human being, didn't exist.

"Does she have dementia?" he asked her, and Gwen was horrified.

"Of course not. She's just sick."

"I'm going to put her in the ICU," he said matter-of-factly. "Pneumonia is lethal at her age," he said within Gabrielle's hearing, and took Gwen out in the hall then to speak to her. They left Federico with Gabrielle, watching over her like a newborn baby, and speaking softly to her, telling her she was going to be all right.

The resident didn't mince words. "This is very serious, given her age. I think you have to be realistic about this. People your mother's age don't usually survive pneumonia. I'm going to start her on an IV antibiotic, but it may not work in time."

"Is there anything else we can do? Something stronger in addition to the antibiotic?"

"We can do inhalation treatments, but they probably won't do much good either." He held out no hope.

"Try anyway. Pretend she's twenty years younger, or thirty. She's normally a very healthy, vital person."

"We'll see what we can do." Gwen wanted to call her mother's own physician, but didn't know the current one's name.

The resident had said they were going to move her to the ICU within the hour, and he was sending a gerontologist to look at her once she was there.

"What kind of doctor is that?" Gwen wasn't familiar with the term. "Is that a lung specialist?"

"No, that's a pneumologist. A gerontologist specializes in geriatric patients, elderly people. It's similar to a geriatrician, but a little broader and more comprehensive to treat the problems of elderly patients."

"My mother will have a fit over that."

But she was sleeping when Gwen got back to the exam room. Federico said she had been dozing since Gwen left. He looked at her with pleading eyes, begging Gwen to save her. She felt helpless, and didn't like the attitude of the resident. He had given up as soon as he saw her mother's age.

"What did he say?"

"They're going to put her in the intensive care unit, and give her a strong antibiotic and inhalant medications. And they've called in another doctor to look at her." She didn't say how hopeless he had made it seem.

Gabrielle stirred then, and looked at Gwen, her eyes bright with the high fever.

"Who is your general doctor, Mother?" Gwen asked her. "What's his name?" Gwen was going to call him and ask him to come immediately. This was an emergency, and Gwen wanted all the help they could get.

"Palmer," her mother answered in a croak. "He died last year. I haven't replaced him. I wasn't sick."

"Do you have a doctor?" she asked Federico, and he shook his head. Gwen was afraid that her own physician might be on vacation after the holiday weekend, and it took weeks to get an appointment with him. She wasn't fond of him either, but her previous doctor had retired two years before and left the practice to the new man. "How did she get this sick?" she asked Federico.

"She's had it for a week, but she only got like this yesterday." At least they were in the hospital now.

They moved Gabrielle to the ICU an hour later. They had already started the intravenous antibiotic in the emergency room, and had done a panel of blood tests, which they said were routine, given her age and how sick she was. Gwen was relieved that the nurses in the ICU were very kind to her.

Federico and Gwen sat next to her bed for the rest of the day, and she slept for most of it. The nurse said the fever had come down. The gerontologist appeared at five in the afternoon. Gwen was prepared to hate him, and was surprised to find that she didn't.

He looked to be in his late fifties, was well dressed in a blazer and khaki slacks, a shirt and tie, he had silver hair and a good haircut. He looked more like a banker than a modern-day doctor. Gwen had been watching them come and go all day with long, greasy hair, in ponytails or to their shoulders, with either five days of stubble or full beards. They all wore scrubs instead of proper clothes, and either sneakers, clogs, or Birkenstocks. None of them dressed like grown-ups in her opinion, but this one did.

He introduced himself as Jeremy Stubbs, and asked to speak to Gwen in the hall after examining her mother. He had a warm smile and a polite, easy manner.

"Your mother has pneumonia, as you know, which is not a good thing at her age. I've been looking at her preliminary blood work. We don't have all the results yet." Gwen was suddenly terrified that they had found something seriously wrong with her, but he surprised her. "She's in remarkably good health, and doesn't seem to have all the ailments her generation is prone to. Low cholesterol, her heart is strong, liver, kidneys, everything is functioning normally. Does she have any chronic health problems?"

"None."

"No arthritis? Dizziness? Does she fall?"

"Never. She's up and down ladders all day long. She's a sculptress and a welder. Her pieces are roughly ten feet tall, and she sleeps in a loft. And no arthritis." Dr. Stubbs smiled at Gwen's report.

"She seems to be one of those lucky people that age doesn't touch. It happens, but not often enough. Maybe her work is part of it."

"She just opened a show at the MoMA a month ago," Gwen said proudly.

"What often happens to people like her is that they go along just fine, and then something like this comes up. It doesn't always turn out well, and most doctors feel that, at a certain age, you just can't fight it. That's not my philosophy. In the condition your mother is in, there's no reason why she couldn't live another ten or twelve years. What we have to do now is beat the pneumonia. I'm going to give her a stronger antibiotic. It may upset her stomach, but it's worth it." It was music to Gwen's ears.

"Thank God for you. Go for it. I was panicked when we got here."

"Let's not panic yet. And she hasn't been bedridden, so if her fever is down, I want to get her up walking, and not just leave her lying down. That's where we get into trouble. And I want to start the inhalants." They walked back into Gabrielle's room together, and she was sleeping again. The doctor checked her fever and it was down. Then he went to tell the nurses about the change of antibiotic, as Federico looked at Gwen in desperation.

"What did he say?"

"He's terrific," she whispered. "He's giving her a stronger medication. He says if we get her out of this, she can live another ten or twelve years." She looked a hundred years old as she lay there, but she opened her eyes and looked at Gwen. "We're going to get you up for a walk, Mother. The doctor wants you to move around."

"There's nothing wrong with my legs. I have a cough."

"Exactly. There's nothing wrong with your legs, so he wants you to use them and not just lie there."

"I'm tired," she complained. "I'll go for a walk later." But if her life depended on it, Gwen was not going to let her off the hook. She got Federico to help her, and they dressed Gabrielle in the bathrobe she'd worn to the hospital, helped her out of bed, and walked slowly down the hall with her IV pole. She was still coughing, but she looked a little better as they walked. "I want to go home," she said, sounding more like herself.

"Not yet. We have to get rid of your cough first."

"I have work to do."

"Then you'll have to get well," Gwen said firmly.

The doctor came back to see her as they walked down the hall, and he smiled at Gabrielle and spoke to her.

"I'm very happy to see you up and walking, Mrs. Waters. You'll get better much faster this way. And we're going to give you some things to breathe that should free up your chest. I want to send you home as soon as possible," he assured her. "We need the beds for people who are really sick." The implication being that she wasn't. She smiled at him for a moment.

"Are you suggesting that I'm feigning illness, Doctor?" she said with a grin and he laughed.

"If you are, we'll find out soon enough and send you packing," he teased her. "There are much better hotels in town than this. I understand you opened a show recently at the MoMA."

"Yes, I did. Have you seen it?"

"Not yet. But I intend to now."

"It's only a small show of recent work," she said modestly.

"I'm sure it's very good." Gwen wanted to hug him as she listened to him, pulling her mother back to life just by treating her as though she weren't a hundred years old and at death's door, even if she was seriously sick. But her own good health and her active life served her well.

They took her back to her room, helped her into bed, and she looked grateful to lie down. She was tired from the fever and coughing, and hadn't slept well for days. The nurse had set up the inhalants while she was walking, and one of them changed the bag on her IV to the stronger antibiotic.

The doctor spoke to Gwen again before he left. "I'll be back in the morning, and here's my card with my cellphone number. If anything worries you, call me. She's doing well for now. I'm hoping she turns the corner in a day or two with what we're giving her. And keep her walking."

"I can't thank you enough," Gwen said, clutching his card.

"There are people this tactic wouldn't work with, but your mother is strong. With good support, her body will fight this." He was reassuring and calm.

"I hope so," Gwen said, looking worried.

"Normally, they keep visits short in the ICU. I've told them to let you and her husband stay with her. Keep her engaged. She needs to sleep too. And I want her to walk three times a day. I want to keep her moving. I'm less concerned about what she eats, the antibiotic will probably upset her stomach anyway, and she's getting what she needs for now from the IV." Gwen thanked him again and he left with a pleasant smile and a wave as he got into the elevator.

They brought dinner for Gabrielle and she picked at it. And at nine o'clock, she went to sleep and Gwen and Federico left to get some rest themselves.

"I'll go back in the morning," Gwen told him. "Come whenever you want to. I like the doctor, don't you?"

"He seems nice," he said cautiously. "Do you think she'll be all right?"

"I hope so," Gwen said earnestly. They were doing all the right things for her now. Usually in most hospitals, they let old people just lie there, the pneumonia got worse, and they died. "We have to make sure she walks three times a day."

Gwen dropped him off in a cab, and then went home to Central Park West. Federico said he would go back that night. She called the nurses several times that night to inquire about her mother, and they said she was sleeping peacefully, and Federico was with her.

Gwen was back at nine the next morning, just as her mother was waking up. She didn't look much better and she was still coughing, but she didn't have a fever, and at least she wasn't worse. Dr. Stubbs came to see her an hour later, and said he had looked at her sculptures online and he thought they were spectacular.

"I do all the welding myself," she said confidently. "Before the foundry casts them in bronze. It's a complicated process."

"I'm sure it is. I'd love to visit your studio sometime." He treated her with admiration and respect.

"I'd be delighted." Gabrielle smiled at him. "You should look up Mr. Banducci's photographs too. They're very beautiful, and more delicate than my work. They're very poignant."

"I will," he promised her, and Gwen followed him out.

"The rest of her blood work is fine," Dr. Stubbs told her. "She still has the pneumonia, but the antibiotic should start working."

"We'll keep her walking," Gwen said, and he looked embarrassed for a moment.

"I feel like an idiot," he said. "I don't go to movies much, but of course I know your name. One of the nurses told me who you are. I don't know why I didn't recognize you. I was focused on your mother."

"That's much more important to me." Gwen smiled at him, and it was nice not to be recognized for a change. She always appreciated anonymity, which she didn't get often. And when she did, it allowed her to be a person and not a star or an object of curiosity. "Thank you for *not* recognizing me," she said, and he laughed.

"Fame must be a heavy burden at times," he said sympathetically, and she nodded.

"It is. I'm really grateful for everything you're doing for my mother, and for your attitude. People, even some doctors, give up on old people when they know their age."

"It's a terrible thing in our society," he agreed, "how we discount people past a certain age, and dehumanize them. They have so much to offer us and teach us. Look at your mother. She's an icon in her field, and still working. I wish there were more like her. It's a question of luck and health, but attitude as well. That plays a big part, maybe more than all the rest." Gabrielle didn't consider herself old.

He promised to come back later that afternoon, and when he did, Gabrielle had taken three long walks by then, her color was better, and she said she was hungry. The antibiotic hadn't bothered her stomach at all. She was a strong woman.

Dr. Stubbs didn't stay long, but he was satisfied with how she was doing, and the inhalants were helping her too. She was breathing better and coughing less.

The following day, she looked stronger and said she wanted to go home. She had too much work to do to just lie around. Her cough didn't sound as deep. She had a long conversation with the doctor about her work, and she looked more like herself by that night. And when he listened to her chest, he was pleased.

"We're winning the battle here, Mrs. Waters. You're improving."

"Good. Then send me home."

"Not yet. But soon. I don't want you to have a relapse. I want the pneumonia cured before you leave." He told Gwen he thought she'd be there all week. "She's a remarkable woman," he said, and Gwen agreed.

Federico stayed longer than Gwen that night. He said he wanted to talk to her mother. When they were alone, he looked at her seriously.

"I want something from you," he said with a stern expression. She could see an Italian drama coming.

"What's that?" she said, smiling at him. She was feeling better.

"Your doctor said you could live another ten or twelve years. And if you do, I want to be married. You've turned me down for almost fifteen years. I've had enough. I want us to be respectable. I want you to be my wife. The nurse asked if I was your husband, and I had to say that I'm your boyfriend. It's humiliating." She laughed.

"I agree," she said quietly with a smile.

"You do? What happened?"

"It scared me when I got sick. I think I'm ready to get married."

"It took you long enough," he said, and leaned over and kissed her. He had been ready to do battle with her. "Should I ask them to call the chaplain now?" She looked outraged at the suggestion.

"Of course not. I don't want last rites. I want a wedding. A proper one. With a nice dress. I haven't gotten married in fifty-eight years, I want a decent wedding. I'm not getting married in this." She pointed to her nightgown, and he laughed.

"When do you want to do it?" He wanted to pin her down now that she'd agreed.

"I don't know. August maybe? That gives us time to plan it." He nodded. He liked that idea. A month before his show.

"It's too hot to travel then. My show is in September. We could postpone our honeymoon until October. Where do you want to go?"

"Paris," she said without hesitating. "It's where we met." She looked girlish for a minute and he leaned over and kissed her again.

"I'm going to hold you to it, you know. You won't get out of this." He was as strong as she was when he chose to be. It was why they got along. They were an even match.

"I don't want to get out of it," she said, smiling at him. "We're engaged!" she said, and they both laughed. "Now you can say you're my fiancé, not my boyfriend."

When they told Gwen the next day, she offered to give the wedding at her apartment, and they liked that idea. They picked a date at the end of August. And they decided to go to Venice, where he was from, after Paris for their honeymoon.

Gabrielle told Dr. Stubbs when he came to see her. "We're getting married," she said with a big smile, "almost sixty-five years after we met in Paris at the Beaux-Arts, we were both students. Federico was only twenty, he's eight years younger than I am. He was barely more than a child then. You'll have to come to our wedding, since you saved me," she told him.

"I'd say we're on the road to recovery if we're planning a wedding." He was pleased with her progress. It was a much happier outcome than many he encountered in his line of work.

Chapter 17

Gwen had ordered all the flowers for the wedding herself. There were garlands of white roses and orchids on all the stairs and over the doors, and arrangements of lily of the valley and tiny white Phalaenopsis orchids on the tables. The scent of the lily of the valley was heavy in the air. Gabrielle and Federico had selected fifty of their closest friends, all of whom had accepted. There were writers, artists, actors, museum curators, gallerists, many of them well known, some not, of all ages. Gwen had organized five round tables in her dining room. The ceremony was in the living room, performed by a minister, and Gabrielle came down the stairs alone in a champagne-colored lace dress, carrying a bouquet of tea-colored orchids. Her long white hair was swept up in a perfect French twist. She looked lovely.

Olivia had come home from France a week early for her grandmother's wedding, and Jean-Pierre was with her. They were both deeply tanned after all the places where they had vacationed in August, with the last week of their vacation on his father's Perini Navi

yacht in Italy. Olivia looked radiant, and her mother and grandmother agreed that they had never seen her happier. And they loved
Jean-Pierre.

Gwen was wearing a navy blue silk Chanel suit and looked very
dignified. She said that she and her mother had switched roles, and
Gwen was playing the mother of the bride. Jeremy Stubbs stood next
to her for most of the festivities. They had had dinner together a few
times since they met in the hospital. He still couldn't believe his good
fortune to be getting to know her. And she was to start pre-production
on her new movie in two weeks.

The groom looked like the happiest man alive as he watched Gabrielle come down the stairs gracefully to where he stood with a
sprig of lily of the valley in the lapel of his formal morning coat. It
was his first wedding and he wanted to do it right, in morning coat
and striped trousers. They exchanged their vows with tears in their
eyes and Federico cried openly when the minister declared them
husband and wife.

The champagne flowed, the lunch was delicious, four musicians
played chamber music for the ceremony and champagne after, and a
livelier group replaced them, so there was dancing during and after
lunch. The guests stayed so long that it became something of a thé
dansant, reminiscent of Gabrielle's youth. They had their honeymoon all planned for October, after Federico's retrospective show.

It was the perfect elegant, intimate wedding, and Gwen's apartment the ideal setting for it. Gwen had invited a few of her friends
from the film world too, who were either major directors or big stars.
She introduced Jeremy to everyone, it was a cavalcade of famous
names and faces all day. And at the end of it, Gabrielle and Federico

spent their wedding night at the Four Seasons like newlyweds and went back to their warehouse on the Bowery the next day.

Gabrielle was back at work that afternoon. Federico smiled at her. He loved knowing she was finally his wife.

On the day of Federico and Gabrielle's wedding, Eileen drove Pennie and the boys to Boston to settle Pennie into Harvard. She had rented a van for everything Pennie was bringing with her, and Max had come along to help. The children had figured out by then that Max was more than just their mother's assistant, and didn't object once they got used to the idea. They liked him, he was nice to them, and fun to be with.

They had catered two weddings that summer, several dinner parties, and were doing a big charity event in New York the following week. Eileen's business was flying, and they were the talk of Greenwich as the hot new event planners and caterers in town. Eileen hardly had time to talk to Jane anymore, but Jane understood and was thrilled for her.

Paul was meeting them in Cambridge with Mathilde after a weekend in Cape Cod, and Mark and Seth were going to drive back to Greenwich with them. Mathilde's boys were with their father for the weekend. The five boys had been having fun together, spending the summer in Paul's new pool and in and out of his house. Eileen was happy for him, and their divorce was going to be final in six weeks.

They got to Cambridge at eleven and to Pennie's dorm assignment in Straus Hall, one of the best locations, near the heart of Harvard Yard. She was to be in a three-person suite, and Paul was shocked when Pennie told him that all the halls were coed. She was going to have two roommates in the suite, and had met them all on Skype. She was distracted and a little disoriented watching all the freshmen students arrive with their belongings and their families to move into the dorms. She saw clusters of boys watching them, several she thought were very good-looking. She had had a text from Tim that morning wishing her luck. She had seen him a few times that summer, and it was still strange to think that they had conceived and lost a baby and almost got married only a year before. It seemed so long ago now. Things had turned out so differently than they'd hoped or planned or feared. For all of them.

Olivia was distant history for Paul now, and Mathilde seemed like the perfect fit. Max was unexpected and an important addition to Eileen's life, and her brand-new business was thriving. And Pennie was standing on the threshold of her future with life rolled out before her like a red carpet as she entered the hallowed halls of Harvard, which was her dream come true. Her life was just beginning with everything she brought to it from the past.

The day was exhausting getting everything hooked up, connected, and put away. Max handled the technology, Eileen and Mathilde put away her clothes, while the boys played outside and waited for them to finish. Paul assembled equipment and a bookcase, and installed a small refrigerator, then helped Max with the stereo and internet to the best of his ability.

Pennie went to a freshman orientation while they were working on her room, and they all went to the family picnic that afternoon. And then suddenly it was time to say goodbye. She clung to her mother for a moment, as they exchanged a look between mother and daughter. Eileen could almost see her take flight with fresh new wings, and prayed that they would hold her and she would make wise choices with her life.

She hugged her father, thanked Max and Mathilde, and ran over to say goodbye to Seth and Mark. Then she disappeared into the building where she would live for the next year, make new friends, and learn what she needed for her future.

The twins climbed into their father's car and they left. Max drove the now-empty van off campus and Eileen cried for a minute. But everything that was happening now was as it should be, in the proper order. It was easier now because Max was with her.

"Are you okay?" He looked at her with a tender smile, and she nodded, wiped away her tears, and blew her nose. Her firstborn had left the nest.

"I'm going to miss her so much," she said sadly, but happy for her.

"She'll come home more than you think. She's going to miss you too." But Eileen knew it would never be quite the same again. The years would fly and she'd be off to her own skies. The time Pennie wanted so much, and waited for, had finally come. She was grown and well on her way.

It was nice being with Max for the drive home to Greenwich. Eileen would have been too sad without him. He was wise for his years, and their age difference didn't bother either of them. It didn't seem to matter at all.

"You know, I hope it's not rude of me to say it," he said cautiously, as they sat stuck in the traffic jam of departing parents, all feeling the same emotions she did, of simultaneous loss and pride. "Paul is a nice guy, but I can't for a second imagine you with him. You're so different."

"We are. We never should have gotten married, or we should have given up a long time before we did. He's much happier now, and so am I. Mathilde suits him much better."

"She's more his style," Max agreed, and smiled at her. Mathilde was milder, less exuberant and energetic than Eileen. Eileen was already missing Pennie, but she was happy with Max. "And do I suit you better?" he asked her.

"It looks like it, doesn't it?" she said with a smile, and leaned over to kiss him. She couldn't have predicted it, or any of what had happened. A year before, Pennie had been pregnant and lost a baby, she'd been married to Paul and thought she would be forever, she was depressed about turning forty, Paul was cheating on her and she didn't know it, and he was madly in love with Olivia. Eileen wondered what had happened to her, and if things had worked out for her too. Life had a way of sorting things out better than one could imagine or plan for oneself. *Everything* in her life had changed for the better in the past year, and her future looked bright.

"Are we all set for the event on Tuesday?" he asked her.

"I think so. I've gone over all the checklists." He was sure she had. He knew her now. *New York* magazine had called her for an interview and said they were the hot new caterers and party planners of the moment. The charity event they were about to do was going to be a big one for them, and would put them in the eye of everyone who mattered in New York. And *New York* magazine wanted to get the scoop first. They were thinking of putting Eileen and Max on the cover in their chef hats and jackets if the event on Tuesday turned out well. The interview was due to come out in October, which was going to be a big month for them, with two more weddings. And two more still coming up in September. They were starting to make real money, and Eileen had found the career she had always dreamed of, just not in the field she expected.

"Would you ever want to open a restaurant?" Max asked her casually, as they reached the highway to take them back to Connecticut.

"Maybe one day, not yet. I'm having too much fun doing catering and event planning." She had thought she would be doing small dinner parties. She didn't expect it to take off the way it had. The Melling wedding had launched them. "Maybe when I'm older," she said about the restaurant with a smile. That had changed too. A year before she was dreading turning forty, and thought her life was over. And instead it had begun again, better than before. Now she felt younger and could see a bright future ahead.

"I'll ask you again about the restaurant in a few years," he said. "When we both grow up, if that ever happens," he said, and they laughed.

Chapter 18

The article about Eileen and Max came out in *New York* magazine in October. The charity event had been a big success. They
were on the cover, back-to-back, wearing their chef hats and jackets.

She'd gotten her divorce papers the same week and it seemed
mildly anticlimactic after everything else that had happened. She felt
nostalgic for a minute and then put the papers away. She was free
now.

Pennie was loving Harvard. They were going up for family weekend in a week. The time had flown since they'd taken her there in
August. She loved her classes, was dating a few boys, and Eileen and
Max had a long list of parties, weddings, and events to cater. The
time had flown since Pennie left.

Gwen was busy on the set of her new movie, but she called her
mother and Federico the night before they left on their honeymoon.
They were going to see Olivia and Jean-Pierre in Paris for dinner.

Olivia was there again, and they had invited her grandmother and Federico to a new restaurant.

Gwen was still seeing Jeremy Stubbs, whenever she got a day off from the movie. He had visited her once on the set and been on Page Six with her when they were seen having brunch at the Mercer in SoHo on a Sunday morning. They referred to him as the "Mystery Man," since no one knew who he was, which suited both of them just fine. They were trying to keep it that way, for now. They were planning to visit Olivia in Paris when they had time. Gabrielle had been right about movies and men.

Federico and Gabrielle drank champagne after they boarded the plane to Paris, and talked about what a success his show had been, and about her next one. Then they both went to sleep so they'd be fresh when they landed.

It was a sunny October day when they arrived. The weather was crisp. They already knew all the places they wanted to go to retrace their footsteps of the past, when they were students in Paris and had met.

They went through passport control and the customs officer looked at Gabrielle in surprise, and pointed to her age on her passport.

"Bravo, Madame!" he said, finding it hard to believe that she was ninety-three years old.

She smiled and shrugged, feeling as young as she had been when she first went to the Beaux-Arts. "It's just a number," she said to him. "We're on our honeymoon," she said proudly. Federico beamed at her, still a handsome man, and she had mischief in her eyes when she looked at him.

"Congratulations!" the officer said to both of them, handing them their passports. They headed for baggage claim at a rapid pace, eager to get started on their honeymoon, as the customs officer watched them go, smiled, and wished them well.

About the Author

DANIELLE STEEL has been hailed as one of the world's most popular authors, with almost a billion copies of her novels sold. Her many international bestsellers include *Moral Compass, Spy, Child's Play, The Dark Side, Lost and Found, Blessing in Disguise, Silent Night*, and other highly acclaimed novels. She is also the author of *His Bright Light,* the story of her son Nick Traina's life and death; *A Gift of Hope,* a memoir of her work with the homeless; *Pure Joy,* about the dogs she and her family have loved; and the children's books *Pretty Minnie in Paris* and *Pretty Minnie in Hollywood.*

daniellesteel.com
Facebook.com/DanielleSteelOfficial
Twitter: @daniellesteel
Instagram: @officialdaniellesteel

About the Type

This book was set in Charter, a typeface designed in 1987 by Matthew Carter (b. 1937) for Bitstream, Inc., a digital type-foundry that he cofounded in 1981. One of the most influential typographers of our time, Carter designed this versatile font to feature a compact width, squared serifs, and open letterforms. These features give the typeface a fresh, highly legible, and unencumbered appearance.